ALICE RUE EVADES THE TRUTH

ALICE RUE EVADES THE TRUTH

Emily Zipps

THE DIAL PRESS
New York

The Dial Press
An imprint of Random House
A division of Penguin Random House LLC
1745 Broadway, New York, NY 10019
randomhousebooks.com
penguinrandomhouse.com

A Dial Press Trade Paperback Original

Copyright © 2025 by Emily Zipps

Dial Delights Extras copyright © 2025 by Emily Zipps

Penguin Random House values and supports copyright. Copyright fuels creativity, encourages diverse voices, promotes free speech, and creates a vibrant culture. Thank you for buying an authorized edition of this book and for complying with copyright laws by not reproducing, scanning, or distributing any part of it in any form without permission. You are supporting writers and allowing Penguin Random House to continue to publish books for every reader. Please note that no part of this book may be used or reproduced in any manner for the purpose of training artificial intelligence technologies or systems.

THE DIAL PRESS is a registered trademark and the colophon is a trademark of Penguin Random House LLC.

DIAL DELIGHTS and colophon are trademarks of Penguin Random House LLC.

Library of Congress Cataloging-in-Publication Data
Names: Zipps, Emily, author.
Title: Alice Rue evades the truth: a novel / Emily Zipps.
Description: New York, NY: The Dial Press, 2025. |
Identifiers: LCCN 2025023536 (print) | LCCN 2025023537 (ebook) |
ISBN 9780593733035 trade paperback | ISBN 9780593733042 ebook
Subjects: LCGFT: Novels
Classification: LCC PS3626.I68 A79 2025 (print) | LCC PS3626.I68 (ebook) |
DDC 813/.6—dc23/eng/20250530
LC record available at https://lccn.loc.gov/2025023536
LC ebook record available at https://lccn.loc.gov/2025023537

Printed in the United States of America on acid-free paper

1st Printing

BOOK TEAM: Production editor: Michelle Daniel • Managing editor: Rebecca Berlant • Production manager: Katie Zilberman • Copy editor: Madeline Hopkins • Proofreaders: Alicia Hyman, Kathryn Jones, Vincent La Scala, and Tracy Roe

Book design by Jo Anne Metsch

The authorized representative in the EU for product safety and compliance is Penguin Random House Ireland, Morrison Chambers, 32 Nassau Street, Dublin D02 YH68, Ireland. https://eu-contact.penguin.ie

To my wife,
who is more than everything

ALICE RUE EVADES THE TRUTH

ONE

Alice has often wished that her job would be more exciting, but performing chest compressions on the love of her life, all alone in the cavernous lobby that serves as her office, isn't exactly what she had in mind. She fumbles with her phone, trying to pull it out of her pocket while still thumping on his chest. She remembers something about doing CPR to the rhythm of the song "Stayin' Alive," so she chants it to herself as she pumps with one hand, frantically dialing with the other.

She's supposed to breathe into his mouth at some point, but she can't remember when. Is it every ten pumps? Every fifty? How many breaths does she do? One? Three? Fuck, why is this so complicated? Why can she remember the jingle from that 1999 carpet cleaning commercial and not how to do CPR?

"Jesus Christ, come on!" The phone rings and rings, like she's trying to reach a pharmacist during their lunch hour instead of 911 in the middle of the night. "Come on!" she yells between chants. "Fucking answer!"

The man below her is still, except for the violence she's enacting on his rib cage. He could almost be sleeping, if she hadn't just watched him wobble and wordlessly fall to the ground, smacking his head with a horrifyingly wet thud.

She braces herself to go in for a breath after this next round. "Stayin' alive, stayin' alive, god I hope you don't have mouth herpes, stayin' alive, stayin' alive."

She tilts his head back, pinches his nose because she's pretty sure she's seen that in a movie, and starts to breathe into his mouth. Of course, that's exactly when the phone connects.

"Nine-one-one, what's your emergency?"

She rips her mouth away from his, stuttering out the address of the enormous office building where she works, managing to say something about *collapsed* and *not moving* and *unsure about the breath-to-push ratio,* possibly something irrelevant and idiotic like *I love him please don't let him die.*

"Stay calm, ma'am," the dispatcher says, and Alice wants to roll her eyes. Stay calm? She's calm! She's extremely fucking calm! She's doing unsupervised CPR on the man she's supposed to marry, singing a fucking John Travolta song at him, breathing her extremely calm air into his extremely pretty mouth like a fucking professional!

The next few minutes are a blur of pumping his chest, hoping she's not cracking any ribs, and somehow having the brain space to wonder if shoving her stale, middle-of-the-night breath into his throat counts as their first kiss. Finally she hears the blissful sound of sirens approaching.

"It's okay," she grunts down at him. "They're here. You're gonna be fine."

He, still unconscious, doesn't answer.

The EMTs come running in, wheeling a gurney between them. It all looks familiar to Alice after watching twelve seasons of *Grey's Anatomy,* and she feels like she's on the other side of a TV screen as they shove her aside and take over, calling out things to each other that she has no hope of understanding.

They snap questions at her—how many minutes has it been, did he hit his head, any symptoms before the collapse—most of which she can't really answer.

"What's his name?" asks the main dude, whose name tag reads COREY J.

Thank god, something she knows. Sending up a silent prayer of thanks to herself for the relatively creepy way she always watches the monitor as he taps his ID on the security turnstile, she confidently says, "Nolan Altman, fourteenth floor."

Corey J. the EMT looks over at her, confused. "What?"

Oops. Shit. "Nolan Altman," she says. Corey J. probably doesn't need to know what floor Nolan works on, or the fact that there begins and ends just about everything Alice knows about him.

They finally finish whatever they're doing and load him up onto the gurney. "You coming?" Corey J. asks, looking back at her as they push the gurney toward the exit.

"Oh, I—" There's nothing Alice wants to do less than go in an ambulance, or to the hospital. *Sorry, Nolan,* she thinks. *It's not personal, but honestly, hell no.* "No," she says. "I'll go, um . . . later."

"Okay," he says, but he gives her an odd look as he shoves the stretcher out the glass front doors.

Once the ambulance pulls away, the lobby is silent, like it usually is at four in the morning, but now it's weird. The paramedics didn't leave any stuff behind, and it's not like Nolan was bleeding or anything, so it looks like nothing happened. It's eerie.

It takes a few moments for Alice to move her body, to lurch back to her place behind the desk, but everything feels wrong. She barely notices her computer, the mouse that only sometimes works, the water bottle she faithfully hauls back and forth each day. She can feel the ghost of Nolan's warm chest under her hands, not rising or falling but horribly, horribly still. She sees the dazzling red and blue lights behind her eyelids when she blinks, hears the squeak of the paramedics' rubber shoes on the marble floor. In the empty quiet in front of her, the memory plays in a gruesome loop: Nolan opening his mouth in surprise and then falling to the ground, the heavy smack of his head on the shiny black floor reverberating in surround sound in Alice's mind.

She has to get out of here, away from the artificial heat and echoing silence of this gaping void masquerading as a lobby, but her overnight shift at the reception desk doesn't end for another three hours, and the building is never supposed to be left unattended. What will the entitled rich men who worship at the altar of capitalism do if they walk into their office and aren't greeted by an exhausted-looking woman paid to be nice to them? Drop dead probably.

Well, okay, bad example.

But she saved someone's life—not just *a* someone, but *the* someone—and she's feeling relatively traumatized. "Fuck it," she mutters to herself. She grabs her purse and walks quickly out of the lobby, the click of her low heels the only sound in the world as the door locks silently behind her.

It's freezing out, somewhere between drizzling and misting, wet enough to leave a film of water on her sweater and her eyelashes. Alice and the small trees along the curb shiver in the gentle breeze, both illuminated only by the faint light spilling out of the lobby's windows. In the darkness Alice almost trips over one of those goddamned ubiquitous scooters that some asshole left in the middle of the sidewalk, but even almost face-planting on the wet ground doesn't get her heart pounding as quickly as when she was in the lobby, kneeling over a prone body.

It takes almost half an hour, but her panic does start to recede. Nolan is officially in the hands of the experts. She did everything she could. She thumped on him in her best approximation of CPR, and she got help. Her own heartbeat slows from a gallop to a jouncy trot, and she can feel something hard unclenching at the bottom of her gut as she looks up at the low, dark clouds obscuring the night sky. For those ten minutes or however long it was, the world had narrowed to just her and Nolan Altman, but now, in the clarity of the frigid air, Alice can see the truth of what happened: A man she had a massive crush on but never technically met passed out in front of her, and she got him help. She did a good job, and now it's done.

She really needs to go back to work.

A few minutes later she slinks back into her spot behind the desk. She's probably going to be fired for leaving during her shift—her boss watches the security camera footage like it's Monday Night Football, and will surely notice her absence. Now that she's less panicked, she feels pretty stupid for leaving, but she's not a time traveler so there's nothing she can really do about it. She shivers as she shakes the rain off her hair, breathes a few times into her hands to warm them up, and then jiggles the mouse to wake up her computer.

She goes through her minimal tasks purely by rote—printing out visitor badges for the day, staring at the events calendar, confirming the time the carpet guys will show up to the fifth floor. The early birds start trickling in around six, the pace slowly picking up over the next hour like usual, although the big rush of people won't hit until after her shift ends at seven. The building houses over thirty different businesses, mostly law and financial firms, which all demand twenty-four-hour access and never use it. Except for Nolan Altman, of course, who shows up between midnight and one in the morning at least once a week.

He's been the only bright spot in her long, lonely nights for the two years she's had this job. Beautiful and serious, with sharp features, pale skin, and jet-black hair, always well dressed, striding into the lobby like it's not the middle of the night. He usually gives her a quick smile, and Alice isn't counting or anything but he's said *hi* four times, *hey* three times, and *how's it going* twice. So. A love story for the ages, she's pretty sure.

She really hopes he lives.

By six-thirty there are always a few people around, but today there seems to be some sort of commotion outside the main doors. Alice squints at it and watches as a group of people bustle in, all of them out of place. It looks like a family, a cluster of people in their sixties and a kid in her late teens, maybe? They're all haphazardly dressed, like they threw on whatever was closest, some with more success than others. The youngest looks almost normal in an Oregon State hoodie and sweats except for two different shoes, but one of the older women seems to be wearing a large men's trench coat over a frilly pink nightgown. They're all wet from the rain that's steadily picked up in the last hour, absently brushing the droplets off whatever they're wearing like true Oregonians.

They're all talking at once, pointing around, and Alice is about to call them over to help when she sees her boss stalking toward her.

Oh shit. Alice gulps. Goodbye, boring job. Goodbye, tiny but steady income. Goodbye, paying rent. It was nice knowing you. "Rue!" he bellows, stomping across the incredibly shiny floor. Goodbye, freshly waxed faux marble. "What the hell were you thinking?"

Alice nervously tucks a piece of hair back behind her ear. Goodbye, enough money for semi-regular haircuts from those hairstylists in training. "Mr. Brown, I—"

"You left the building unattended!"

"There was an emergency," Alice says weakly. She's not sure why she's even trying. Brown is a fucking asshole and always has been. He won't give a shit about how she low-key might have saved someone's life. All he cares about, as he has said repeatedly, is *her ass in her chair all night.* He even tried to tell her not to go to the bathroom when she first started working here, which, like, on a ten-hour shift? Yeah, no.

"A tenant, Nolan Altman, he collapsed, and I had to give him CPR," she says, and out of the corner of her eye she sees the lost family all snap to attention and start to rush over to them.

"I don't give a shit—" Brown starts to say, but the woman in the trench coat and nightgown interrupts him with a loud cry.

"Oh my god, it's you!" She reaches over the desk and grabs Alice's face in her hands, which is so startling that Alice forgets to recoil, allowing the woman to get a freakishly strong grip on her cheeks. "You saved my baby boy!"

Oh god. Oh *god.*

"Oh," Alice says, managing to slide her head back and out of this woman's hands. "No, I just—"

"They told us at the hospital that you saved his life," the woman sobs, grasping at Alice's hands now, giving them a superhuman squeeze.

"It's so romantic," the college student gushes. "Saved by your girlfriend."

Okay, honestly, what the fuck? Alice chokes. "Girl—what?"

"Oh, don't worry, sweetie, the cat's out of the bag!" the nightgown woman says, patting her firmly. "No need to keep it a secret anymore—the EMT told us that his girlfriend saved him, and that's you!"

What the actual hell is going on? Alice had always assumed that the *Grey's Anatomy* rumor mill was exaggerated for TV, but maybe it's all true? Fucking Corey J. the EMT!

"No," she says firmly, needing to nip this in the bud. "No, there's been a misunderstanding."

The nightgown woman, who Alice figures must be Nolan's mom, has somehow come around behind the desk and Alice finds herself enveloped in an enormous mom hug. The woman is round and soft, and the feeling of being pulled into her makes something bereft and primal rise up inside Alice's chest, an echo of a cry she'd learned to ignore years ago. The words catch in her throat, just for a second.

"You should be proud of your employee," the other older woman says to Brown, looking at him a bit shrewdly. "She single-handedly saved the life of one of your most successful, um . . ." She stops for a second, clearly searching for the right word. "Clients?"

"Tenants," Alice hisses at her, and the woman takes the suggestion much too loudly.

"*Tenants,* who happens to be her boyfriend, and my nephew."

"Oh," Brown says, awkwardly shuffling his feet. Alice can tell that he's not quite sure how to go about firing her in front of this family, especially now that one of the men is vigorously shaking his hand and the mom is sobbing all over Alice's favorite shirt, babbling about how Alice is a hero. "Err, right,"

Brown finally says, backing away from the desk. "Uh, good work, I guess."

"I—thank you?" Alice gingerly pats Nolan's mom on the back. She's torn between needing to clear up this whole girlfriend thing immediately and wanting to wait until Brown's out of earshot. The family angle is definitely the only thing keeping her employed right now, and she's not about to look a gift horse in the mouth.

"Come back to the hospital with us," Nolan's mom says, tugging at her. "He'll want to see you when he wakes up."

"Oh no. No, no, no," Alice says quickly. He certainly will not want to see her when he wakes up. He doesn't know her name, and probably couldn't pick her out of a lineup. She's pretty sure he doesn't spend all week breathlessly waiting to catch sight of her. She can't imagine how weird it would be to wake up after an aneurysm or whatever this was and see the loving faces of your entire family plus someone you can barely place.

Also it's a hospital. Alice doesn't do hospitals, not anymore.

She absolutely cannot go with them, but Mr. Brown is still standing there, staring at her. "My shift isn't over," she says weakly.

"I'm sure your boss can cover for you," the shrewd woman who is apparently Nolan's aunt says, something almost evil in her eye. She'd clearly heard Brown gearing up to fire Alice, and she's obviously not having it. Alice quickly slots her into the category of "chaotic good" and can't help but like her. "Right, Mr. . . . ?"

"Brown," he says quickly. "Robert Brown."

"Mr. Brown," the aunt says smoothly. "I'm sure you won't begrudge letting, um, this lovely young woman visit her boyfriend in the hospital with us."

Please, lady, Alice thinks, *make it more obvious you don't know my name.*

"Of . . . of course not," Brown stutters. "I can, uh . . . I guess I can sit here until the day-shift girls come."

"Girls?" the college student asks, her head tilted. "Do you employ children here, Mr. Brown?" He stares at her, obviously not computing, and Alice tries not to laugh. She wishes she were actually dating Nolan. His family is clearly hilarious. "Because if they're adults," she goes on, eyes narrowed now in a clear challenge, "I think the word you're looking for is 'women.'"

"Uh, right," he manages, surrendering to whatever is happening right now. "Women. Right. Well, Rue, off you go."

He clearly can't get rid of the family quickly enough, and Alice is too stunned to come up with an excuse to get out of this hospital visit that doesn't include *yeah, no, we've never actually spoken, please blame Corey J. the gossiping EMT.* She'll have to break it to them outside, or in the car or something. Maybe at the hospital, like right outside the doors so she doesn't have to go in?

Nolan's mom pulls her out of the building and neatly shoves her into an enormous SUV that's been parked in front of a fire hydrant this entire time. Alice finds herself wedged between the mom and the chaotic aunt in the middle row of seats, while the college student clambers over her to sit in the back row and the two men who Alice can't tell apart settle into the front.

"Listen," Alice tries to say, but they're all talking at once, their voices overlapping as they finish one another's thoughts in what seems like three different simultaneous conversations, all over the thumping sound of the windshield wipers. "I'm sorry, I don't know how it got to this point, but—"

"It's okay," Nolan's mom says, absently patting her cheek while the men in the front debate the fastest route to the hospital. "We didn't know about you either, sweetheart. But that's our Nolie, isn't it? Such a private boy! He's always kept his girlfriends as far away from us as he could. Worried we'd scare them off, I bet!"

"No," Alice says for what feels like the millionth time. She's not sure when the right moment to dump this news on them is, if there even is a right moment. It's definitely not now, when they're halfway through the drive to the hospital, the college student aggressively shouting directions from the backseat and the driver resolutely ignoring them, but this seems to be spiraling very quickly out of control. Alice waits for a red light and once the car has come to a stop she takes a deep breath and, in a miraculous second of quiet, says in her loudest, clearest voice, "I'm not his girlfriend."

She expects that to be that. She's ready to tell them everything—well, maybe not everything. They probably don't need to know about her stalkery crush on their comatose son. She'll tell them it was all a misunderstanding, a literal game of telephone gone wrong from the dispatcher to the EMT to them, and hopefully it'll be a funny part of the story they tell one another in the years to come, once Nolan is awake and healthy again.

But that's not quite what happens.

"Oh sure, Marie's told us all about that," Nolan's mom says, waving a dismissive hand. "Labels like that are for old people, or something, I don't know."

The college student, ostensibly Marie, leans forward, her face now way too close to Alice's. "They're outdated," she says, a long-suffering tone in her voice. "I keep telling you, Mom, we've progressed beyond the need for labels and binaries, like, as a society."

Alice wants to scream. She's as bisexual as the next person, but this is not some highly evolved plea for implied polyamory or whatever. She literally does not know this man!

"But whatever you call it," Nolan's mom says, talking smoothly over her daughter, "knowing that he has you in his life made all of us breathe easier this morning. We're always so worried about him being alone and working so much."

"Oh god," Alice mutters. Great. This is just great.

The mom wraps her arm around Alice and pulls her into a side hug as the SUV barrels down the narrow street. Alice feels like she's in one of those inspirational videos where an orphaned animal is adopted by a mom of another species; she knows this isn't her mom, not anywhere close, but she can also feel herself going limp and submissive in her grasp. Once again, she fails to respond quickly enough to tell the truth.

"He had someone there for him," the chaotic aunt adds from Alice's other side. "Knowing that he had someone he loved there with him in those last moments—he's going to wake up, I know he is, but if he doesn't—well, that's a real comfort to us."

Fuck.

Fucking fucking fuck!

What the fuck is she supposed to do now? Say, *Sorry to break it to you, but if your beloved son/nephew/brother dies, the last person he ever saw was a complete fucking stranger? He spent his nights working by himself in his office and he died in the lobby, completely alone except for the receptionist who didn't properly know how to perform CPR?*

"Is he—is he going to wake up? What did they say?"

"We don't know," one of the men says from the front seat.

"They said we have to wait and see. Maybe Van will know more when we get back. She was going to make some calls."

Alice takes in a deep, shuddering breath.

Okay, she can handle this.

If he wakes up, she'll be able to drop the bomb on them because they'll be so elated that he's alive that her lie won't even register on their radar. And hey, maybe he'll be so grateful to her for saving his life that they'll fall in love for real, the lie forgotten, and this will end up being the most overdramatic meet-cute in the world. Right? Alice has read romance novels; she knows how this shit works.

And if he doesn't wake up . . . well. Is letting them believe this white lie really that bad? Letting them think he had company and comfort in his last weeks, last moments?

"This is kind of awkward," she manages to say, Nolan's mom's arm still around her. "But he never actually told me any of your names."

Not a lie, technically.

Marie laughs out loud, and Alice steels herself. She can do this. Just until he wakes up.

Or doesn't.

TWO

Alice walks toward the hospital, blankly following Nolan's mom, who is apparently named Barbara but insists that Alice call her Babs. Alice personally would rather be called almost anything other than Babs, but, sure. To each her own slightly infantilizing nickname. His Aunt Sheila is absolutely booking it inside, and Alice and Marie are practically running after them to keep up while the men park the car.

Alice almost balks at the entrance to the hospital. She hasn't been in one in over a decade, not since she was nineteen, and she'd honestly hoped to never cross the threshold of Portland Grace, or any other hospital, ever again.

But here she is, about to go in not for her own dad, but for someone she's never really met. Or, well. For his family, she guesses. For Babs and Aunt Sheila and sweet Marie and the two boomer men she's still struggling to tell apart. She takes a deep breath—one last breath that doesn't smell like sterile plastic and antiseptic—and she forces herself inside.

They ride up to the fourth floor, and Aunt Sheila bolts out of the elevator before the doors are fully open.

"Alice, what's your last name?" Marie asks as they breathlessly stride out of the elevator in a futile attempt to catch up. "I need to find you on Instagram."

Oh definitely no. Alice's Instagram is basically a graveyard, but it has a suspicious lack of Nolan on it. "I don't have one," she lies, resolving to delete her account at the first opportunity. "But it's Rue. Like rue the day."

"Alice Rue." Marie scrunches up her nose. "That's so cute I almost hate it," she says and Alice, for the first time today, laughs.

"Hey, we can't all be Altmans," she says, and Marie grins, pretending to flip her hair. The move is slightly compromised by the two different colored Crocs she's wearing, but something about her energy is infectious anyway.

God, Alice would love to be an Altman.

Marie links her arm with Alice's, which makes Alice almost stumble in surprise. She doesn't have what one might consider friends and she's so painfully single she seems to have hallucinated an entire relationship, so it's been a minute since she's touched anyone. Marie doesn't seem to notice, still grinning as she says, "Well, none of us are going to rue the day we met you, I'll tell you that much."

Alice laughs again but this time it's fake, high and way too loud. Alice is going to rue the day she was fucking born, that's for sure. She's moderately confident that Nolan doesn't have any social media, but now she's paranoid about it. She's spent many hours searching for Nolan on Instagram without finding him—she's not a stalker, she's simply insanely bored at work and also maybe very lonely—but what if he does have one? Alice is clearly not going to be on it, and, shit, what if there's another girl pictured? Oh god, what if he really has a girlfriend?

How did a simple, private little crush get so complicated? It's enough to make her regret maybe saving his life altogether.

Marie pulls her down the long hallway, and Alice tries to repress the flashbacks dancing between her eyes, the way her gorge is rising at the familiar fluorescent lights, the steady whirs of the machines, the squeak of comfortable nursing shoes on linoleum. It's all as familiar as breathing and she hates it with every molecule in her body.

"He's in here," Marie says, pushing Alice into the last room on the right. The first thing Alice sees is Nolan in the bed. He's in a gown, with an oxygen cannula in his nose. His hands are flat at his sides, and the blanket is tucked under his armpits, unnaturally smooth. Purely by habit, Alice's eyes flick to the monitors, but then she drops them. His vitals are none of her business. Besides, she can tell the important thing from looking at him. He's still not woken up.

He looks terrible, pale and wan under the thick black hair that Alice has always loved. Something clenches in her chest. This is the man she's been pining after for 751 days, and this is how she's meeting his family, learning how his mom brushes the hair out of his face, how his aunt bustles around the room like it needs fixing. This is her first sight of him outside of his tailored suits, and it's all wrong. Nothing is supposed to be this way.

It becomes very clear, between one heartbeat and the next, that Alice absolutely cannot handle this. Not him lying motionless in this bed. Not the hospital, not the loving mom, not the little sister hanging on her arm. None of it. She can feel the old signs of a panic attack forming behind her eyes, signs she hasn't felt in years. The world is closing in around her; her chest feels too tight and her brain too swollen for her skull, just like when she was a kid, standing in this same building.

She turns on her heel, ready to flee, plan be damned, but she crashes straight into a wall that has a surprising amount of give.

"Oomph," the wall says. "What in the—"

The wall is gripping onto her arms now, and the small part of Alice that isn't consumed with panic registers that the wall is probably a person.

"Hey, are you okay?"

Certainly the most compassionate wall Alice has ever met, with a pleasantly gravelly voice, like the owner doesn't use it much. The hands on her biceps are big and strong, somehow holding her up but still gentle. The wall smells amazing, a combination of cologne and a slightly feminine shampoo that cuts beautifully through the ubiquitous stench of hospital disinfectant.

A tiny corner of Alice's mind clears, and she realizes that the wall is quite possibly the most stunning butch she's ever seen.

She looks like Nolan—same coloring, same square jaw, same strong nose, same devastating cheekbones—but softer where he almost veers into hawkish. Marie looks like Nolan watered down, but this person makes Nolan look like the one who is a faint copy. She's tall and solid, wearing an extremely stereotypical flannel shirt tucked into dark jeans.

"You okay?" she asks again, and the way her dark brown eyes bore into Alice's is way too much for Alice's poor bisexual brain.

"Yes," Alice manages, shoving the panic as far down as she can. Each breath smells like butch now, and Alice closes her eyes for a second, letting it ground her. "Sorry. Yes."

"Van, this is Alice," Babs says. "Nolan's girlfriend."

Van's eyebrows shoot up and she abruptly releases her grip on Alice's arms like Alice's sweater was about to burst into flames beneath her palms. "Girlfriend? Nolan?" She looks around, almost like she's double-checking that she's in the right room. "Seriously, *girlfriend*?"

Alice swallows. Van looks skeptical about all of it—the existence of a girlfriend and said girlfriend being Alice—and that's very much a bad thing. Or, is it? Alice, lost in a butch haze, can't quite remember if she wants to be found out or not.

"Isn't it just like Nolie to keep such a sweet girl from us," Babs says, shaking her head and patting her son fondly on the leg over the blanket. "He's such a funny boy sometimes."

Marie rolls her eyes. "Can you blame him, Mom? The last time he let you meet someone, you asked how fertile the women in her family are."

Alice, still more than halfway to a panic attack, chokes back a laugh.

"What?" Babs says, for all the world like that's a normal thing to have done. "It was only a question."

"We hadn't even ordered drinks yet," Marie says with the kind of exasperation only teenagers can muster, and Alice finds her attention sliding away from the family drama and back to Van, like the woman is some sort of magnet.

Van looks at Alice again, like she's taking an X-ray with her eyes. Alice feels Van's gaze slide over her reddish-brown hair, which after the night and day she's had, and the number of times it's been wet in the rain, is more oily frizz than careful wave. Van's eyes take in what must be dark exhausted circles under her eyes, dropping down to her body—twenty pounds heavier than Alice would like it to be—and her clothes, all of which were bought off bargain basement sales racks at least four years ago and are, in a word, uninspired. Alice knows that she absolutely does not look like someone who should be dating any tenants of the office building, not to mention one as well-dressed as Nolan.

"Alice, this is Van, Nolan's sister."

Well, yes, Alice had guessed, based on the same-face situation, but still good to get confirmation. "Right," she says, like maybe Nolan had mentioned having a sister during one of their many dates. Two sisters, in fact. "Van. Of course."

"Van, honey, did you reach your neurologist?"

Van tears her suspicious eyes away from Alice, and Alice tries not to be obvious about her relief. She's still only about an inch away from losing it, and being scrutinized by the hot butch doppelgänger of her forever crush is certainly not helping to make any of this less complicated.

"Yeah, for a minute. She said basically the same thing as the one here." She says a bunch of words in a row that Alice recognizes separately but has no idea what they mean when put in that order, and one that sounds like "hippopotamus," which surely can't be right. Luckily Alice isn't the only idiot in the room; everyone else makes confused noises until Van translates. "All we can do is wait and see."

Babs sighs. "Oh, my poor boy," she whispers, and strokes his hair.

Alice drops her gaze as Babs starts to cry. Fuck, she really shouldn't be here.

Marie and Aunt Sheila both fold in on Babs, murmuring words of comfort. Van stays where she is, her hands scrunched into her front pockets like she doesn't know what to do with them.

Alice obviously doesn't know her at all—that's kind of the whole deal about right now—but something about the clearly gay sibling standing so outside the family dynamic, so apart from the womanly display of grief but not out parking the car with the men . . . damn. Alice is trying not to get any deeper in with this family than she already is, but Van's very presence is gripping at the edges of her rib cage with something that feels an awful lot like maybe Alice was the one getting CPR.

THREE

By eleven in the morning, Alice is so exhausted that she's not sure she can keep her story straight anymore. She works from nine at night until seven in the morning, and she's usually asleep within an hour of getting home. And it's not like today has been calm or normal in the slightest.

She's sitting in one of the plastic chairs in the waiting area, trying to figure out how to get the hell out of here without blowing her cover, but her brain is moving too slowly to come up with any actual plans.

It feels like each of her blinks is taking longer than normal, which explains how Van is somehow able to come and sit next to her without her noticing.

"Hey, no offense," Van says, "but you look dead on your feet."

Alice looks over at her, trying and most likely failing to scowl. "That's probably a very offensive thing to say in a hospital," she hears herself saying. But, oh shit! Bad Alice! Don't make dead people jokes to the person whose brother is in a coma right now. "Fuck. Sorry. I didn't—"

But Van cuts her off with a laugh, something low and deep that feels oddly private. "You're good, Allie."

"Alice," she quickly corrects, and Van nods her apology.

"Right, sorry. Alice." She drops her head back, rubbing at her eyes. "I knew that. Alice, wonderland, et cetera. Long morning."

"Yeah," Alice says softly. "No worries." Van's eyes are closed, so Alice lets herself take in Van's broad shoulders, her long neck, her delicate ears, the sharp lines of a recent haircut at the nape of her neck. For the first time, she actually thinks about the fact that most humans are not awake at four in the morning and Nolan's family must have all been woken up by a phone call from the hospital, grabbing whatever clothes were nearest and bolting. "Probably not the best wake-up call you've ever had?"

Van lets out a sarcastic little chuckle, dropping her hand and opening her eyes again. "Yeah, can't say I recommend it," she says. Alice wonders if her voice is a little hoarse because she's tired, or if that's how it always is.

"Fucking Nolan," Van says, shifting to lean forward now with her elbows on her knees. Alice narrows her eyes, trying to figure Van out. She sounds irritated now, almost pissed, which is a stark departure from everything that's happened so far. "God, he's always had the worst timing."

Alice is apparently way too tired to filter herself. "In fairness, not sure there's ever a good time for a traumatic brain injury."

Van looks over and gives Alice a wry smile. "Well, yeah. But today, tonight . . . it's the first night of Chanukah. Big deal for our family."

Alice tries to pretend like she knew Nolan is Jewish and when Chanukah is and also remembered that Chanukah exists.

"Oh right," she says, probably too quickly and definitely too loudly. "Yeah. Slipped my mind, I guess. So weird!"

Overkill, possibly.

"Whatever," Van says. "I mean, it doesn't matter, but I was going to—whatever. Anyway." She shakes her head a little bit, like a horse trying to dislodge a fly. "Listen, my mom said you work nights?" Alice nods. "You must be exhausted."

Alice tries to smile but she's pretty sure it comes out as a grimace. "Understatement."

"Let me take you home," Van says, smoothly standing up. "You should get some rest."

"Oh no, I can take an Uber," Alice says, standing too, letting this be the motivation she needs to get the hell out of here. "I don't live nearby."

Van looks horrified. "Yeah, no. No way am I letting my brother's girlfriend slash savior take an Uber home after being awake all night." Alice opens her mouth to protest again, but Van clearly isn't having it. "I have to pick up my dog anyway," she says, taking Alice's elbow and steering her back toward Nolan's room.

"Hey, Mom? I'm going to get Frank from Sarah's house and drop Alice off to get some sleep. I'll be back later."

Alice tilts her head in confusion. Frank? Van said dog . . . Is her dog named Frank? Alice can't decide if that's weird or charming.

"Ugh, Sarah," Marie mumbles, wrinkling up her nose in distaste. "Poor Frank."

Alice blinks over at her. It's the first unkind word she's heard the teenager say. Alice is surprised, and looks at Van to gauge her reaction to the judgment about her choice in dogsitter, but Van is almost smiling.

"Down, girl," she mutters to Marie, whose face breaks into a genuine smile.

"Okay, sweetie," Babs says from where she's perched on the foot of Nolan's bed, obviously accustomed to ignoring snarky, good-natured asides between her children. "Come, give me a kiss, and drive safe."

Van obediently walks over and drops a kiss on her mom's cheek. Alice looks away.

"Alice," Babs says, something almost stern in her voice. "Come here, honey."

Alice shuffles forward and lets Babs envelop her in yet another hug. She's so tired and overwhelmed and confused that it feels like all her emotions are right up at the surface, and she's horrified to feel the first prick of tears in her eyes.

"It's going to be okay," Babs murmurs, clearly mistaking where Alice's emotions are coming from. "He's going to wake up soon. I know it."

Alice says something back, she's not sure what, and lets Van guide her out of the room. All she feels is Van's hand on her lower back as she stumbles down the long hallway, into and out of the elevator, and out the main entrance. Alice blinks at the natural light, even though the sun is—as always—dimmed by the layers and layers of heavy clouds in the sky. She feels like she's tilting off her axis, but Van's hand is steady as she wordlessly directs Alice toward her car.

"God, is this how bright the daytime always is?" Alice asks, squinting up at Van. It never gets that bright in Portland in the winter, but still. "I feel like a fucking vampire right now."

Van laughs, a deep chuckle that rumbles in her chest more than it escapes out of her mouth.

They walk for a while until Van unlocks what looks like the world's oldest station wagon. It probably began its life as white, but it's now a sort of road-grimed beige, and it's way boxier than anything made in this century. Alice loves it. She settles into the passenger seat, the worn leather embracing her like a favorite jacket, soft in all the right places. The car smells like Van, like she's hotboxed it with her very essence.

Alice doesn't have a car. She takes the bus or MAX light rail everywhere, or Uber when she's desperate and has a hankering for credit card debt. She hasn't sat in the front seat of a car in ages. She takes in the little bits and bobs scattered around, things that mark this car as Van's territory, as an extension of Van herself. The water bottle and thermal mug in the cupholders, the energy bar wrapper and exercise band at Alice's feet, the little wooden turtles with the swaying heads on the dashboard.

As Van starts to drive, Alice is forcibly reminded of being a little kid, how safe she always felt in the backseat of her dad's car at night, when the streetlights would whoosh past and she'd fall asleep to the soft lull of her parents in the front seat, the seatbelt digging into her neck and the window cold against her forehead.

But this isn't her dad's car. This shouldn't feel safe, shouldn't be sending her back into that feeling of peace. Alice is in quite possibly the most absurdly precarious position of her life, alone in this car with a literal stranger who thinks Alice is someone she isn't.

She knows she should take this moment to tell Van the truth, to clear things up with the person who seems like the most suspicious, and possibly most levelheaded Altman. Tell her that she doesn't want to make Babs and Aunt Sheila sad but the whole thing is a giant misunderstanding, and help!

But Alice can't stop thinking about Van's hand on her lower back, Van holding the elevator door for her, Van making sure she's getting home okay, Van easing up to each stop sign and red light with the gentlest application of the brakes Alice has ever felt.

It's been so fucking long since anyone has taken care of Alice that she'd almost forgotten what it feels like. She never wants to get out of this car, this cocoon of warmth and comfort, this embodiment of security that has been so far out of her reach for so long.

She doesn't say a thing.

Van doesn't take her home right away. She crosses the Ross Island Bridge and then turns south, pulling up at a little house in a cute middle-class neighborhood near the river that Alice has never been to, and tells Alice to wait in the car. She disappears inside for a minute before emerging with an enormous skinny white dog on a leash. The dog is positively prancing, his narrow butt dancing around with joy at seeing Van, and he's wriggling like a puppy. But he's clearly not a puppy, because he's tall as fuck. He would easily come up to Alice's hip, and he's all legs and elbows, with floppy ears, light brown speckles, and an enormous grin. His tongue is lolling out of his mouth as he shamelessly rubs his side against Van, and Alice is climbing out of the car before she can decide if it's a good idea or not.

"Thanks, Sarah," Van is saying to the woman standing in the doorway, who Alice was too distracted to notice. She's short and pretty, with long blond hair and a thick white sweater dress. "I appreciate it."

Alice is an expert at people watching—there's not a lot to do, otherwise, when you're a receptionist with no friends and no one to actually talk to. She prides herself on her ability to read people and relationships at a glance, and she wouldn't have needed the *ugh* tip-off from Marie to clock them as exes.

From the way they're standing weirdly far apart, Sarah with her arms crossed over her chest like a shield, the tension thick in the air between them, they might as well be shouting that they used to see each other naked, but they haven't done so recently enough to make dogsitting normal. Alice wants to ask, but it's none of her business. Although if she's pretending to be, like, Van's future sister-in-law, maybe it's exactly her business? Fuck, but this is the kind of messy confusion that makes her need to confess everything immediately.

As soon as Sarah closes the front door, Van turns and leads the prancing dog/pony toward Alice. "Alice, allow me to introduce you to Frank," Van says, and Alice can't help but grin at the formal introduction. She decides the name is charming.

"Hello, Frank," she says. "Nice to meet you." She holds out a hand and Frank wiggles himself into a sit and then offers her a paw. Alice's heart explodes as she bends down to shake it. "Oh my *god*."

"Good boy, Franko," Van says with a grin, patting his head. "Very nice manners."

"Quite a gentleman," Alice agrees, and Van laughs.

"We'll see if you say that the next time you're over at Mom's and he tries to sit on your lap. He thinks he's a lapdog but he has the boniest ass on earth."

Alice laughs, trying to ignore the part about being over at Babs's house. She's really not ready for that.

Van gets Frank into the car, letting his muddy feet stomp all over the towel draped across the backseat, while Alice returns to her spot up front. Van hands over her phone, Alice types her address into the map, and Van wordlessly drives her a little north and a lot east. They pass by Alice's favorite food truck after a few minutes, and Alice points it out to have something to say in the slightly awkward silence, even though it's not open yet. "That truck has the best bao." She gestures at it, and Van dutifully slows down to look.

"I've never been to it."

"Oh," Alice says, not quite sure how to keep this conversation going. "Well, add it to your list."

"Noted," Van says, and Alice lets it go. She tries not to think about bao. She should probably be hungry, but she's too tired for that.

Alice sinks deeper into herself as they turn in to her neighborhood. It's not a bad place to live—there's nothing particularly wrong with it—but it's certainly nothing like Sarah's neighborhood of cute little traditional Portland Craftsman houses. It's nothing like where Nolan must live.

"I know it's probably not what you were expecting," she starts as they pull up in front of Alice's apartment building, one of many out here on Division between Eightieth and Ninetieth, but then she trails off. Her eyes skate over the peeling paint on the side of the building and the overflowing dumpsters in the wet parking lot before dropping down to her hands, clenched hard in her lap. "It's nicer than it looks," she says to her hands.

It's not, really.

It's quiet, and Alice looks over to see Van staring at her like she's trying to see through her. Alice shrinks a little, trying not to get consumed by her dark eyes. There's a long quiet beat, and then Van runs a hand through her hair. It looks thick and straight, and Alice wonders how much heavier it must be than her own thin frizz.

"I don't know what Nolan told you about the family," Van finally says, her voice so soft Alice can barely hear it. "But he's the only one . . . we're not all rich. Just . . . just him."

"Oh." Alice hadn't considered that. There hadn't been time

to consider anything, of course, but no, she'd definitely assumed that his whole family was top-floor-financial-firm people. Though this nineties-style station wagon certainly isn't giving off custom-tailored-suit vibes.

"I mean, we're all fine, but Nolan is, uh . . . I don't know. Dad calls him the retirement fund."

Alice wonders just how rich Nolan is, how recently he got that way. She wonders where he lives, what his lifestyle is like. What car he drives. If he helps his parents out with their mortgage or rent or whatever. She's guessing, from the twist of Van's mouth, that she might not like the answers to those questions. She wonders, for what is definitely the first time since he dropped onto the pristine floor of her lobby, and quite possibly the first time since she saw him 751 days ago and fell in love, if he's a nice person. If she would have liked him, if they'd ever had the chance to talk to each other. If he'd like her.

He said *how's it going* to her twice but he never waited for her to answer.

"I think I might know less about you all than you think I do," Alice says carefully. She's trying really hard not to lie, even though she knows it won't matter. Betrayal is betrayal is betrayal, and none of them are going to remember her exact words when the truth smacks them in the face, but something about knowing she hasn't said the lie outright makes deceiving them five percent easier for Alice to live with. At this point, she'll take what she can get.

"Okay," Van says, her face easing again. She smiles, and Alice tries not to be captivated. "We can work on that."

Alice gets out of the car, planning to lean down and wave goodbye, but Van is getting out too. "We'll walk you up," she says, opening Frank's door.

"Oh, you don't have to—" Alice starts, but Van is already striding toward the front door of the building.

What is it with these Altman women and walking so damned quickly? Alice has to nearly jog to keep up. "You and Frank seem well suited," she says as she fumbles for her keys. "Long-ass legs."

Van makes a quiet sound in her chest that Alice can't quite parse, and then Alice is pushing the door open. She feels incredibly awkward as Van and Frank follow her up the two flights of stairs to her third-floor apartment. What exactly is the protocol for when your fake-boyfriend's hot sister and her dog walk you to your door after you leave his hospital room? Alice obsessively reads advice columns but somehow this particular scenario has never come up.

"Um, this is me," she says when they finally reach her door. She's not sure what to do with her hands so she ends up weirdly tapping her knuckles against the doorframe.

"Okay," Van says, but she's not turning to go.

Maybe she's literally waiting for Alice to get inside. Excessive, but kind of nice. Alice sticks her key into the lock and jiggles it back and forth, rocking the knob in a very choreographed move that she does every day but hasn't thought about in years.

"Wow." Alice can hear the smile in Van's voice. "You really need to make love to that thing, huh?"

The laugh that throws itself out of her chest feels almost hysterical. Today has been so much. Too much. Alice is one sex joke away from a complete and total meltdown.

The key sex works, and the lock slides open. Alice turns the knob before looking back at Van in triumph. "Door orgasm achieved." She wrinkles up her forehead as she thinks. "Doorgasm?"

"Doorgasm," Van says, nodding seriously like they've settled an important point at the UN General Assembly.

Alice bites her lip, looking down to stare at how Van's scuffed sneakers stand out against the stained brown hallway carpet. "Well, um . . . thank you. For the ride. And, uh. Everything."

"Of course."

There's a beat, and Alice looks up into Van's eyes.

Big mistake.

Van is looking at her like she's fragile, a breath away from shattering into a million pieces. Van is right.

"Are you okay to be alone?" she asks, her voice softer than it's been all day.

Alice can't help the way a laugh turns into a hiccupping sob somewhere behind her vocal cords. Van has no fucking idea how good at being alone Alice is.

Van takes a step forward, clearly interpreting Alice's wet eyes and erratic emotional state as a *no*.

"I'm fine," Alice gasps. "Just overtired, I think."

"Okay," Van says slowly, clearly not believing her for a second. "Well, it's been a rough day for Frank too." Alice stares at her, confusion cutting neatly through the swirls of darkness in her chest. The dog seems to be the only one who had a nice, non-traumatic morning. She supposes hanging out with your mom's ex could be triggering for a dog of a certain emotional intelligence, although the way Frank's tongue is currently lolling out the side of his mouth doesn't exactly make him seem like a candidate for Mensa.

But then Van says, "I think he might need a hug," and, oh.

Alice is horrified to feel tears slipping down her cheeks. She hasn't openly cried in front of another human being in thirteen years and she'd hoped to never do so again, but here she is, fucking weeping in front of a total stranger. She brushes them off, pretending it's not happening. She focuses on the dog, trying to convince herself that Van isn't there.

"Is that so, Frankie? Do you need some affection?"

Van must signal to him, because he sits and then lifts both front paws off the ground, for all the world like he's offering her a hug.

This is the most confusing and complicated day of Alice's life. She saved someone who might die anyway, gained a fake-boyfriend who might be a jerk, and is now lying to a half dozen of the nicest people she's ever met, including someone who might possibly be her dream woman.

She drops to her knees and wraps her arms around Frank. He rests his paws on her shoulders and nuzzles his face into her hair, somehow managing to lick the inside of her ear on the first try. It makes her laugh and squirm, but she doesn't let go of the hug for a few long breaths. Frank smells surprisingly good, and he's warm and soft under her hands. When she pulls back enough to scratch him behind the ears, he closes his eyes in bliss and his tongue falls out the side of his mouth again. She doesn't even care if he's leaving muddy paw prints on her shoulders.

"Thanks, baby," she says to him, and it's only when Van makes another little sound that Alice remembers that she's there. That Van is watching her cry into her very tall dog's neck.

Alice hauls herself to her feet, swaying a little until she catches herself on the doorframe. She doesn't miss the way Van's hands twitch, like she was ready to spring into action to catch Alice like some action hero.

God, they should make butch action heroes.

"Here," Van says, pulling something out of her pocket and

handing it to Alice with what might possibly be a tinge of shyness. "My cell is on there. Call or text when you wake up, or if you need a ride back to the hospital or anything."

Alice nods, sliding the card into her own pocket. It's still warm from the heat of Van's body, and it burns against Alice's thigh.

Alice watches as Van and Frank turn to go, as Van pauses at the top of the stairwell with slightly pink cheeks to say, "Um . . . sweet dreams, Alice."

FOUR

Alice doesn't seem to be fired. The day-shift receptionists ask her incessantly about what happened when she shows up to relieve them, but Mr. Brown doesn't make an appearance. She'll take that as a win.

Being alone in the lobby after everyone else leaves seems eerier tonight. It had freaked her out for her first week or two of the job, until she got used to being the only awake human on the entire block, completely unprotected should some sort of murderer come on a receptionist-killing rampage. But tonight Alice can't stop thinking about the fact that if she were to have a clot in her brain, no one would find her until morning. She'd die completely alone.

It's not like she wouldn't be alone if she had a coronary at home either, but she spends most of her time at home asleep, so it's not where she does most of her existential rumination on the fleeting nature of life.

Alice tries to pass the time like she normally does—alternating between mystery and romance novels, watching cooking competitions on her phone, half-heartedly flipping through the community college bookkeeping course list for the millionth time—but none of it holds her attention.

It feels like hundreds of years pass before the front doors open a few minutes after six in the morning. Alice looks up, ready to greet whatever white-collar breadwinner hates sleeping, but the words catch in her throat, because the person striding inside is unmistakably Van.

It's almost déjà vu. How many times has Alice seen Nolan walking in those doors, wearing a nearly identical face? How many times has she breathlessly watched him cross the empty lobby, wondering if he's going to nod to her this morning, or maybe even say hello? How many times has she watched the way the fancy lights glint in his thick black hair?

But of course, Van isn't wearing a bespoke suit and dress shoes polished to a shine. She's wearing dark jeans and a green quilted jacket, and what look suspiciously like work boots. Instead of a briefcase or bag, she's carrying two coffee cups, and she's not walking toward the security turnstiles, but instead heading directly to Alice.

"Hey," Van says as she approaches the desk. Her voice is quiet, but it still echoes off all of the marbled surfaces.

"Hi," Alice manages to say, wondering if this is some kind of apparition her brain has invented to cure her of boredom.

"You, uh . . ." Van looks nervous. She's shifting from foot to foot, and she doesn't meet Alice's eye. "You didn't text."

"Oh," Alice says softly. She'd stared at Van's business card for probably an hour around three in the morning, memorizing the way it read TOTAL BODY PHYSICAL THERAPY above VANESSA ALTMAN, DPT, all in a sort of inoffensively bland peach color. She'd input Van's number into her phone, but no. She had not texted.

"I didn't have your number," Van explains, carefully placing one of the coffee cups on the desk between them. "But I figured I might find you here."

"Good guess." Alice looks closely at her. Van looks haggard. Alice wonders if she slept at all, if something has happened to Nolan. She wonders where Frank is.

"I, um, I brought you some tea. Herbal, 'cause I know it's almost the end of your night." She nudges the cup closer to Alice, and Alice's heart does a flippy melty thing that she decides not to think about at this particular moment.

She's not supposed to have anyone behind the desk, ever, but she gestures to the spot next to her. "Do you want to sit?"

Van nods, walking around the ridiculously large desk and perching on the high stool next to Alice. She moves like she's used to being a bull in a china shop, like she's always about to break something, which confuses the hell out of Alice because so far Van seems to be the most careful, gentle, body-aware person she's ever met.

"Thank you," Alice says softly, taking a sip of her tea. It's chamomile and something else soothing . . . lavender, maybe? There's honey in it, and it's the perfect temperature. "This is amazing."

Van takes a sip of her own drink, something almost bashful in the tilt of her head.

"I didn't want to overstep," Van finally says, and Alice is reaching out before she can stop herself. The instant her hand closes over Van's wrist, Van's entire body stills.

Two of Alice's fingers have landed on the cuff of Van's jacket, and the other two on the smooth skin of the back of her hand. It's not possible but Alice is pretty sure she can feel Van's thudding heartbeat.

"You didn't," Alice says, staring hard at Van's face until Van finally turns to look at her. "Really."

A slow smile grows across Van's face, but it doesn't start at the corners of her mouth. It starts with a softening of her eyes, and it seems to almost float down her face, smoothing her cheeks and easing a muscle in her jaw, before her lips finally tug up, and Alice catches a hint of dimples. She's so pretty that Alice can barely breathe, although in fairness some of that is probably from the feeling of Van's skin under her fingertips, the scent of Van's body slowly filling the sterile space behind the desk.

"Is there any news on Nolan?"

Something shutters behind Van's eyes. She drops her gaze again, reaching for her coffee with the hand Alice was just touching. "No," she says quietly. "No change. I was there all night."

"I'm sorry," Alice says, and it's only when Van looks at her a little weird that Alice realizes that's a strange thing to say about your own boyfriend. She tries to correct. "You must be exhausted."

Van nods. "I was on my way home to sleep, but I wanted to see how you were doing."

Jesus fucking Christ. This was a terrible idea from the start—not that it was even Alice's idea—but the deeper she gets with Van, the more Van thinks about her and takes care of her, the harder it's all going to get. She absolutely cannot keep doing this. She can't. Alice gathers her courage, takes a deep breath, and starts to bail. "Van, I need to tell you . . . things with me and Nolan, they weren't . . ." She trails off, not sure how to say it. It's only been twenty-four hours but that already feels so impossibly long to have kept the lie going. She tries again. "I don't know how to say this . . ."

"It's okay," Van says, and this time she's the one putting her hand on Alice's arm. It's a fleeting touch, she doesn't leave it there like Alice had, but it messes Alice up just the same. "I don't need to know the details."

Alice huffs out a breath. Why won't any of these damn Altman women let her finish a goddamned sentence? "That's not it."

"Look," Van says, and there's something harder in her voice than Alice has heard before. "Nolan and I have never seen eye to eye on . . . well, a lot of things. But how he treats women, that's always been, um." She scratches at the back of her neck, clearly trying not to badmouth Alice's boyfriend right in front of her. "A difference," she finally says. "But you—knowing he finally got his shit together enough to be with someone like you—that's . . ." She bites her lip, takes a sip of her coffee, runs a hand through her thick hair. "Honestly it's the first thing I've admired about him in a long time."

Fuck.

"And my mom, she's so happy to meet you. For real. She's always believed, deep down, that Nolan is, like, a good guy who will settle down with a nice girl like you, get married, give her grandchildren, all that shit."

She grimaces at Alice, and Alice hears everything she isn't saying. The way Babs must have put all of her eggs in Nolan's basket, never expecting her gay daughter to have those things, to give her those grandchildren. Marie's too young and Van's too queer, so it all fell on Nolan. Who is now an inch from death.

"And now you're here, and she's like, he did it! We're so close!" Van twists up her lips a little bit. "Everyone is so pleased he finally ended his eternal fuck-boy phase. Honestly, if he weren't in a coma, I think they'd be throwing him a Welcome to Monogamy party."

Alice tries to laugh, but she's pretty sure she sounds more like a dying farm animal. Eternal fuck-boy phase? Great. Simply, absolutely the best. Of course Alice's fake-boyfriend ends up being quite possibly the biggest player in the world. Alice isn't exactly anyone's dream girl, she knows that—poor, uneducated, sarcastic as shit, unwilling to laugh at jokes that aren't funny, not hot or skinny—and Nolan is sounding less and less like someone who'd pick her for her winning personality.

It doesn't matter, not in the grand scheme of Nolan's life, or even in the delicate balance of maintaining this fiction for the family, but if Nolan wakes up, the odds that he falls madly in love with her are getting slimmer and slimmer.

And making the truly wonderful situation worse, now not only are his parents and his aunt thrilled that Nolan settled down with her, but Van is too? Even Van wants to believe this absurd fantasy, that her fourteenth-floor brother found himself in a relationship with a dowdy, impoverished receptionist? Even Van feels closer to her brother and more settled knowing that he had Alice these past few months?

Fuck Alice's entire fucking life.

After only a few more minutes, Van leaves to get some rest, and Alice spends the rest of her shift with her head in her hands, trying to figure out how she—a person who prides herself on being realistic, responsible, and pessimistic—landed in this absolutely ridiculous scenario. It's certainly the most out-of-character thing she's ever done, going along with this ruse that can only end in loss and disappointment.

Besides the shame of inventing a romance out of a single scrap of eye contact, Alice is now full of information about

Nolan she never wanted, and she's starting to feel something beyond embarrassed—ashamed, maybe, or even disturbed—about the enormous crush she's been harboring for so long despite knowing nothing about him except that he never stopped to chat with her. Would Nolan ever have seen Alice as anything other than a frumpy ornament in his otherwise pristine lobby? If she'd gotten another job, would he even have noticed she was gone?

She wonders why he regularly comes into the office in the wee hours of the morning; she'd daydreamed that he was deeply dedicated to some clients in Japan or something, but maybe he was running away from one-night stands, preferring to leave after sex rather than have an actual conversation with a human woman. She wonders what his days are like, his nights. His friends. The women he actually dates.

She should have walked away from this mess immediately, hopped out of the moving SUV if she'd had to. It's always mattered to her that she stick to her guns, be fiercely independent, so she tries not to think about how easily swayed she's been by Aunt Sheila's snark, Marie's hope, and Babs's soft hugs. How little it took to make her stay and lie.

Stuck behind her desk, lonely and exhausted, she definitely tries not to think about Van at all. She doesn't want to think about Van's kind smile, her understanding eyes, her broad shoulders and long legs, her gentle touch, her dykey outfits and cologne, her enormous dog, or her beat-up station wagon.

She's trying not to get too deep with Van in particular, but apparently that message hasn't traveled from her brain to her body, because her fingers type out and send a text before her shift ends. *I'm going home to sleep, but could you come get me on your way back to the hospital this afternoon?*

FIVE

Babs isn't at Nolan's bedside, which eases some of the clenching pressure in Alice's chest. Marie seems to be on duty this afternoon, along with the man who is either her dad or her uncle. Alice really needs to figure out which one is which, but even face-to-face with this one, she's pretty sure she wouldn't be able to pick him out of a lineup of other sixty-year-old white guys. Dad/Uncle is reading the newspaper—a real, physical newspaper—and Marie is buried in a terrifyingly large textbook with headphones on. Alice belatedly realizes that it's almost Christmas, so Marie's probably in finals.

Van was right; talk about bad timing.

It's pretty awkward. Dad/Uncle isn't a talker like Babs is, and Van seems significantly quieter around her family than she is with Alice alone. Marie is the only one who seems like she could bridge the uncomfortable silence with light chatter, but she's so deep in what looks like biology that Alice honestly isn't sure she knows that Alice and Van showed up half an hour ago. Alice leans against the wall, listening to the nurses in the hallway gossiping about the uppity medical residents, and wishes she'd brought a book.

Finally a nurse comes in to check on Nolan, but she doesn't have any updates to share. Van asks a question that Alice doesn't understand, and the nurse gives an equally incomprehensible answer. Alice hadn't realized physical therapist training involved so much neurology—Van clearly knows a lot—but it kind of makes sense.

"His vitals are steady," the nurse translates for Dad/Uncle when he looks up from his newspaper. "No changes today."

He frowns at her. "At what point is it a concern that he hasn't woken up?"

The nurse looks uncomfortable. Alice is pretty sure the answer is "already," but clearly the nurse doesn't want to be so blunt about it. "It's hard to say," she hedges, and Alice tries not to smile. She's had some bad experiences, of course, but overall, nurses are the bright spot in the hospital. "Each patient is different."

Van huffs out a breath, clearly not finding this vagueness as predictable as Alice is. As a PT, Van must not be a stranger to this type of cover-your-ass hedging that is so common in the ICU, but maybe this is her first experience as a family member instead of a provider, hearing it rather than saying it.

Maybe this is her first experience with someone she loves being stuck in the liminal twilight between life and death. That thought, for the first time, makes Alice want to take care of Van right back. Of Nolan's entire family. Her thoughts are somewhere between bitter envy and *oh, sweet summer child,* but mostly she wants to smooth the worry lines burrowing into Van's forehead, the slight shake of Dad/Uncle's newspaper, the pinch of Marie's hunched shoulders.

"I'm going to take him for another MRI now," the nurse says, starting to unhook Nolan from all of the equipment.

"How long will that take?" Dad/Uncle asks Van in an undertone, almost like he doesn't want the nurse to know that he doesn't know without asking.

Van looks over at the nurse. "Brain only?"

The nurse nods.

"With and without contrast?"

She nods again.

Van turns to her older male family member. "Probably around forty minutes," she says. She scoots her chair neatly out of the way as the nurse starts pushing the bed out of the room and says to her, "No pacemaker, metal jewelry, or implants."

The nurse nods a final time to Van in thanks, and wheels Nolan out the door and down the hall.

It's weird in the room without him, without the bed. It makes Alice think about what will happen if he dies, about the huge gaping hole in the middle of the room, everyone standing around the edges and staring at where he should be.

Unable to handle it, Alice abruptly straightens up. "Who needs coffee?"

Somehow the word *coffee* seems to cut through Marie's music. Her head snaps up, and the dark bags under her eyes explain why she says, "Oh my god, me," with such fervor.

Alice has never had finals, but, damn. Seems rough.

Dad/Uncle—Alice is pretty sure Dad? At least fifty-four percent sure—wants some too. Van doesn't put in an order but rather stands herself, unfolding her long legs and easily towering over Alice. Alice is only five foot three, so it's not that it's hard to be a lot taller than she is, but something about Van's height, or maybe her proximity, makes her feel startling every time. "I'll join you," Van says in that deep voice of hers, and Alice blinks quickly, trying to keep it together.

"Great," she says, her voice strangled, like Van wasn't one of the things she was trying to escape from.

Van leads the way down to the cafeteria on the first floor with her ridiculously fast strides. She must have been here before because she goes directly to the coffee without looking around. Alice grabs a couple shrink-wrapped pieces of banana bread before joining Van, who is already double-fisting, and making herself and Marie enormous cups.

This whole work-by-night, lie-by-day thing is surprisingly exhausting.

Van pays for all of it, which makes Alice feel itchy. It shouldn't—Van clearly has a good job and it's not like Alice can afford to go around blithely buying things for other people—but it does. Alice hates being poor, hates having to track her money so obsessively that she knows she would have had to skimp on something else this week to compensate for the extra twelve dollars if Van hadn't paid. She hates, judging by how quickly Van whipped out her wallet, the way she rolled her eyes at Alice's feeble attempts to reach for her own, that Van already seems to know that about her.

She hates how clearly Van sees her. It's not just dangerous for this lie, but for how it feels like Van could destabilize Alice's entire life. She's never really been one for wanting to be seen. Not like that. Not for a long time, anyway. She doesn't feel at all ready for someone like Van.

After they bring everything back upstairs, Van suggests that she and Alice drink theirs out on one of the tiny hospital balconies to take advantage of the four seconds today without rain. The closest one is empty, and Alice isn't sure they're supposed to use it without a patient in tow, but Van slides the glass door open without hesitation, and Alice figures Van probably knows what's what.

It's not a particularly nice view—they're looking out over parking structures in front of the backdrop of the interstate—and Alice is immediately shivering in her oversize sweater, but it means every sip of coffee won't taste like rubbing alcohol, so Alice would settle for much worse.

They sit down in two chairs on either side of a small round table, and it's quiet for a while, other than the rush of cars on the wet surface of I-5 three stories below. Alice slowly unwraps a slice of banana bread and sets it between them.

"Is Marie in finals?" she asks after a while.

"Yeah," Van says, breaking off a piece of bread. "Last one is in a few days. Her professors are mostly letting her take them from here, which I guess is nice, but means she isn't getting extensions."

"Rough." Alice watches as Van looks around for a napkin and then settles for wiping her greasy fingers on her pants. "What's she studying?"

"That's kind of the million-dollar question," Van says, squinting as she looks over at Alice. "Or, well, whatever this degree is costing everyone. Hundred-thousand-dollar question. Dad wants her to major in business, but she wants theater." Van shrugs. "Still up in the air who's gonna win."

"Theater, wow." Alice tears off a piece of the bread and eats it. It's too oily, but it's nice and soft inside. A chocolate chip melts on her tongue. "That sounds fun, but I mean, definitely not practical."

Van makes a little humming noise to show she heard, but she's carefully not making eye contact with Alice as she takes what feels like a pointed sip of her coffee. "That's the thing, I guess," she eventually says, which is wildly unhelpful.

"The . . . thing?"

"Is college supposed to be practical, or, like, you know. Intellectually interesting and challenging?" She shrugs again, but not like she doesn't care. More like she wants Alice to think she doesn't. "Is the goal a trade and a salary, or to grow as a person?"

Alice doesn't mean to pick a fight with the kind, compassionate, super-hot sister of a guy who might be dying, she really doesn't, but she finds herself pulling a face anyway. "I mean, seems a little wasteful to spend a hundred thousand dollars to grow as a person and put on plays, doesn't it? Like, you can do that on your own time."

Van finally looks over at her, but this time her gaze is hard in a way it hasn't been since the moment Alice was first introduced as Nolan's girlfriend. "What did you major in?"

A familiar shame rises up in Alice, and as usual, she sharpens it and uses it as a weapon. "I didn't go to college," she says, trying to sound like it's something she's proud of, like it was a choice. "I made my own way."

"Oh," Van says softly, and the cruel parts of Alice relish the way she looks uncomfortable. Van clearly went—Alice is pretty sure you can't be a physical therapist without it—and Nolan must have too. So that's all three of them; maybe they're not rich, but that puts them in an entirely different class of life circumstances than Alice.

"It's not that I think you have to be in college to grow and challenge yourself," Van says softly. "I don't think that, at all. But I also . . . I don't know." She takes a sip of her coffee, clearly stalling as she thinks of how to say it. "Marie has the rest of her life to have a career, to be practical. She's only eighteen. I wish she could . . . you know. Be a kid for a little longer. Do things because she loves them and they challenge her, not just because one day they'll help her make more money."

Alice forces herself not to retort right away. She tries to be thoughtful, like Van. To consider everything Van has said, and especially to consider what she hasn't.

"It's hard," Alice says softly. "To grow up too quickly."

Van's head snaps over to her, seemingly against her will. She's staring hard at Alice, her eyes a little narrowed. She opens and closes her mouth without saying anything, and Alice wonders if Van is feeling the way Alice often has since yesterday morning, like the two of them already know each other in ways no one else has bothered to.

All Van says is, "It is," but Alice knows she hit it on the money.

Van—gay, butch, dykey Van, sister of the handsome and wealthy Nolan who might or might not be an enormous jerk—grew up too fast, and now she wants better for her baby sister.

Alice wonders what her life would have been like if she'd been a Marie, if she'd had a Van.

Alice shouldn't be surprised that Van walks her into work that evening, not after she followed Alice up those two flights of stairs at her apartment, but she is. Van gallantly tries to open the front door for Alice, and Alice really should tell her that you need a badge at this hour.

"What the hell," Van says, shaking the glass door by the metal handle, and Alice doesn't bother to stifle her laugh. She wordlessly swipes her badge after giving herself a moment to enjoy the visual, and Van nearly falls over as she gives another sharp tug but this time the door easily swings open, sending her tripping backward.

"Fuck!"

Alice holds out her hands, laughing, grabbing onto Van to keep her upright.

"Sorry," she chortles. "I couldn't help it."

Van mutters something about abuse while she straightens her shirt, but she's clearly trying and failing not to smile. "After you," she says, holding the offending door open with an eye roll and an overdramatic sweep of her arm, and Alice slides inside, still grinning.

She takes a few steps across the lobby but stops in her tracks when she sees who's in her seat behind the computer.

"Mr. Brown," Alice says, resuming her slow walk toward the desk. "This is a surprise." She tries to keep her face neutral, but she knows what's coming. The only reason he would be here in person is so that he can fire Alice.

She looks back to where Van is standing and looking a bit confused. "Uh, Mr. Brown, let me introduce you to Van Altman. Nolan Altman's sister."

Van nods at him, and he nods back.

"We just came from the hospital." Hey, if Alice is going to torture herself for the rest of her life for lying to Van and the Altmans, she might as well milk it while it's happening.

"I see," Mr. Brown says slowly. "And, um, how is Mr. Altman doing?"

"Stable," Alice says at the same time as Van says, "Still unresponsive."

Alice looks over at Van quickly. She's always hated that question, *How is he doing?* It's so invasive. Like, I'm sorry, but just because you asked doesn't mean I have to share all the gory, intimate details of this person's disintegrating body with you, near-stranger.

"Stable but unresponsive," she says.

"Well, I, uh . . ." He looks awkward, and Alice isn't sure if she wants to ask Van to leave or not. Honestly it might be nice to get a ride home after being fired. Maybe hug Frank again. "I moved the schedule around, so you should go home," Mr. Brown continues, looking pained at having to say it. "You start on the early day shift in the morning."

There's suddenly a loud rushing in Alice's ears, so she's not sure she heard him right. "The . . . the early day shift?"

"Seven to three," he says. "With Delilah."

"Um, wow," Alice says, gorgeously articulate as always. "This is . . . wow." Then, because she's been burned too many times before, she clarifies. "Do you mean only for this week, or . . ."

"Permanent," he says, his voice gruff. "Unless you don't want—"

"No!" Alice takes an involuntary step forward. "No, I definitely want it. Thank you, sir. So much."

He gives her a quick nod. "Seven," he says. "Don't be late."

"I won't." She grins at him, and turns to Van, her eyes screaming with happiness. The day shift! The fucking day shift! No more overnights, no more living like a vampire without seeing Portland's best approximation of daylight, no more breakfast for dinner. No more sitting behind the desk all alone—the early day shift has two receptionists at all times. She'll have someone to talk to, actual visitors to direct to various floors. Things to do with her time. People to watch.

"Oh, and, Rue?"

Alice turns back to him.

"Wear something nice tomorrow. Local news wants to interview you."

An icy wave of realization slams the joy right out of her. "Oh," she says, her mind reeling. There's a catch. Of course there's a fucking catch, and it's a doozy. The day shift is for the good press of saving Nolan. And that press is only good because apparently she's his girlfriend. Lying to his family is one thing—one horrible, awful, express-lane-straight-to-hell thing—but lying on the news? That's a whole other beast. Someone is going to figure it out. His real girlfriend, or someone he banged the other night, or a friend of his; someone is going to bust this story right open. And not only will Alice then be well and truly fired, but the Altmans will never forgive her.

Van will never forgive her.

"Uh, Mr., um, Brown, was it?" Van is stepping forward now, reaching out and clasping onto Alice's elbow like she could tell how quickly Alice was spiraling. "Of course I want Alice to be recognized for what she did in saving my brother's life. But the family would prefer that his name not be used. To protect our privacy in this difficult time. You understand."

Oh god. Alice sags into Van, letting Van's grip hold her up.

She absolutely does not deserve this woman, with her quick brain and steady stare, the way she's wearing Brown down in a second. The way she's leaping to Alice's defense when Alice most certainly doesn't deserve it. Van probably does want privacy for her family, but she also likely saw the color drain from Alice's face, the way Alice started to sway on her feet, and there she went. Doing that butch superhero thing again.

"Of course," Brown says, obsequious and deferential. Alice is pretty sure he doesn't know that Van and the rest of the Altmans aren't nearly as rich and powerful as Nolan is, and she's certainly not going to tell him. The longer he's afraid of them, the longer she has a job. "I'll take care of it."

"Great," Van says. "I'll look forward to seeing the coverage." She looks at Alice then, her hand still tight around Alice's arm. "Drive you home?"

Alice nods, her throat still tight.

They say goodbye to Brown and walk out of the lobby, neither daring to say anything until they're back in the station wagon, the doors shut behind them.

"Holy shit," Alice says, blinking quickly. "Did that just happen?"

"Hmm." Van turns the car on, buckles her seatbelt, and then pulls out into the street. "Did you really just get promoted off the night shift and told you're going to be locally famous? Yes."

Alice doesn't say the other part: *Did you just save my ass from public ridicule?*

"Let's celebrate," Van says, looking over at Alice. "Or, well. I'd say I'll buy you a drink, but I need to go home and let Frank out."

Alice should say *okay*, should say, *It's all right, you can take me home.* She should say *raincheck.* But instead she says, "Do you have drinks at your house?"

Van looks over at her with surprise and something that might be happiness. "I sure do."

She drives farther north than Alice ever goes, eventually pulling into the driveway of a two-story duplex a few blocks away from a park. Alice gets out, savoring the quiet street until she shuts the car door behind her and she hears a few excited barks from inside the house.

"Hey, Franko," Van calls as she and Alice walk up the front steps. "I brought you a friend, buddy!"

She unlocks the door but turns to look at Alice before she opens it. "He's usually good, but he's been alone for a while today so he might jump up on you."

"That's fine," Alice says quickly. She could definitely use some full-body contact—it's been years—and if it has to come from a dog again, so be it.

Van opens the door, and indeed a blur of wriggly white fur, whipping tail, and pink tongue launches itself at her and then at Alice. Alice can't help but laugh as Van tries to pull Frank off her, but Van can't get a hand on his collar because he's so excited about seeing them. It's not until he puts both gigantic paws on Alice's chest and enthusiastically licks her neck that Van grabs him and hauls him backward.

"Get off, Frank. Down. Sit. Frank, sit!"

"Damn," Alice says, laughing. "He's so tall."

Something in Van's eyes seems to darken and turn predatory as she watches Alice wipe off her throat. It's a few beats too long before she manages to say, her voice sounding oddly tight, "Yeah, he's ridiculous."

After a significant amount of time petting and complimenting Frank, they finally get him to back up enough for them to walk inside. It's small and a little cluttered, and it feels like the inside of the station wagon. Lived in, well used, loved. Completely and utterly Van. Alice follows Frank into the living room, taking in the big brown couch, the TV mounted over the fireplace, what looks like a handmade wooden coffee table, and an enormous dog bed. The blue area rug is scattered with chew toys and there's a big exercise ball in the corner. She can see out a window to what looks like a sizable, wet, green backyard. Nothing matches, but it all works perfectly together.

Alice never wants to leave.

"Sorry it's messy," Van says, her voice shy.

Alice shakes her head, flopping down on the couch. "This is, like, the best place I've ever been." Frank hops up next to her and immediately sticks his tongue deep into her ear.

Van scoffs, heading into the small kitchen that's separated from the living room by a half-wall, like they used to be separate rooms but Van HGTV'd it to create a sightline. "You need to go to some better places."

Alice gets off the couch with a grunt, walking over and placing her hands flat on the countertop dividing the two spaces, staring hard at the back of Van's head as she rummages in the fridge. "Van," she says softly. Van takes a second to respond, freezing for a beat at something in Alice's tone, or maybe how close she is. She finally turns, and it's only when she's looking right at Alice that Alice says it. "This is a great place." She's careful to speak slowly, to make sure her words have weight to them. "If I were imagining my dream house, it would look a lot like this."

Van breaks eye contact, staring down at the can of beer in her hand. "It's, um . . . I only live in the downstairs. I rent out the upstairs."

Alice doesn't say anything, but her mind is reeling. Van owns it? Alice will never own property in her life, that's always been very clear to her, and Van is saying this place that she owns, with a backyard and a cozy living room and rental income, isn't something absolutely incredible?

If her brother weren't in a coma—and Alice weren't fake-dating him—she'd try to smack some sense into Van.

Van takes a small step forward, the counter now the only thing between them. "But, um, thank you. I, uh . . . I worked hard on it."

Alice grins at her. "Fucking finally," she says, trying to soften it with a laugh. "Finally something you're admitting to being proud of."

Van shrugs one shoulder and Alice almost rolls her eyes. Girl *cannot* take a compliment.

Alice decides that being chill is overrated. "Van, seriously. You're a doctor. You own a house and a car. You take care of your parents and your sister. And me." Alice gives it a quiet beat, watching as Van blinks quickly. "You have the world's tallest dog."

That gets a laugh out of Van, albeit a slightly wet one. "I do, yes."

"You have a lot to be proud of, Van," Alice says, almost a whisper. "I hope you know that."

Van presses her lips together, like maybe she's trying not to smile, or possibly not to cry. She takes a couple of deep breaths and then she looks up, pushing a beer across the counter to Alice. "You and my brother," Van says softly, her eyes big and serious. "He doesn't deserve you."

SIX

Alice's phone rings during her first lunch break. She actually gets a lunch break on the day shift, which is wild to her. She and Delilah each get half an hour to themselves, to go anywhere and do anything. Delilah, who is tall, Black, young, and infinitely cooler and happier than Alice, says she usually goes to the coffee shop down the street, so Alice does that today too, positively bouncing through the freezing rain to get there. It's called Fresh Grounds, and Alice definitely can't afford anything there except black coffee, but the thrill of being out in the daytime, on a lunch break, means that the six-dollar lattes next to bumper stickers that read KEEP PORTLAND WEIRD don't even piss her off like they usually would.

Or, well, not as much as they usually would anyway.

She's sitting in the corner of the shop, eating the sandwich she packed this morning and sipping her fresh black coffee, when her phone rings. She pulls it out of her pocket and frowns at it. The name flashing across the screen is ISABELLA, and Alice hasn't actually talked to her in . . . jeez. Years.

"Hello?"

"Alice! Hi! It's Isabella."

Alice blinks. She knew that, but she guesses *hello* is kind of an impersonal greeting for your one and only cousin, even if the last time you talked on the phone to her was probably right around puberty. They stay in touch well enough, thanks to social media and the occasional text, but a phone call? It might as well be 1999.

Alice decides to fake it. "Oh my god," she says, her voice weirdly high. "Wow, Isabella! Hi!"

"Oh my god is right! That's exactly what I said twenty minutes ago when I saw your face on my flipping TV! On the news for saving some guy's life?"

"Oh," Alice says, her face coloring. She's glad Isabella can't see her right now. The interview had been heinously awkward, with Alice trying very hard not to actually say or confirm that Nolan is her boyfriend. The reporter had clearly thought she was nuts, and just as clearly hadn't wanted to be there. The camera guy had been leering at her, and the whole thing had made her skin itchy. "Yeah," she mumbles, "it's been an intense week, I guess."

But, wait. Isabella lives in Texas. The bored reporter was from a local Portland news station. How the hell did Isabella see it? There's a pause as Alice's mind whirs, and she takes in the sounds of a cartoon in the background and the high-pitched voices of Isabella's two little kids squabbling. She's never met the kids, but she's seen approximately a billion pictures of them on social media. They seem cute, or whatever. Normal.

"Listen," Isabella finally says, and her voice sounds a little different now. Maybe concerned? "I'm sorry I didn't reach out before, I'm literally the worst person alive and I freely admit that, but Henry and I moved back to Portland a couple months ago for his work—the mushrooms are better here, I guess—and I want to see you. I meant to text you before, I swear I did, but seeing you on TV this morning felt like a signal from Portland Jesus that I can't wait another minute. Can you come over for dinner tonight?"

Alice's brain short-circuits. Isabella lives here? Has for months? With her husband and her kids? Alice has had family here for months, and they didn't even bother to reach out, to send a text or DM to say hi?

And what the heck do mushrooms have to do with anything?

Alice squeezes her eyes shut. She will not cry in this fucking overpriced hipster coffee shop that is doing anything but keeping Portland weird. She will not let this bother her. Isabella never called from Texas, so why should Alice have expected her to do so from a few minutes away? Isabella has a ton of family on her dad's side; she never needed Alice like Alice needed her.

"Um, things are pretty up in the air with Nolan and everything," Alice manages to say into the phone, hoping her voice doesn't shake. "I think I'm going back to the hospital after work today."

Isabella says something but her voice is muffled, like she's holding a hand over the phone. Alice thinks it might be, "Sebastian, stop hitting your sister."

"What hospital is he at?" Isabella asks, her voice clearer now even as the kids get louder. Alice suspects Sebastian may not, in fact, have stopped hitting his sister.

Alice lets out a puff of air. "Portland Grace."

"Fu—*fudgsicle*," Isabella says, and Alice can't help but laugh.

"Pretty much, yeah."

"Al, how are you doing? Really?"

Alice lets out a long, shuddering breath. Isabella and her family moved away when Alice was eleven, but when they were little they'd been inseparable. Isabella is one of the only people in the world who knows what Alice's life has been like. Who could make a decent guess of what walking into that hospital is doing to her.

"How about Sunday?" Alice hears herself saying. Today is Friday, she's pretty sure. "I could come over Sunday."

"Good," Isabella says, the sound of a toddler wailing now blaring in Alice's ear like a siren. "Sebastian, I said stop hitting— Okay, I gotta go because my child might be a sociopath, but I'll text you the address, okay? Come whenever. Prepare yourself for some light chaos. Sebastian! That's it, you lost a sticker!"

"Okay, I'll—" The wailing cuts abruptly off, and Alice is left holding her phone in her hand, her elitist coffee slowly cooling in front of her.

SEVEN

A few hours later, Alice is washing her hands in the bathroom at the end of her shift. The thought of having so much daytime left on this lovely, cold Friday—and then a whole weekend where she won't need to sleep during the day—is so foreign that she honestly has no idea what to do with herself. Well, when she's not expected at the hospital all the time, that is. Delilah invited Alice to happy hour sometime with her and some of her friends, and Alice knows she should say yes to what is honestly a ridiculously kind invitation, but it's been so long since she's done anything like that she worries she's forgotten how. The night shift took so much from her, and she had so little to give in the first place.

She walks back out into the lobby and stops short at the sight of Babs and Aunt Sheila standing at the desk, chatting with Delilah. Aunt Sheila catches sight of her and waves her over, and it's only when Alice takes a few more steps that she sees Van, hovering behind her mom with her hands in her pockets like she's worried about taking up too much space. She looks devastatingly handsome in her thick jeans and the same familiar quilted green jacket, and it's probably Alice's imagination but she's almost convinced she can smell Van's cologne from ten feet away.

"Alice, honey, there you are!" Babs says, holding out her arms.

Alice's heart stutters as she closes the distance between them and lets Babs wrap her up in what Alice is quickly coming to realize is her signature squeeze. The woman must be part boa constrictor; she's not very muscular at a glance, but she has some kind of hug-related super strength for sure.

Once Babs releases her, Aunt Sheila gives her own hug—less tight but still affectionate—and then it's awkward. Woman code means Alice should hug Van, but the part of Alice's brain that is screaming about how hot Van is makes her think she should probably keep as much physical distance between them as possible.

Van doesn't take her hands out of the pockets of her jacket, and she and Alice end up sort of nodding at each other from very close by. It's not Alice's finest moment.

She makes it worse by failing to say anything kinder than, "What, um, what are you all doing here?"

"We came to get some things from Nolie's office to decorate his hospital room," Babs says, taking hold of Alice's arm like maybe she knows Alice is a flight risk. "After that we'll all stop by his condo before going right on over to the hospital together, okay, dear?"

Oh no. Certainly not. Aside from the whole Alice-does-not-know-this-man of it all, what even is a condo? Alice definitely would have referred to his place as a house or an apartment, so thank goodness Babs said it first. Although they're all looking at her weirdly, and Alice's heart sinks as she realizes what they're expecting from her. "Oh, I would love to help," she says quickly. "But I don't have keys to his, um, condo. We hadn't gotten to that point yet." This is true, of course, because she figures that if Nolan had made a list of people to give his house key to, she'd probably be somewhere on page eighty-nine, between a fictional character and a long-dead U.S. president.

"Oh," Babs says, and Alice mentally wipes off her brow. Whew. Close call.

But then, fucking Aunt Sheila chimes in. "Well, I'm sure his condo board can let us in."

Shit. So close. Alice resigns herself to this happening, and hopes they know where this condo is, because lord knows she doesn't.

"Okay," Alice says, hoping she doesn't sound robotic. Or terrified. "Great."

Delilah, meanwhile, is handing out guest passes to the upstairs offices like they're golden tickets. "Alice has told me so much about all of you," she gushes before winking over at Alice. Alice has told her as little as possible, because she doesn't want to lie to the person who will hopefully be her new friend, but she can tell that Delilah is covering for her. It makes something in her chest thrum, the knowledge that there is a human being in the universe who would cover for Alice, maybe even actively enjoy her company, and not because they think she's dating their attractive and comatose family member. It's been over a decade since Alice has had someone like that. Even after this all inevitably ends with the Altmans, either because Nolan is dead or because he wakes up and the truth comes out, Alice hopes she'll get to keep Delilah.

Alice takes a little peek at the pass Delilah has handed Aunt Sheila, unsure if Delilah tilted it over at the perfect angle for

Alice to see the suite number on it because she knows Alice is a huge fucking liar, or if the flourish is simply part of her customer service charm.

Either way, Alice now knows they're headed to suite 1403. "Great," Alice manages to say again, this time through gritted teeth. "Up we go."

She follows as Aunt Sheila makes a beeline for the elevator and then pushes the button like a thousand times until it arrives. They all pile in, and as the doors close and the elevator climbs, Alice anxiously picks at her fingernails. What if there's a picture of him and some other girl in his office? What if they run into someone who was out last week with Nolan and his secret gay boyfriend Rolf? That would be extremely fucking bad, right?

Babs and Aunt Sheila talk a mile a minute about how much nicer this building is than where his last office was, while Van is silent, opening and closing her hands like they've fallen asleep or something. Alice wants to curl up under her arm, lean against her broad chest, and close her eyes for the next week or so.

But instead the elevator dings, the door opens, and much too quickly, Aunt Sheila is blazing a trail into the suite marked HAYES AND ASSOCIATES. Babs goes right up to the receptionist, introducing herself as "my sweet boy Nolan's mother" and asking her to let them into Nolan's office. The receptionist is—of course—a young woman, prettier and thinner and much better dressed than Alice. Alice pulls down on the bottom of her black sweater and tucks her hair back behind her ears, cursing herself for never learning how to properly put on makeup or use a curling iron, skills Nolan probably values and this woman certainly has.

The receptionist is gushing over Babs in a second, coming

around the desk to hug her, happening to demonstrate that she looks great in a pencil skirt, can walk in four-inch heels, and has perfectly swishy hair. She looks like the kind of person who vigorously exercises before work, which Alice has always hoped she would be if she had the time and money, but has a sneaking suspicion she would not.

There is absolutely zero reason Nolan Altman would ever pick Alice over someone like this, even if he were too lazy to hit on someone more than ten yards away from him.

Babs introduces her to Aunt Sheila and Van, which is polite but pointless because this office is fancy enough that even the receptionist has a nameplate on her desk. KERRY ANDERSON, it reads, in perfect white font.

"And this is Alice. Nolan's girlfriend."

Kerry blinks. "Girl—*girlfriend?*" There's panic in her perfectly lined eyes now, and Alice doesn't need to be an expert at reading people to tell exactly what's going on.

Kerry and Nolan totally fucked.

Recently.

Not frequently enough for her to think *she* was his girlfriend, but certainly enough for her to have thought he was single.

"Don't worry," Alice says, trying to stave off a public spectacle and end this interaction as quickly as she can. Now not only is Alice lying to the Altmans, she's also making this perfectly nice stranger think she's a homewrecker or something, and that doesn't feel awesome. "No one knew," Alice adds, which is a bit of an understatement, but technically true.

Kerry blinks at her, and Alice can practically see the millions of things running through her brain—probably an advanced calculus of her own sexual history with Nolan, her knowledge of his tastes, and all of the ways Alice falls short of his usual standards. Her eyes linger on Alice's hair, her waist, and Van takes a step closer to Alice, clearly reading the same vibes. She's right up behind Alice now, like a bodyguard. Alice can see in her peripheral vision that Van is still opening and closing her hands, and she wonders if she's doing it to intimidate Kerry.

"You look familiar," Kerry says slowly, not nearly as friendly as she was before Babs said the *g*-word. "Have you been up to visit him before?"

"No," Alice says, trying to not fidget, trying to channel Van's steady strength into her own bones. "I work at the desk downstairs. And, um. You know. Coming up might have seemed, like, unprofessional?" Alice figures that's sort of not a lie. As visiting him upstairs would have involved a few minor felonies—breaking, entering, and she's pretty sure a stalking charge would stick—*unprofessional* may be generously vague, but no one could say it isn't true.

"Wait. You're the one who saved him, aren't you?"

Alice shrugs. She's getting more and more uncomfortable with that term, because he's still not, like . . . super alive. She tries to sound dismissive and casual as she says, "I mean, I gave him shitty CPR. The doctors at the hospital are the real heroes." That's laying it on a little thick, but Babs wipes a tear from her cheek, so Alice figures maybe it landed okay.

Kerry looks at Van, her eyes running up and down her body the same way she'd evaluated Alice. "And you're Nolan's . . . sister?" The slight pause before *sister* makes Alice's hackles rise. Kerry didn't say it in an affirming way, like she was checking in about Van's pronouns. No, she meant it as an insult, like Van's handsomeness is a bad thing, that her masculinity is something to be judged instead of drooled over.

Alice opens her mouth, unsure what she's going to say but positive it won't be nice, but Van talks first. "Listen, Cherry."

"Kerry," Kerry corrects. She's still looking at Van in that way that straight girls sometimes do when they see a butch—critical and low-key homophobic even while they pretend to be friendly. Alice feels herself straightening up and moving between them in a vain attempt to shield Van's tall, broad body with her own. Even butch superheroes deserve protection.

Van's voice is harder now, even as her hand comes up to Alice's elbow and closes over it with exquisite tenderness. "Can you show us to his office, please, Cherry? We don't have a lot of time."

"Of course," Cherry Kerry says, clearly deciding against pushing it in front of Nolan's mom and his girlfriend, who is either very magnanimous or unbelievably oblivious. She pulls a key out of a drawer and starts to walk down the hallway. "Follow me."

They all do, and Cherry unlocks an office at the end of the long corridor. She opens the door and leads them inside, and Alice almost trips over her feet. One wall is entirely windows, and Alice has never seen Portland from this high up before. It's beautiful, even in the last dregs of winter daylight. The rain is more of a heavy mist right now, so it feels like she's standing inside of a cloud. The city looks gray and cold in the kind of way that makes Alice want to curl up in the corner with a mug of tea and a romance novel, Frank on her lap and Van next to her, steady and solid and warm.

"Thanks, Cherry," Van says, and Alice chokes at her dedication to the bit. "We've got it from here."

Cherry looks pained, but she nods and backs out of the office. "Let me know if you need anything," she says, but her eyes linger on Alice before she closes the door after herself.

Babs and Aunt Sheila are already poking around, touching everything on Nolan's bookshelves—mostly technical manuals and unlabeled three-ring binders—and leaving fingerprints on his massive glass desk. Alice steps farther into the room, taking it all in and pretending she's seen his belongings before, like she's not desperately searching the office for clues that will help her pull off this ridiculous charade.

But she's pretty sure, as she swivels her head around, that she's shit out of luck. It's a minimalist office, all glass and steel. It's decidedly impersonal—the only thing Alice gets from it is that Nolan is rich and wants people to know it. He doesn't have any photographs or notes from satisfied clients, and all of the clothes and knickknacks scattered around are pretty generic: a mug from the company, a Portland Timbers bobblehead, a black raincoat hung up on a hook on the back of the door.

Alice walks over to a wall with two framed diplomas, glancing up at them out of the corner of her eye. The smaller one is from the University of Southern California, awarding a bachelor of science to Nolan H. Altman in the area of finance.

Alice files that away in her very meager mental folder called *Nolan Facts*. Nolan went to USC. Nolan's middle name starts with an *H*. So does Alice's; two weeks ago she'd have thought that made them soulmates.

The bigger diploma is from USC too, this one commemorating him for his master's in business administration.

That's an MBA, right? Okay. Two different finance degrees from California. No wonder he has a rich-person office and a rich-person desk and a never-ending series of rich-person suits.

No wonder he fucked Cherry.

No wonder his dad wants Marie to major in business too. No wonder Van doesn't.

"Alice," Babs says, holding up a mug from next to his enormous Mac desktop. "This reminds me. Have you been in touch with any of his brothers?"

Alice blinks. Brothers? What the hell! How many fucking children does this family have? What the actual shit is going on right now?

"B-brothers?" she stutters.

The mug says what looks like EX in a weird font, and has a white cross inside a blue shield. It's absolutely incoherent to Alice. Ex what? Ex-brothers? Alice feels like reality is tilting out from underneath her, her mind spinning like a hamster trying to outrun a predator using only its squeaky, utterly useless wheel. What the hell is an ex-brother in a family of only sisters?

"She means his fraternity brothers," Van says into the awkward silence. She gestures at the mug. "From Sigma Chi."

"Oh," Alice says, forcing out an extremely unconvincing fake laugh, her brain plopping sideways off the hamster wheel. "Right. Of course. Sorry, brain fart. Yes. His brothers. From the, uh, fraternity. Of brothers."

Alice doesn't know shit about fraternities except what she's seen in movies. Everything is always exaggerated, of course, but it's never seemed like those dudes are, like, super great. She files the words *fraternity, sigma,* and *chi* away in her brain, noticing the way they slide without her permission from *Nolan Facts* into a subfolder simply labeled *Unfortunate.*

"No, I, um, I haven't been in touch with them." Definitely not a lie.

"Okay," Babs says, placing the mug down reverently. "I'll see if I can reach Iron Allan."

Alice decides not to worry about what in the world an Iron Allan is. The enormous windows start to feel threatening, like Alice is about to tip out of the building and careen down fourteen stories to splat on the cement below. "I'm going to, um, check on something with Cherry," she says, backpedaling quickly out of what has become a very claustrophobic room. "Be, uh. Be right back."

Alice tries not to think about how every new fact she learns about Nolan makes her like him less and less, how foolish she feels for spending 751 days pining over someone who probably wouldn't have ever given her the time of day, and who she might have hated even if he had. She's feeling more and more idiotic for attaching herself to him, even by evasion and omission. What do they think of her, these strong, badass Altman women, for hitching her wagon to a guy like him? What will they think of her—how will their faces fall, their arms cross over their chests, their jaws hang open—when they learn it was all a lie?

She quickly walks down the hallway, breathing fast, but in her panic she forgets that the only way out of this suite is right past Cherry.

"Hey, Alice," Cherry says, stopping Alice from her attempt to blow past the front desk. "Can I talk to you for a second?"

"Sure," Alice says, not bothering to hide her grimace. What today definitely needs is a one-on-one conversation with the tall, flawless goddess who very recently fucked her fake-boyfriend, and is maybe his actual girlfriend.

"Listen," Cherry says, tucking a strand of blond hair back. "I, um, I didn't know he had a girlfriend."

She doesn't say out loud she slept with him, probably in case Alice really is the most oblivious person in the universe and hasn't figured it out yet. But they both know what Cherry means—she didn't know he had a girlfriend when she hooked up with him—and she looks so horribly guilty and torn up about it that Alice sighs. None of this is Cherry's fault. Not her perfect hair or her skill at being femme or the fact that Alice's enormous lie of omission is making Cherry feel like shit. "It's okay," Alice says softly. "I don't—I'm sure it was before anything, um, happened between us."

Because, of course, everything that has ever happened in human history happened before her and Nolan, seeing as there is no her and Nolan.

Cherry opens her mouth like she's going to protest, but Alice shakes her head. "Seriously. Don't worry about it, okay? I'm not . . . it's not a problem, Cherry."

"O . . . kay," Cherry says. "And it's Ker—"

"Alice." Van's voice comes through the hallway, sharp and clear, and Alice both hates and loves the way everything in her chest suddenly loosens, letting her fully exhale for the first time in what feels like half an hour. "You okay?"

"Yeah," Alice says, turning quickly. "I'm good."

Van is glaring at Cherry now, who mutters something about going to the bathroom and positively scurries away, her towering heels clicking hurriedly on the floor as she flees Van's scrutiny.

"I'm sorry," Van says, her eyes softening as soon as they land back on Alice. "You shouldn't have had to—Nolan shouldn't have . . ."

"Hey." Alice holds up a hand, surprised by how close together they're standing. She could so easily lay her hand on Van's chest. "It's okay."

"It's not." It comes out of Van with more force than Alice expected. Alice's eyes drop to Van's hands, still opening and closing.

Van takes a step to the side and sinks down, half sitting on the corner of Cherry's desk, gripping the edges of the wood with her long, strong fingers.

"It is, though." Alice moves even closer, letting herself talk softly, at eye level with Van for the very first time. "Like, I get it. She's . . ." She sighs. "I mean, you saw her. She's hot. There's not . . . I don't think there's a single person in the world who would turn her down for me."

It's quiet for a long moment, and Alice immediately regrets her words. Would Nolan's real girlfriend, someone serious enough to be hanging out with his mom while he's in a coma, really be cool with him fucking Cherry on the side? Likely not, but Alice simply can't muster the effort to pretend to be mad right now. Cherry and Nolan haven't done anything wrong. The only liar here is Alice H. Rue, and all said liar wants to do right now is curl up on Van's strong chest and fall asleep to the comforting thump of her heartbeat.

Something in Van's perfect face settles, like she's made a decision. "Yes," she says softly. "There is."

After a few beats of Alice trying not to fling herself at Van, swallowing down everything she shouldn't be feeling and definitely shouldn't be saying, Van moves off Cherry's desk. She drops heavily into a chair tucked over to the side for waiting clients, and Alice sinks into the one next to her. Babs and Aunt Sheila must be checking Nolan's desk for secret compartments or something, with how long they're taking in a room that clearly has nothing personal in it. Van looks over at Alice. It feels a little like she's trying to distract Alice from what she's just admitted when she says, "Do you like working here?"

Alice takes the bait, silently agreeing to the vibe change.

"The night shift was awful. I hated that. So today, being on the day shift—that was much better," she says, shrugging. "But it's still . . . you know. Not thrilling or anything."

Van nods. "If you could have any job in the world, what would it be?"

"Like, if I could go back in time and change my whole life, or starting from right now, with who I am?" Alice is almost positive you can't become a whale scientist with no degree, a C+ in ninth-grade biology, and never having actually been on a boat.

"Starting from now."

Alice considers for a moment. It's been a while since she's thought about anything more than making it through to her next paycheck. "I used to work at this pediatric dentist's office, before they closed the practice," she says slowly. "I really liked that. There was always something different to do: filing, scheduling, inventory, cleaning, lots of kids to talk to. I mean, most of them were miserable, because who likes the dentist." Van laughs. "But, yeah, that was the best job I've ever had. I'd love to do something like that again. Somewhere busy, with people, where I feel like my contributions matter."

Van hums a little, like what Alice said is important enough for Van to let it sink in. Like Alice said something meaningful, not some babble about a job she hasn't had in years.

"Do you like your job?" Alice asks.

Van smiles, and Jesus fuck, she's so pretty. "Yeah," she says softly, and Alice wants to crawl into her lap. "Honestly, I only got into the field because it was respectable, you know, one of the only things I thought my parents would approve of and I wouldn't hate, but it turns out I love it."

Alice can picture it perfectly. Van's strong hands, her calm voice, her steady presence helping people work back from knee surgery or broken hips or stiff necks.

"Good," Alice says, looking deeply into her eyes for way longer than she should. "I want you to be happy."

"You too," Van says, and it looks like she means it.

EIGHT

Back in the lobby, Van begs off going to Nolan's condo, saying she's tired and she'll meet everyone at the hospital when they're done. Alice didn't think that would work—Babs is on a fucking mission—but Babs immediately looks concerned and starts talking a mile a minute about how Van needs to get home and rest immediately. It's a lot, and it makes Alice wish for a mom so badly.

"I'll go with you," Alice says when she can get a word in edgewise, immensely grateful for the opportunity to not have to fake her way through his house. Or condo, rather. She still needs to google what that is. Anyway, she's pretty sure she got away with not having visited his office before (the two of them care deeply about professionalism) or knowing about his family (he's kind of a dick), but she definitely would have seen his place.

He doesn't seem like the type to deign to visit her tiny studio out on Division, and he definitely seems like the type to want to get laid. There's no way around it. She would need to be very, very familiar with his bedroom. Which, now that she thinks about it, makes her feel weird. This whole family thinks she had sex, repeatedly, nakedly, with their favorite son? Who is now in a fucking coma? And that's basically the only thing they know about her? It makes her feel squicky, and she'll very happily skip over that part, thank you very much.

"Well, let's all go over the weekend then," Aunt Sheila says, helpful as ever. "Let's go see our boy now."

"Gee," Alice says, resigning herself to being foiled at every damn opportunity. "Great plan, Aunt Sheila."

The next night, Alice has just stepped back inside Nolan's hospital room with Marie when she hears a familiar voice speaking softly to the Altmans, and Alice snaps her head over to the far side of the bed. Babs, Aunt Sheila, the interchangeable dad and uncle—Alice needs fucking flashcards, honestly—and Van are all scattered around the room eating mediocre Chinese food out of take-out containers. It's a raucous Saturday night if Alice has ever had one. Alice and Marie have just returned from plundering extra napkins and chopsticks from the cafeteria, and there's a woman in the room who wasn't there before. She looks over at the doorway at the sound of their footsteps and immediately springs to her feet.

"Alice? Little Alice Rue Rue? Is that you?"

Alice's throat is suddenly tight and she feels like she's a little kid again, small and afraid and stuttering on the doorstep, unwilling to walk into the room unless Lupe holds her hands out and gives her that safe smile. "Lupe," she manages to choke out. "Wow."

Lupe, a short Black woman with strong arms and more

wrinkles than Alice remembers, quickly crosses to the doorway. Alice shoves the chopsticks into Marie's hands before she's enveloped in Lupe's arms.

She smells exactly the same. Alice tries to swallow her tears.

Lupe pulls back after a long moment, cupping Alice's face in her hands. "Look at you!" She's beaming, but her eyes are wet too. "You're all grown up!"

Alice tries to laugh, like maybe this is all casual and fun. Running into an old friend! "Yeah, thirteen years will do that to you."

"Has it really been that long?" Lupe slides her hands down to squeeze Alice's arms. "It feels like last week."

Alice nods. "And also like a hundred years ago."

Lupe nods too, sad and knowing. "What are you doing here, sweetheart?" She looks around the room. "Are you . . . is Nolan a friend of yours?"

Alice presses her lips together. She doesn't want to lie to Lupe. Every time a new person thinks she's dating Nolan, it's torture, but lying to Lupe feels way beyond the pale. "Um, not exactly," she mumbles, hoping that's vague enough to serve as both telling the truth to Lupe and upholding the lie to the other six spectators, all of whom are watching with profound interest.

But it backfires. The hours Alice had spent staring at Lupe's face when she was younger means that now she can see how Lupe is trying not to visibly crumble. "Oh, sweetie," Lupe whispers, clearly taking that to mean Nolan is more than a friend, rather than less. "Not again. I'm so sorry, honey."

Alice blinks. She can feel all of the Altmans staring at her, Van's eyes almost burning her with a confused tenderness Alice absolutely cannot handle.

"Alice, Pastor Lupe, you know each other?" Babs asks once it becomes clear that Alice isn't able to respond, one hand on her takeout and the other resting on the blanket next to Nolan's ankle.

Lupe nods. "I've been the ICU chaplain here for almost thirty years. I spent a lot of time with Alice and her parents," she says, like that will explain things to Babs. Like the Altmans know anything about Alice's parents, about this hospital. About Alice at all. Lupe gives a little laugh as she says, "The number of card games this girl put me through!" She pats Alice on the shoulder with a loving, maternal smile. "I haven't been able to stomach a game of Go Fish since."

Lupe's phone buzzes and she apologizes, excusing herself from the room. Alice tries not to look at anyone, but she finds herself sending what must be a particularly pathetic and pleading look over to Van, because Van picks up her kung pao chicken immediately. "Let's get some air," she says, standing up and absorbing Alice into her orbit as she walks slowly and deliberately out of the room.

Marie wordlessly picks up the container of lo mein and a pair of chopsticks from where she'd dropped them onto the counter, and presses them into Alice's hands as they pass. Van usually walks with such a quick stride, but Alice finds herself slowing down to match Van as Van heads to the same balcony as before, sliding the door closed behind them and settling into a chair. She doesn't say anything, simply eating her chicken in silence and letting Alice take the lead.

Alice plops into the other chair and tries not to think about how Van is quite possibly everything she's ever wanted.

Van's almost done with her kung pao by the time Alice is ready to talk.

"Both my parents died in this hospital," Alice says to her lo mein, aiming for casual and probably hitting a tone closer to robot-about-to-fucking-lose-it. "My mom when I was eight, and my dad when I was nineteen."

"Alice," Van says, tender and so gentle.

Alice doesn't look up. She can't. She can't possibly face the expression she knows Van must be wearing. The horror, the pity, the sorrow. She's spent most of her life avoiding that look, and she knows seeing it on Van's face—Van, who means more to her after a few days than most people in her life ever have—will break her.

Alice refuses to be broken.

"They were in a fire when I was eight, while I was at a sleepover." Alice recites the facts to her noodles like she's reading them from a book, like she's memorized them from someone else's life. "The apartment was really old, not up to code. The smoke was extra toxic, I guess. My mom was in the hospital for a month, but she didn't make it. My dad lost a lung, and he was pretty sick for the rest of his life. He was always in and out of here. He got lung cancer when I was in middle school and died when I was nineteen."

"Alice," Van says again. "*Alice.*"

Alice shakes her head. Her chest feels tight and there's tension mounting in the center of her forehead, a sure sign that her body wants to cry. She squeezes her eyes shut, forcing her tears back down with iron will, desperation, and twenty-odd years of practice.

"Alice, look at me," Van says softly, moving to kneel in front of Alice. She takes the lo mein out of Alice's limp grasp, placing it on the little table between their chairs and resting both her hands on Alice's thighs.

Alice focuses on the pressure of Van's hands on her, not heavy but solid. Present. Grounding. She blinks a few times and then lets her eyes skim over Van's face.

There's the look, almost exactly like she knew it would be.

"I am so sorry," Van says, but there's something firm underneath the pity and softness, something Alice hasn't seen before, like Van means it, like it matters. "I'm so sorry that happened to them. To you."

Alice shakes her head. "It's okay," she tries, but Van says, "No," and her hands tighten.

Her fingers twitch on Alice's legs. "We've been dragging you here with us, every fucking day, and this is . . . god. The worst place in the world for you. I'm so sorry. I don't—I can't imagine."

Alice clears her throat, hoping her voice won't break. "It's okay. I mean, yeah, it's hard to be here, but it's okay. I'm not . . ." She doesn't know how to say it nicely, how to say that in the grand scheme of things, watching Nolan die doesn't really feel like watching her parents die, because she didn't fucking know him and quite frankly if he had dropped dead in his apartment she would have grieved for a few weeks and then moved on to a new fixation to distract herself from her lonely, disappointing, shitty life.

"It's not the same," she finally says. "I can handle it."

"You don't have to," Van says. "I can come to your place, call you. We can keep you updated without you having to be here."

This is exactly what Alice has been looking for. It's an out, finally a reason to back away without having to tell the truth, without hurting anyone. She can say, *Yes, thank you for caring about my trauma,* and moonwalk right on out of this situation.

She expects to feel a rush of relief, a release of all of the lie-induced tension she's been carting around, but she doesn't.

Something that certainly isn't relief is surging up from her gut into her throat, screaming at her to stay, to cling as tightly as she can to Babs, to Marie. To Van. As shitty as evading the truth makes her feel, leaving the Altmans—leaving Van—is abhorrent. Staying makes her a truly horrible person, but she can't let them go, not yet.

"I don't want to intrude on family stuff," she says carefully. "But it seems like your mom is happy that I'm here." She's not proud of blaming Babs for her staying—it feels closer to lying than anything else has so far—but the churning dread in her stomach at the idea of backing away has left her with no other choice.

Something flickers across Van's face, something that would maybe be frustration if she let it. "You don't need to be reliving your trauma just to make my mom feel better," she says, almost in a whisper. "You don't—you don't owe her anything. She's not . . ."

She's not your mom, she means.

Yeah, Alice is quite clear on that, thanks.

She closes her eyes, shoving down the unspeakably selfish, awful, evil thought that if Nolan dies and her lie is never found out, maybe Babs could be, though.

"Your mom is a really nice person and has been really kind to me," she says, opening her eyes and immediately wishing she were still looking into her lo mein instead of at Van's beautiful, chiseled, caring face. She stares at the little white scar on Van's cheek, right above her faint dimple. She tries not to wonder what it would feel like under her fingertips. Her lips.

"I want to do whatever I can to make this horrible situation easier for her," Alice says, which is completely true and not the complete truth. It's not why she's putting herself through this. Not entirely, anyway. Not anymore.

The fucked-up thing is that the nicer Babs is, the more earnestly Van cares, the closer Alice feels to them, the more she lies to them. The harder she works to stay. Not to victim-blame, but if they were worse people, she wouldn't be lying to their faces, technically or otherwise. If Van weren't so kind right now, weren't kneeling in front of Alice like Alice is the most important, precious thing in the world, Alice would have stopped, dropped, and rolled right out of here. She wonders why *Jerry Springer* isn't still on TV; this would make a great episode. America would love to hate her.

"What can I do?" Van is still kneeling in front of her, her hands hot on Alice's thighs. This has been quite possibly one of the least sexy conversations Alice has ever had—for some reason talking about her dead parents and unresolved trauma has never really done it for her—but she can't help but notice how intimate this is. Not just emotionally, not just how Van seems to be holding Alice's feelings with a steady, gentle, caring pressure, like Alice deserves kindness and isn't a terrible liar, but physically, too. It's intimate how close Van is. How big her hands are, how long her fingers, how Alice's legs have fallen open to allow Van to ease her torso between them.

You can get up, Alice thinks. *You can let me take a breath without smelling your skin. You can take your hands off me. You can wrap me up in your arms and never let go.*

"I mean, I won't say no to more hugs from Frank," Alice says, because she can't say anything else.

Van might hear everything else, though, because her smile is still sad when she says, "Deal."

NINE

On Sunday morning, Alice takes a deep breath and knocks on Isabella's front door. She's clutching a bag of bagels from the grocery store, sure she should be bringing something better but she doesn't get paid until next week. She'd have liked to bring something for the kids, little toys or whatever, but she's not exactly sure how old they are and she doesn't know if Isabella is going to be the type of Portland parent who needs everything in their house to be perfectly organic and made out of undyed recycled free-trade rainforest wood. Alice assumes they don't sell that hippie shit at the dollar store.

The house is cute, two stories and narrow. It's surprisingly close to Van's duplex, up in North Portland near the St. Johns Bridge. It had taken two buses and over an hour to get here from home, making Alice more grateful than ever for the way Van has been shuttling her all around the city the last few days.

The front door opens, and there she is. Isabella. Alice's only living family member. She doesn't look a thing like Alice; her dad is Persian, and she has his thick black hair and warm brown skin. She's only a few months older than Alice, but she already has some streaks of gray in her hair and a few lines at the corners of her eyes.

Damn, Alice thinks. *Having kids really does a number on you.*

"Alice!" Isabella pulls Alice into her arms, and Alice is too stunned to do anything but loosely hug her back.

She's tugged inside the house, and it smells so much like Isabella's childhood home that Alice is instantly transported back in time as she toes her shoes off in the hallway. Back when Alice's mom was alive, both families would gather at Isabella's at least once a week for a meal, Alice and Bella spending hours lying on the floor of Bella's bedroom, playing games and watching Disney movies on VHS while Bella's dad cooked. Alice would come home with Bella after school whenever her mom had to work late, mainlining snacks and doing homework at the kitchen table under her aunt's watchful eye.

Then her mom died, and the visits dried up. Right when Alice needed them the most, the invitations stopped coming, and her dad was too sad and sick to notice.

And then Isabella's family up and moved to fucking Texas, and Alice was alone with a dad who couldn't breathe.

Alice follows Isabella through the house, barely hearing Isabella's idle descriptions of the rooms they're passing through, trying to push down the pain of those first years when she lost not only a mom but an aunt, an uncle, and a cousin so close she might as well have been a sister. She tries not to let the smells of the kitchen Isabella leads her to—cumin, turmeric, and roasted meat—remind her of her uncle's cooking, of those long days of childhood innocence. One of Alice's therapists—her least favorite one, who smelled like cabbage and had an insulting framed quote on his desk that read EVERYTHING HAPPENS FOR A REASON—had suggested that Isabella's mom was grieving her sister too much to be able to see Alice, who looked so much like her mom, and that maybe her aunt resented her dad for surviving when her mom didn't. Alice suggested that her aunt should have fucking gotten over it and not left an eight-year-old child alone, adrift, without a real mom or a backup mom. Her therapist suggested some yoga and crystals for her anger. Alice fired him soon after, and it turned out his quote was right; it *was* for a reason.

Anyway. She never did quite get the hang of yoga, but she's pretty good at trying to shove all of her resentment back where it belongs, and she tries to flex that muscle right now. Namaste.

The move to Texas wasn't Isabella's fault, Alice silently reminds herself as Bella rambles about the botched installation of her new fridge; it wasn't her decision to abandon Alice to face middle school and a dying dad by herself. Isabella was only a kid too. Sure, she didn't call when she moved back—and sure, there are phones in Texas that she definitely didn't use for the last twenty years—but she called now. And she's always texted on Alice's birthday, commented on her infrequent posts.

Alice needed her back when everything was falling apart, yes, but she needs her now too. She's willing to give it a shot.

Two small children come flying into the kitchen, both holding on to the same toy.

"Mommy," the bigger one screeches, "Hazel took my truck!"

"No!" the little one screams. "Miiiiiiiiiine!"

"Okay," Isabella says, reaching down between them and prying the truck out of their tiny but eerily strong fingers. "Now it's my truck. Say hi to your Auntie Alice, please."

Alice blinks. Auntie Alice? Technically she's their cousin—first cousin once removed, Google told her earlier this morning. She never expected to be anyone's auntie.

But then again, she never expected to be anyone's fake-girlfriend either, so this week is full of surprises. "Hi, guys," she says, looking down at them. "How's it going?"

They both stare up at her, dark eyes and trembling lips. She can tell they're each only one small indignity away from throwing a massive fit, so she submissively breaks eye contact, hoping that will feel like a win for them.

"Sebastian," Isabella says, placing the truck up on the counter where neither can reach it. "Can you tell Auntie Alice how old you are?"

The bigger one seems to really think it through for a while. Alice isn't sure if he's running the math on his age or on whether or not she deserves the information. "Sree," he finally allows, holding up three little fingers.

"Thhhhree," Isabella says to him. "Try it."

"Thhhhree," he repeats, thoroughly dousing his sister in a healthy amount of spit.

"And how old is Hazel?"

"One and a half!" He holds up two fingers, but he's got the spirit of it for sure.

"Wow," Alice says. "You're pretty grown up."

"Yeah!" He turns around and runs off, shouting, "Legos!" with Hazel toddling behind him. Well, he's grown up enough to know when he's done with a conversation, which honestly is a skill Alice admires.

Isabella turns to Alice, a wry look on her face. "So, those are my spawn." Alice laughs, and Isabella smiles at her. "Henry's at work, some sort of mycological emergency, I don't know, but he'll be back in a bit. He can't wait to meet you. Come, sit down. Coffee?"

Alice sits on one of the stools tucked under the kitchen island. "My . . . cological?" she asks, beyond confused. "And yes to coffee, please."

"Mushrooms," Isabella says, her back to Alice as she grabs two mugs from a high cabinet. "He's a scientist. I don't understand a bit of it, but the man loves a good fungus."

"Oh," Alice says faintly. "Sure." She wishes a mushroom emergency were the weirdest thing to happen to her this week, but it's barely cracking the top five.

Isabella puts a warm mug of coffee in front of her, and Alice gratefully wraps her fingers around it. It was freezing on the buses, and she's chilled through. "Thanks. I just moved from the night shift at work to the day shift, so my sleep schedule is super fu— Um, messed up."

Isabella laughs at her failed attempt to not curse. She quickly puts together a few plates of bagels and scrambled eggs, pulling bacon out of the oven and strawberries out of the fridge. She drops two small plates on a low table in the living room, but the kids don't notice and she doesn't seem to mind. "They'll find it when they're hungry," she says, coming to sit up next to Alice at the island. "They're grazers."

"Like you," Alice says, remembering how Isabella's dad always had food out—yellow rice or kebabs or peanut butter—and how Isabella was sort of constantly eating but never actually ate a full meal at once.

Isabella's eyes crinkle up as she smiles at Alice. "I'd forgotten I used to do that," she muses, almost to herself. "That's . . ." She trails off, looking closely at Alice. Alice wonders what marks of the years Isabella is seeing on her face, how old and haggard she looks from a lifetime of too much responsibility and not enough money.

"I'm really happy to see you," is what Isabella finally says, her nervous, rambling energy seeming to ease a bit, and Alice lets herself smile back.

"Me too."

"So," Isabella says around her first mouthful of scrambled eggs. "Tell me about this guy! He, like, dropped dead in front of you and you heroically saved his life or some ships?"

Alice wonders if she heard right, or maybe if she, like Nolan, is having some sort of serious brain malfunction. "Some . . . ships?"

"Oh," Isabella says with a laugh. "When Sebastian was born, Henry and I decided to pull a *Good Place* and say words that sound like curses. Ships, muck, hitch, grass. Whatever. Shiitake is his favorite, for obvious reasons, and it—very embarrassingly—became habit."

Alice laughs. "I love it."

But Isabella grimaces. "Yeah, I did too, until my boss overheard me last week saying, 'Ships ships ships I dropped my coffee, oh muck me.'"

She drops her head into her hands as Alice positively cackles.

"Pretty mucking humiliating," Alice manages to say, which makes Isabella snort, and Alice absolutely loses it.

Once they've both stopped wheezing, Alice asks, "You're still in PR?" and Isabella nods.

"Communications, yeah. Same difference. Making sure everyone and their mom who hears about our company thinks about sunshine and rainbows." Alice thinks that's kind of like being a receptionist, but probably much better paid. She and Isabella are both the smiling face at the doorway, the woman pretending she's not being friendly and enthusiastic for a paycheck but instead because this is truly the best building/company in the universe!

"Okay," Isabella says, taking a sip of her own coffee. "You and this dude. Spill."

"Uh . . ." Alice picks at her bagel. "I mean, there's not much to tell. He collapsed, I did CPR and called 911, then the EMTs came."

"Wow, way to make something so badgrass sound boring."

Alice snickers at *badgrass,* but shrugs at the rest of it.

"So wait. You guys were dating?"

Alice takes a questionably large bite of bagel to buy herself some time. This is a direct question. Either yes, they were dating, or no, they were not dating. There's really no way to slide past this one like she's slid past all the others.

And also . . . wait.

She has to lie—or, well, whatever she's doing. Omit, maybe. She has to omit to Nolan's family because she decided not to hurt them while he's dying, and she has to omit to her boss so she'll stay on the day shift. But Isabella isn't an Altman, and she isn't Mr. Brown. She doesn't know any of them.

Isabella is the one person in the world Alice could tell the truth to.

Before she can chicken out too much, before she can seize onto the fear that what she's doing is so terrible that Isabella will kick her out of the house, this sweet family reunion over before it truly began, Alice painfully swallows a lump of dough and shakes her head.

"Funny story about that, actually."

Ten minutes later, Isabella's eyes are wide, her jaw slack with surprise. She's been frozen like that for Alice's entire story, her breakfast forgotten and her coffee growing cold. "Jiminy cremini, this is the craziest ship I've ever heard in my life."

Alice grimaces. "It's . . . um. Well. Definitely the most confusing situation I've ever been in, that's for sure."

"So, okay," Isabella says, rubbing at her forehead. "Let me make sure I got this right. You've literally never spoken to this man, and his whole enormous family thinks you're his, like, serious girlfriend, and you're just . . . faking it and hoping you don't get found out?"

"I mean, when you say it like that it sounds insane."

Isabella laughs, something high and almost hysterical. "How else could you put it?"

Alice shrugs. "I guess I figured . . . they were so happy to think that he was settling down, that he was with someone who cared about him. I didn't . . . I didn't want to make any of this harder on them. If it makes them feel good to believe that, I guess I hoped it wasn't hurting anyone."

Isabella's eyes get softer, some of the wild energy draining out of her. "I get that," she says, her voice caring now, something maternal in it. She drops her hand on top of Alice's and squeezes. "I do. But what about if he wakes up?"

Alice breaks her bacon into tiny pieces. "Originally, I figured they'd be so happy he was alive that they wouldn't really care about me. But now . . ." Her lips twist up. "Now I don't know. We've gotten closer than I thought we would. Especially me and Van. I don't know, I think she'd be . . . it kind of feels like she, sort of . . ." She trails off, grimacing. She's not sure how to say this. "I think she, like . . . cares."

Isabella's voice is gentle. "About you?"

Alice nods. "Yeah. Like, separate from my relationship to Nolan, or whatever. You know? Like, his mom cares about me because of what she thinks I meant to him, but for Van, maybe . . . it's not about him. Or not all of it. I think some of it's about me."

Isabella almost laughs, shaking her head. "Holy everything, Al. I mean, I know my life is basically a boring suburban mom cosplay right now, but, wow. This is all . . . *holy ships,* you know?"

Alice chuckles, taking a bite of bacon. "Tell me about it. A whole mucking flotilla of ships."

After a couple more plates of bacon and one toddler meltdown, Alice finds herself led into the living room to sit on the floor with Hazel and Isabella. Hazel is playing with magnetic tiles while Sebastian is enjoying screen time, so mesmerized by some show on his iPad that Alice is pretty sure he hasn't blinked in literal minutes.

Isabella has spent the last five minutes incessantly demanding that Alice show her a picture of Nolan, which has resulted in Alice trying to figure out Marie's Instagram handle.

"I wonder why he doesn't have an account," Isabella says, leaning over Alice's shoulder to look while half-heartedly stacking some tiles.

"Probably to keep all of the women in his life from finding out about each other," Alice mumbles.

"Woof. Nice boyfriend you've got there, Rue Rue."

"Tell me about it. You should have seen the receptionist at his— Oh! That's her. Okay." She clicks on Marie's profile, and bless her oversharing generation, it's public. Alice only has to scroll for a minute or two before she sees familiar faces. She clicks on the picture, and yup. There they all are. It's everyone she's grown to know in the last five days, and honestly it's weird to see Nolan standing up among them instead of lying silently between them. Van had mentioned Chanukah, but it seems like they must celebrate both, since in the picture they're all wearing thick Christmas sweaters, posed in front of a decorated tree.

"That's him," she says, handing the phone to Isabella.

"Daaaaaamn, girl," Isabella says, grinning. "Your fake-boyfriend is hot!"

"Thank you. I picked him out myself."

Isabella zooms in on Van and Marie, standing side by side. "That's the sister?" she asks, pointing at Marie.

"Yeah. Both sisters."

"Where is— Oh. I see. Sorry, I thought that one was a dude."

Alice tries not to ruin things by getting frustrated. Straight people can be so freaking narrow sometimes. "That's Van."

"Huh," Isabella says. Then, after a beat, "She's hot too."

Alice swallows, something in her throat suddenly thick. "Yeah."

Isabella hands the phone back, but there's something pointed and knowing in her face that Alice is absolutely sure is going to become very, very dangerous in the future.

Only a couple minutes later, when Alice is focused on making the magnetic tiles into a star, Isabella seems to get uncomfortable, some of the nervous energy from before popping back up. She's shifting more than is warranted by the soft living room rug underneath them. "Hey, I, um . . ." Isabella looks down at the tiles in her hands, putting them together with way more focus than is required. She lets out a loud, long breath, and then she finally looks up at Alice. "I have to apologize."

Alice blinks a couple times. "For . . . what?"

Isabella seems like she's almost going to laugh, but not because something is actually funny. "For everything," she says, her voice quiet and serious. "I didn't . . . I think back when I was a kid and we moved away, I didn't really get it. I didn't fully understand what you were going through, and I had all these other cousins in Texas, and I . . ." She bites her lip, and Alice wonders if she's going to say *forgot about you.* "I had this whole new life," Bella finally says. "And I didn't understand that you didn't too."

That punches Alice in the gut a little bit, but she gets it. Kids are self-centered. It was Isabella's parents' job, her mom's job, to remind her about Alice. To not have yanked her away from Alice in the first place.

"You were a kid," Alice says, leaning forward. "You couldn't have been expected to—"

But Isabella cuts her off, a wry smile on her face. "I haven't been a kid in a long time, Alice."

Well, she's not wrong.

Alice waits, wondering what's coming next. She's honestly furious that Bella didn't reach out when they moved back, and she's curious to hear what Bella's going to say about it.

"It wasn't until college that I really started to look back and be like, okay, what the actual muck, you know? Like I put all of the pieces together, and only realized then that what happened was so messed up, that my mom totally dropped you and your dad, and that I had been, like, a horrible cousin."

Alice shakes her head, more out of polite habit than honest disagreement, but Isabella keeps going. "But instead of reaching out then and being like 'Wow, that was messed up, let's be friends again,' I think I got . . . ashamed." She's twisting her fingers. "I felt so shitty about how I'd ghosted you that I was too embarrassed to reach out. So I didn't."

Alice can tell from the fact that she cursed, actually said *shitty* instead of *shippy* or whatever, even with Hazel right there on the rug with them, that she means it.

"I've regretted it, always," Isabella says, looking right at Alice. "And I know this doesn't make up for it, but I really . . ."

She takes another long breath, like she's bracing herself. "If you could ever forgive me, I'd really like to be close the way we used to. You're my family, and I don't want it to be weird anymore."

She looks like she might cry, and Alice has been through a lot of surprises this week, but this is the one that makes tears come to her eyes.

She could have a cousin again. Family, again. A person who loves her, who's there for her, who might even have Alice over for Thanksgiving and Christmas, invite Alice to her kids' birthday parties and bring over food when Alice is sick. Someone who could know Alice well enough that she wouldn't always have to explain herself, someone who would know to never leave a candle burning in an unattended room, or smoke a cigarette in front of her. Someone who could be her best friend again.

It isn't hard to find forgiveness. She needed Isabella back then, but she wants her now too.

She reaches out, pulling her cousin into a side hug that should be awkward, but isn't.

"It's already done," she says, and Isabella squeezes her back until Hazel drops herself into Alice's lap like a wrestler, all pointy elbows and sharp knees and suspiciously wet diaper.

An hour or so later Alice is due to leave for the hospital, but instead of letting her look up the bus schedule, Isabella insists that Alice text Van to see if she's home. "It's a fifteen-minute drive to Portland Grace from here, and you said she lives nearby," Isabella insists. "Why not try to save yourself an hour on the bus if you can?"

Which is how Alice finds herself waiting in the kitchen,

shoes and jacket on, for Van to pick her up from her cousin's house.

She hopes that Van will simply text from outside when she's there, but she has a sinking suspicion that Van "I'll walk you up a bunch of flights of stairs" Altman doesn't quite have that move in her repertoire.

And, lo and behold, there's a sharp, crisp knock on the door.

Alice opens it, but Isabella is immediately elbowing her out of the way. Van is there, tall and solid in the freezing rain.

"You must be Nolan's sister Van," Isabella chirps, neatly shoving Alice a few steps backward into the house. "I'm Isabella. Please, come in."

"No," Alice starts, but Van is already stepping inside, careful not to drip too much water on the floor as she pushes her hood back.

"Nice to meet you," Van says, holding out a hand that Alice has to imagine is ice-cold and wet. Isabella takes it enthusiastically, and Alice is forcibly reminded of how easy it was to make friends as a kid with Isabella by her side. Bella did all the work, Alice following like a quiet shadow and reaping the benefits by tagging along to everything Bella was invited to.

"You too," Isabella says, something dangerous glinting in her eye. "Alice has been telling me all about you and your family."

Van shifts, and it's the first time Alice has ever seen her look anxious. Actually, come to think of it, Van looks a little pale, the circles under her eyes heavier than usual. Alice wonders if she didn't sleep well.

Alice wonders what her bedroom looks like, if Frank sleeps in the bed next to her.

"I didn't realize Alice had family in town," Van says, looking between them. "And so close by."

"Oh, that's because I'm a total grasshole. We moved back from Texas a couple months ago but I was so frantic dealing with the kids and new jobs and everything that I didn't reach out until now."

Alice can see Van's mouth moving over the syllables of *grasshole,* but before she can ask, said kids come up to them.

Hazel immediately pulls on Isabella's hand, and Isabella sweeps her up onto her hip. Sebastian is staring hard at Van, his iPad dangling from his hand. "Are you a boy or a girl?"

"Sebastian!" Isabella's eyes go wide as she shushes him. "That's not polite—"

"It's okay," Van says, crouching down to look at Sebastian with a slight wince. "What's your name?"

"Sebastian."

"Sebastian. That's a cool name. My name is Van. Like a minivan."

Sebastian giggles, clearly as enraptured with Van as his auntie is.

"I'm a girl," Van says, "but that doesn't really matter, does it? Because no matter if you're a girl or a boy or both or neither, you can still have friends and eat snacks and play games and have fun, right?"

Sebastian seems to be considering for a while. No one says anything, letting him chew on it. Finally he nods a little bit, clearly approving of this new information. "Wanna see my room?"

"Oh heck yes." Van goes to stand up but she wobbles a little bit, sinking back down immediately. Alice grabs onto her arm, her fingers slipping on the wet, slick surface of her raincoat as she helps tug Van back upright. "Thanks," Van says, studiously not making eye contact with Alice. She quickly toes out of her boots and Sebastian offers her his hand. She takes it, wordlessly following him as he leads her into the house, giving her a grand tour that he certainly didn't offer Alice.

"Well," Isabella says, watching them go. "I guess Sebastian's a fan." Hazel starts wiggling, and the instant Isabella puts her down, she toddles as quickly as she can after Van and Sebastian. Isabella laughs. "Got it, make that two fans."

Alice laughs because she should, and also because some part of her is relieved to see someone else falling so quickly under Van's spell. It makes her feel better; yes, she's hopelessly bisexual but also Van is clearly as magnetic as Hazel's tiles.

Alice listens to the sounds of Sebastian narrating his room to Van, and she's never been jealous of a preschooler before but she is now. She wishes she could be the one hand in hand with Van, showing off her bedroom and all her favorite things, the sole focus of Van's steady gaze and warm, easy smile.

TEN

It takes half an hour to extract Van from Sebastian's clutches, but they finally succeed through a winning combination of bribery (Legos) and distraction (more Legos!). The promised fifteen-minute drive to Portland Grace later, and Alice and Van are stepping inside the ICU, raincoats dripping. Babs and Marie are sitting in Nolan's hospital room, which looks different today. The mug from his fraternity is prominently displayed on the little table next to his bed now, plus what looks like every single other personal item from his office. The bobbleheads, even a stress ball that Alice is absolutely sure he got from some mandatory HR training. Aunt Sheila had pulled it out of the back of one of his desk drawers with a crow of triumph most suitable for a win on the battlefield, and is now clearly showing it off like some kind of trophy.

Finally, the décor shouts to Alice. *Some tiny indication that he's a person and not just a finance bro robot!* It's like Babs and Aunt Sheila have created a shrine to the person they think he is, but since it's populated only with these few meaningless bits and bobs from his office, it has the opposite effect on Alice. Without his suits and his job and his diplomas and his women . . . Alice still has no idea who Nolan actually is, and she's becoming worried that maybe it's not about *when* she learns more about him, but *if* she does. If there's actually anything more to learn, or if she's seen what there is to see, and this meager shrine is the best anyone could do for him.

Alice wonders what would be in her hospital room if the roles were reversed. What would Isabella pull out of her studio to cozy up the sterilized space around her bed? The dusty paperbacks from her side table, the old Christmas ornaments from her mom, her favorite big blue mug, the photos of her and her parents smiling, back before the fire?

Is there anyone whose life wouldn't look pathetic, distilled down into depressing hospital decorations?

There's one other big change in the room: Nolan's comatose form is now covered with what looks like a hand-knit blanket, which Babs keeps stroking as she sits by his head. The blanket is bursting with color—all deep reds and bright yellows and liquid blues—and it should make the room feel brighter but all Alice can focus on is how it makes Nolan look paler.

Ideally he'd be getting pinker and pinker each day, but his face still has that grayish, ashen sheen she remembers all too well from her dad's last few months. It's not a super alive color, and honestly the blanket is making it worse.

"I love this blanket," Alice gushes to Babs. She's very purposely technically not lying about being his girlfriend, but she's definitely cool with lying about other shit. A girl has to get by somehow, right?

"Thank you, honey," Babs says, looking up with those big

eyes that Alice is pretty sure haven't been fully clear of tears since Nolan collapsed five days ago. "I knitted it when I was pregnant with him."

Alice tries not to picture it. Young Babs, curled up on a couch, knitting around her enormous belly, hoping her child will turn out to be worthy of these bright, vivid colors, to be as bold and warming as this blanket.

Nolan doesn't strike Alice as a bright-colors person—he's always worn very traditional suits to work, and his office was basically monochrome. He feels more like an expensive slate-gray cashmere blanket than this riot of handmade color.

This blanket feels a lot more like Van than like Nolan.

But, then again, what the fuck does Alice know? Never having actually talked to him or anything.

"It's beautiful," Alice says. "What a wonderful gift."

"I have mine in my dorm," Marie says. "It's water themed."

Babs gives her youngest a sad smile. "My little Marina."

Alice blinks. Okay, so Marie's name is maybe Marina? Seems like a weird time to be learning Marie's actual name, but okay. Sure. Marie's a cute nickname for Marina.

Nolan, Vanessa, and Marina.

Alice almost laughs at how ridiculous it is to think of Van as a Vanessa. She's not a Vanessa. She's not anything but a Van. Blunt and to the point, unique, surprisingly soft, butch as the day is long. She turns her head, about to ask Van how old she was when she started going exclusively by Van—and by the way, why does her business card say Vanessa instead—but she stops short at the expression on Van's face.

It's pinched, something painful in the clench of her jaw, years of buried hurt in the way her shoulders are inching up toward her ears. Alice rewinds the conversation in her mind, trying to pinpoint what could have happened. They were talking about the blankets. Nolan has one, and Marie does too. She's about to ask about Van's, but then she glances between Van and Babs, who are very studiously not looking at each other, and clocks the way Marie looks at Van and then guiltily drops her eyes.

Oh.

Van doesn't have one?

She must not be very subtle—in fact, she's pretty sure her jaw is hanging open as she stares between them all like she's watching a horrifying tennis match of unresolved family trauma—because Babs says, "Nolan and Van didn't care as much for theirs. I've held on to Nolan's for him, and Van gave hers away years ago."

A muscle jumps in Van's jaw, but she doesn't say anything.

It's so painfully awkward that Alice considers leaping out the window.

"Why don't you guys go get some food and fresh air," Van finally says, looking at her mom and Marie. "Alice and I can hold down the fort for a while."

It's, of course, forty degrees and raining, but like all born and bred Portlanders, both Babs and Marie look excited by the idea of going outside. They troop out, and the instant the door closes behind them, Van sags down into the chair next to Nolan.

She looks so fucking exhausted that Alice has an absurd urge to drop into her lap, to cradle Van's head to her chest, to stroke her hair until Van falls asleep against her.

But of course that would be weird, wildly inappropriate, and quite possibly unwelcome, so Alice forces herself to sit down in the other chair, the one across the bed from Van, and hold on to her own hands to keep them to herself. She doesn't know what to say—to Nolan, to Van, about what just happened, about all of the history that Alice doesn't understand but is influencing everything happening in this room—so she doesn't say anything.

It's maybe three or four minutes, functionally an eternity, before Van says, "It was pink."

Alice blinks a couple of times. She was going through her monthly budget in her head, trying to figure out if her small raise from the day shift will mean she can afford to buy a couple more fresh vegetables a week, so she's a little lost. "What was?"

"My blanket," Van says, finally looking up at Alice. She's holding the edge of Nolan's blanket, rubbing the soft yarn between two of her fingers. Alice can't tell if she's jealous or disgusted. Or both. "It was all pink. She was super pumped about having a girl, I guess." She gives a tiny shrug, so small Alice wouldn't have noticed if she hadn't been staring so hard. "I wasn't quite what she'd expected, I guess."

She grimaces up at Alice, almost like she's trying to make it seem like a joke, but nothing has ever been less funny.

Alice swallows, hard.

"Anyway," Van says, raising her shoulders again, this time like she's trying to shrug it off, to let the heaviness roll off her like it doesn't matter, even though Alice can still so clearly see the pain in her eyes, in the set of her mouth. "We got in a huge fight the summer after my sophomore year of college. A cousin was getting married and Mom was trying to force me to wear a dress to the wedding. I was living in Corvallis in this amazing, nasty group house with all my gay friends, deeply involved with the queer community on campus, finally coming into my own, you know, all that cliché shit of figuring out who I was and how I wanted to look." She gives Alice a wry smile, and

Alice's heart melts. She'd love to go back in time to meet baby butch Van, see the light in her eyes when she first tried on a suit or men's jeans, when she cut off her hair and saw herself in the mirror for the first time. "And then I came home for the summer, to this bedroom designed for, like, I don't know. Barbie's grandma."

Alice almost does a spit take.

Van actually smiles at her. "I mean, white lace and pink everywhere. Walls, décor, everything. And then this fucking hideous pink blanket on the bed, a tangible representation of everything my mom hoped I was going to be, you know? Like she put all of her girly, ballet, pigtails, shopping spree, low-fat-diet partner dreams into every fucking stitch, right?" She shakes her head, and Alice can't help it. She stands up and walks around the bed, sitting down on the edge right in front of Van. Nolan is behind her now, no longer between them. She's close enough to touch Van, but she doesn't.

Van doesn't say anything about it, but something might loosen in her face at Alice's proximity. "And anyway, I . . . I lost it. I told her I wasn't wearing the fucking dress and I hated the fucking blanket and no matter what I wore or what I slept under, I was never going to be straight and she needed to open her eyes and meet the kid she actually had instead of trying to force me to be the kid she wanted."

Alice's hands are on Van before she's finished talking. One on her shoulder, one gently brushing the side of her face before dropping down and squeezing her arm.

"Anyway. She donated the blanket to Goodwill or something, I don't know. And now we just . . . don't talk about it."

"Van," Alice breathes, but Van shakes her head.

"It's okay. I mean, it's fine. I'm still, like, you know. Part of the family. She didn't disown me or whatever. We . . . she'll be perfectly nice to whoever I'm dating but call them my friend. That kind of shit."

Alice squeezes Van even tighter. She can't imagine being disappointed in Van, wanting Van to be anything other than the brilliant, kind, gentle, beautifully queer butch that she is.

"I never came out to my dad," Alice offers softly, knowing there's nothing she can say to make this any better, to ease three decades of Van's pain. Van's eyes flicker up in that way queer people's always do when someone overtly comes out to them, even if they already suspected. That way that says, *Hey, I see you. You're one of mine.* Alice nods back in that way queer people often do, the tiniest motion of her head that says, *I know. We're one of each other's.*

"My mom died when I was too little, obviously, but my dad . . . By the time I'd guessed that I might be bi, in high school, he was already so sick. I didn't want to risk it, you know? Like, what if he wasn't okay with it, didn't want me around anymore, and then there was no one to take care of him?"

One of her hands is still on Van's arm, and Van brings her own hand up to cover Alice's, trapping it in her warm grip.

"So I didn't," Alice says, simple and true. "I've always wondered what he would've said. If he'd like who I am."

"There's no way he wouldn't," Van says, her voice a little thick. Alice shakes her head—Van is literally perfect and she was just talking about how her own mother hasn't gotten with the program—but Van clenches her fingers around Alice's until it's right on the line between pleasure and pain. "He'd be so proud of you, Alice."

Proud of what? Alice wants to say. Working these jobs she hates, still in the same apartment she's been in since he died, living every day like it's *Groundhog Day* and she's waiting to be woken up from the most boring, tedious dream on the planet? Lying to Babs and Aunt Sheila and Marie to get a tiny bit of comfort and care in return? Touching Van every chance she can while she's pretending to be halfway in love with Van's brother?

Alice is pretty sure there's not much to be proud of.

But Van doesn't need to hear any of that. "Everyone in your life should be proud of you," Alice says instead. "You're the best person I've ever met."

Van's lips press together, and Alice guesses that Van's inner monologue might sound pretty similar to hers right now.

Minus the enormous, ridiculous lie, of course.

They don't say anything else, but Alice doesn't move away, doesn't pull her hand back, until Babs and Marie come in.

ELEVEN

"Okay," Babs says, clapping her hands together three days later. Alice has just gotten to the hospital after work, and it's officially been an entire week that Nolan's been comatose, that Alice has been a part of this clan. "Let's head over to his condo before the sun sets."

It's clearly a shift change—all the women stand up, and the men both settle into the chairs, each with an iPad already open on his lap. Alice doesn't know what it is about middle-aged white men and their iPads, but it seems like the kind of true love that she thought only existed in storybooks.

The women head out of the hospital, and after a great deal of back and forth, they decide to all pile into Aunt Sheila's Honda Civic, which has a smaller backseat than Van's Volvo but is less likely to cover all of them in a fine but thorough layer of dog hair.

Alice finds herself wedged between Van and Marie in the back, insisting on yielding the seats with more leg room because she's several inches shorter than both of them. Plus, the prospect of spending ten long, quiet minutes pressed up against Van, shoulder to shoulder and thigh to thigh, well. It won't be the worst thing that's ever happened to Alice.

However, it ends up being a little less tender than all that. It turns out Aunt Sheila drives like maybe this is her first time ever behind the wheel. It's a short drive—they're not even crossing a bridge because apparently Nolan lives in a high-rise building right on the river in the Pearl District—but Aunt Sheila manages to bump over two curbs, use the horn four times, and almost crash into seven other cars. Despite her seatbelt, Alice is careening back and forth between Van and Marie like a Ping-Pong ball, but no one is making so much as a muttered comment.

Alice figures they must all be used to it.

She can't help but think about how gentle a driver Van is. She wonders what Babs and her husband drive like, if Van is so careful because of, or despite, whatever fresh hell this is.

They finally pull into a garage underneath an extremely fancy, very tall building that looks like it's glass all around, and the second Alice steps out of the car she has an absurd urge to cross herself, like she's survived some great journey.

She's also immediately grateful for Aunt Sheila's compulsive power walking because Alice doesn't have to pretend to know where she's going. She falls into step with Van, who is once again moving more slowly than Alice would have expected, able to follow Aunt Sheila without tipping anyone off that she's never been here in her life.

They get into an elevator and Alice carefully positions herself in the corner farthest from the buttons so she doesn't have to know which floor they're aiming for. Babs pushes the button marked 19, and Alice commits it to memory. Nolan Altman, fourteenth floor at work, nineteenth at home.

Not like Alice Rue, who is in the lobby at work and a third-floor walk-up at home.

The elevator spits them out into a hallway that's nicer than anywhere Alice has ever lived. Aunt Sheila practically sprints down it, calling out over her shoulder to Babs that she doesn't remember which door is Nolan's. Alice wonders why she doesn't slow down and wait for Babs, but who is she to interfere with someone else's process?

Babs and Marie stop in front of the door marked 1912. "It's this one, Aunt Sheila," Marie says, beckoning for her aunt, who is several doors past them by now, to come back. "Remember, it's the year the *Titanic* sank."

"I don't do boats," Aunt Sheila says, shaking her head at Marie as she gallops back to them. "You know that, Marina."

Next to Alice, Van snorts, and Marie mutters, "I mean, I wasn't suggesting we, like, get on the boat. 'Cause, you know, it's literally at the bottom of the ocean."

"Poor Leo," Alice says as quietly as she can. "He totally could have fit on that door."

Marie snickers and Van hums "My Heart Will Go On" as Babs enters the code the condo board gave her into the front door, because apparently this building is too fancy for keys. Keys are for peons, obviously. Plebs. Idiots who carry things and put them in things and might even have to jiggle them back and forth.

Alice remembers the word *doorgasm,* the way Van had stood so close to her outside her apartment, and feels her cheeks warming, her fingers twitching out to brush against Van's.

There's no chance of a doorgasm here. The mechanical lock makes a whirring sound, and then Babs opens the door. They all trail in after her like ducklings and Alice makes sure Van goes in front of her so no one will see Alice looking around to get her bearings.

They walk down a long, kind of narrow entranceway, turn left, and holy shit. Alice stops short. Like, she knew Nolan was rich. She knew from his office, from the outside of this building, from the way the hallway from the elevator looked like it was ripped right out of a catalogue, but, holy shiitake mushrooms, nothing in her entire life prepared her for this.

She's standing at the edge of a large open space that makes up living room, kitchen, and dining room, and it's glass all the way around. They're so high up that she's looking out over the entire city. The rolling hills of west Portland are straight ahead, and to her right is a glass wall overlooking the river, the park, and the Fremont Bridge. There's a huge fireplace that draws her eye—got to be fake, right?—and the furniture is all black or white and sleek. The whole kitchen is incognito, with a fridge that's pretending to be a cabinet, and cabinets that are pretending to be walls. Not a handle in sight. Alice has the absurd thought that maybe they're all controlled by an app or something, like he points his smartwatch at the kitchen and the fridge springs open and a plate magically lifts itself from a cupboard and floats down to the counter.

There's not a single cooking implement out, only what she thinks is either an espresso machine or a torture device. It has so many knobs and pokey things sticking out of it that the idea of having to use it before having any caffeine makes her armpits sweaty. Everything is clean. So clean. Too clean. It smells like . . . nothing.

"Oh man," Marie says. She's over on the side of the living room that doesn't face the river, and Alice belatedly tries to look less gobsmacked.

You've been here, she chants to herself. *You've been here. You've had sex here! You've seen this!*

"I forgot he has a whole-ass balcony," Marie says, and Alice tries to pretend like she knew that. Of course he has a whole-ass balcony. Why wouldn't he. Who doesn't, really?

She looks around the room, taking in how angular and impersonal everything is. There's abstract art on the walls but Alice doesn't know shit about art so she's not sure what it's telling her about Nolan or his taste. There's not a single photograph or keepsake or knickknack that looks like it wouldn't have been put there by someone staging the apartment for selling it. Like, if this were a model apartment, would anything have to change?

Seems like maybe no.

Alice tries not to think about Van's house, about how the worn, overstuffed sofa and the exercise ball and all of Frank's toys made it feel so much more welcoming than this space. Alice would be afraid to touch anything here—and god forbid if she had to eat or drink on that very uncomfortable-looking white sofa—but at Van's she felt immediately at home. At Van's she wanted to help with the dishes, put her feet up and watch TV, coax Frank's bony butt into her lap, and here she finds herself backing up until the kitchen counter is digging into her side, trying her best not to break or breathe on anything.

"Alice, why don't you and Marie go into the bedroom and gather whatever you think he'd like to have when he wakes up," Babs says. "His slippers, a book, whatever's in his nightstand. I'm sure he wouldn't want us old ladies rummaging through his things."

Right, right. The bedroom. Where all of the sex happened. Alice wonders if he has bunches of condoms and lube in his bedside table, if that's what his mom is afraid of finding.

Oh god. Or what if he has, like, a sex swing in there? Oh fucking fuck, what if everyone but Alice knows that he's super into some very specific kink, and this whole time they've been like, *Damn, Alice is really into eating spaghetti with her toes while being boned!*

This lie was a bad idea when it was all PG and sad, but Alice absolutely one hundred percent will not be able to handle it if it gets R-rated. Certainly, positively, hard pass on that.

"Sure," Alice says, her throat dry. "The bedroom. Let's, uh. Yup. Let's go. You and me, Marie. Na. Marina. Altman. Marina Altman."

Marie looks at her like she's having a stroke. "You good, Rue?"

"So good," Alice says, too loudly. She realizes that Marie is waiting for her to lead the way, and Alice wishes that she'd been assigned this task with Aunt Sheila, because she'd already have blazed the trail. There are two possible ways to go, both back through the entranceway. There had been a split left or right, and they'd gone left to get to the living room. So probably right? Okay. Alice can go right. Righty-ho, then.

She walks back out of the open space, confidently doing what she hopes is sauntering but sounds more like stomping, off in the direction she hopes is correct. And lo and behold, a bedroom!

Fucking genius, Alice thinks. *I'm a master of my environment. I'm a born liar. I should join the goddamned CIA.*

Although . . . the room is kind of small. And sure, there are floor-to-ceiling windows but they're pretty narrow. And there's not a bathroom attached, which seems odd.

Marie makes a confused sound from behind her. "Uh, isn't this the guest room?"

Shit. Alice mentally retracts her application to the CIA.

She's never been on an airplane and only speaks English, so honestly she's probably not their top choice of recruit. That's fine. Apparently being a receptionist has more subterfuge than she can handle anyway.

"Yes," she says, laughing way too nervously. "*Obviously.* I just wanted to, um, make sure there wasn't anything in here we wanted to grab. You know. On the way to the real bedroom. The one I've, um, you know. The big one."

Marie gives her a strange look, and Alice needs to fucking get it together. Marie is really, really not stupid, and Alice is being really, really weird right now.

Alice turns on her heel, back into the hallway. She tries to use her peripheral vision to take in her options, and, aha! Bingo.

She strides forward through an open door, and almost trips over herself when the first thing she encounters is a closet literally bigger than her childhood bedroom. It doesn't have doors or anything, it's just there. This is clearly what people mean when they say "suite"; Alice had thought it meant a bathroom attached to the bedroom, but no. Apparently for rich people it means three entire huge rooms, one for sleeping, one for dressing, and one for pooping.

The closet is rows and rows of suits and dress shoes, shirts and pants hung crisply on fancy hangers, ties rolled up in little dividers like this is a fucking department store. It's completely full, even though Alice knows her entire wardrobe, including winter coats, scarves, boots, and all, would take up maybe a fifth of it.

"Ugh," Marie says from behind her. "I'd kill for this closet."

Alice wonders if maybe Nolan did, in fact, kill for this closet. Like, how does a human even get this rich without making a bargain with the devil?

The bedroom is past the closet, and Alice tries not to look at the big bed with the unfriendly white duvet and white pillows propped up on the headboard. There are two nightstands, one on each side, and a TV mounted on the opposite wall.

Alice doesn't know what side of the bed Nolan sleeps on. Ugh, crap. Which one will have the condoms? She needs to save Marie from seeing that, but also . . . who will save *her* from seeing it?

Alice pokes her head into the bathroom—holy enormous shower, Batman—and conclusively decides that this is an absolutely terrible way to get to know someone. She wonders why there's never been a dating show with this premise, where the two strangers explore each other's bedrooms before going on a blind date. It would be a disaster, which probably means it would get seven or eight seasons at least.

"Why don't you take the bathroom," Alice suggests to Marie, mostly to get her out of eyesight, "and I'll start in here."

"Cool," Marie says, and Alice takes in a deep breath, squaring her shoulders.

Here we go.

Into the nightstand of a stranger.

She starts with the one closer to the window. She wouldn't want to sleep on that side of the bed herself, because it might feel like she was going to roll out of bed and down nineteen stories. She prefers to imagine a sturdy body between herself and the window. She tries to picture Nolan there, but in her mind he's lying flat on his back, hands at his side, his skin a sickly gray. Nope. No sleeping next to what is functionally a corpse, no thank you.

Although, of course, then her brain unhelpfully puts Van there instead. Alive, vibrant, looking over at Alice and grinning in a way Alice has never seen, something predatory and hungry, like she's going to reach over, pull Alice into herself, and absolutely ravish her.

"Nope," Alice says out loud, trying to force that vision out of her mind. "Absolutely not."

"What?" Marie calls from the bathroom.

"Nothing," Alice says quickly. *Fucking get it together!*

She opens the top drawer, and it's ... weird. A couple chargers for different kinds of phones, four kinds of ChapStick, some travel-sized lotions, sets of hair ties and bobby pins in different sizes and colors. Face wipes, gum, a box of tissues. It's all weirdly generic, like it doesn't belong to the same person. It's almost like ...

Alice slams the drawer quickly, shutting her eyes and breathing rapidly through her nose. It's okay. He's not really her boyfriend. None of this is real, so it doesn't matter that he has an entire pharmacy available for the random girls he sleeps with on the regular, with a variety of ChapSticks and hair ties for them to choose from.

She's not sure if the drawer is the most considerate or most skeezy thing she's ever seen in her life.

She doesn't bother to open the drawer below it. This is clearly not the side he sleeps on.

She walks around the bed, careful not to touch it for some reason she's deciding not to interrogate at this particular moment, and aha. This top drawer is clearly his. A notebook and some pens, a few expensive-looking watches, the remote for the TV, mints, what Alice is pretty sure is a wireless charge pad for his phone, a small flashlight, rewards cards for Starbucks and Whole Foods, a bottle opener shaped like a naked lady, a biography of some old white man CEO who is smiling up at Alice from the cover with dead eyes and a prominently receding hairline. She pulls out the notebook, a watch, and the creepy book, setting them on the bed. She can bring this successful plunder back to Babs.

She closes that drawer and moves to the bottom one, letting out a big breath before she opens it.

It's—yep. Okay. It's the sex drawer. It's not that she wants to look at it—she's all for sex and stuff, but *eww* at wading through a stranger's sex drawer—but she needs to know if there's something she needs to know. Luckily, it seems pretty vanilla, all things considered. Condoms—lots of condoms—lube, tissues. A little vibrator and what Alice is pretty sure is a butt plug, a set of leather handcuffs. Nothing weird. Nothing Alice would have to do a lot of research to figure out anyway.

Great.

Honestly, best-case scenario.

And anyway, it's not like she needs to bring any of that to the hospital.

She walks away from the bed, hugely relieved, and finds Marie in the closet, staring dumbly at all of his clothes.

"Overwhelmed?" Alice asks, and Marie nods, her jaw still slack. "I don't think I'll ever get used to how big this is," Alice says honestly, and Marie laughs.

"Me neither. Maybe let's aim for, like, pajamas and a bathrobe? I don't think he's going to be needing work stuff right away."

Alice considers saying something. Considers taking Marie's hand in hers and softly saying, "*Sweetheart, you need to start preparing for what happens if he doesn't wake up,*" but she doesn't.

Van wants Marie to still be a kid, to grow up slowly. To keep sleeping with that blanket her mama made her, to stay innocent for as long as she can. So if she thinks her brother is going to need pajamas and a bathrobe because he's about to wake up, well. That's okay.

Alice can try to find some pajamas.

TWELVE

Alice is so busy trying to use her powers of mind control to keep Aunt Sheila from crashing the car that it takes her way longer than it should to realize they aren't driving back to the hospital. It isn't until they're on the Broadway Bridge, fully halfway across the river, that Alice looks over at Van. "Wait, where are we going?"

"Oh right," Van says, smiling. "I forgot you haven't been to the house."

"The . . . house?"

"Our house," Babs says from the front seat.

Oh. Shiitake.

Okay. This is probably fine. Right? Going to Babs's house, seeing where Van and Nolan grew up, being surrounded by their knickknacks and evidence of the really nice life they had until a week ago, spending more time with Van outside of the sterile, extremely unsexy vibes of the hospital? It's harder than it should be not to flirt with her over her brother's graying body, but in a dim, cozy living room? Or, god forbid, in a bedroom?

Yeah, no. Possibly the tiniest bit not fine.

"Jeez, Mom," Marie says, leaning forward to look at Babs. "Did you even ask, or are we, like, kidnapping Alice right now and forcing her to participate in a religious ceremony against her will?"

Alice blinks a couple times. "Wh-what?"

Van laughs, and Babs clucks her tongue at her youngest. "It's just Chanukah, Marina. Stop being so dramatic."

"But did you ask?"

"Alice is family," Babs says, her voice firm. Alice forgets how to breathe. "Of course she's coming for Chanukah."

Marie, clearly unaffected by this life-changing proclamation, rolls her eyes as she settles back into her seat. "Alice," she says, her voice performatively loud. "Would you like to join us for a belated Chanukah celebration tonight?"

Alice can see Babs rolling her own eyes, and it would be hard to miss the bleating sound of Aunt Sheila laughing. "Um, I've never celebrated Chanukah before," she admits. "But as long as that won't mess anything up, then, yeah. Sure. I'd love to."

"It's not, like, a religious thing," Van tells her, her voice soft. "It's mostly food and candles."

Alice finds that confusing—Is Chanukah not, in fact, a Jewish holiday? And does that not, by definition, mean it's religious?—but she nods anyway. She doesn't need to roll up looking ignorant, even if it could be understandable that Nolan hadn't given her the full-on Judaism primer yet.

It's not a long drive, although Alice vows to never, ever be driven over a bridge by Aunt Sheila again, not as long as she lives. Aunt Sheila finally navigates into a neighborhood Alice doesn't know too well, one of the lovely old middle-class neighborhoods on the east side, full of well-loved Craftsman houses with small porches, slightly muddy lawns, basketball hoops, and surprising pops of color on their columns and front doors. She pulls into the driveway of a two-story house with light blue siding. The roof is steeply pitched, so the rooms on the top story must have sloped ceilings, their windows poking out cheerfully to look over the street. The front porch is framed with two squat columns, and there are two tall, slightly gnarled trees in the front, their bare branches dripping in the winter rain.

It's a perfectly Portland house, the kind Alice used to dream about owning one day. She and her dad would drive around when she was in middle school, back when they both thought he'd get better one day, and they'd pick out their favorite house, sometimes after a fearsome debate. They'd park in front of the winner and spin elaborate stories of how they'd decorate it, where their bedrooms would be, what kind of pets they'd have, who would have to mow the lawn in the springtime.

Alice hasn't let herself dream like that in a long time.

She and the Altmans pile out of the car and walk briskly up to the porch, their only concession to the rain the little turtle hunch of their heads into the collars of their jackets that, for everyone in Portland, is as natural as breathing. Alice already likes this house much better than Nolan's apartment, but she has to admit that accessing your place without getting rained on does sound pretty appealing.

Babs unlocks the front door and they all head inside. Everyone takes their shoes off in the foyer, and Alice does the same, enjoying not having to pretend that she's been here before. For once, she can look around the way she wants to, take things in without straining to see from her peripheral vision.

It's clearly an older house, not open concept or anything,

but from the living room she can see into the dining room, and the kitchen is around the corner from there. Like Van's, it's clearly lived in, cluttered with furniture but clean, and it's cozy but with more of a Pinterest or white-mommy-blogger twist. There are signs on the wall with cursive mantras that say things like HOME IS WHERE THE HEART IS and FAMILY, surrounded by posed photos of all three kids.

All of the furniture is nice but well used, like they bought it new fifteen years ago. It looks like the kind of house that's seen three children born and raised, and Alice loves it, even though Babs is clearly not happy with the state of it, striding through the living room and barking orders at Marie and Van like a drill sergeant about what to clean up first.

There's a door off the living room that Alice assumes is a closet, but Van opens it, and Alice catches a glimpse of a small bedroom before an enormous, gangly, white spotted animal flings itself out of the room at Van, all wriggling elbows and wet tongue.

"Hey, Franko," Van says, letting him jump up on her and scratching his face. "Hey, buddy."

"Frank!" Alice didn't consciously move, but she's suddenly right behind Van, and Frank is snuffling at her ears. "My favorite gentleman! I didn't know you'd be here."

"Oh yeah." Van pushes him down, where he makes enthusiastic circles around them, his tail smacking into Alice's thighs like a happy propeller. "He wouldn't want to miss Chanukah. Would you, boy?"

Alice grins down at him. "Now I'm picturing him in one of those little hats—what are they called?"

Van laughs. "A yarmulke? Good lord, that would be so freaking cute. Can you imagine?" She cups her hand over the top of his head, approximating what it would look like, and yes. It's quite possibly the cutest thing Alice has ever thought about. Frank gives them both a huge doggy grin, his tongue drooping out the side of his mouth, and Alice can't help it.

She drops down to her knees and opens her arms, and Frank wiggles his way into them. It's less a hug than her holding on to him while he tries to stick his nose all the way down into her eardrum, which is much louder and wetter than Alice would have imagined, but it's still perfect.

After only a minute of dog cuddles, Sergeant Babs orders Van and Alice to gather "the Chanukah supplies" from the garage, and Alice isn't sure what "Chanukah supplies" are—hopefully some little hats for Frank—but she nods and follows Van until something in the hallway stops her in her tracks.

"Oh. My. Fucking. God." Alice's eyes are bugging out. "Vanessa Altman. You have some 'splaining to do."

Van rolls her eyes and puts both hands on Alice's back, pushing her forward. "I said no detours."

"This isn't a detour," Alice protests, digging her heels in and refusing to be moved. Of course they both know Van could easily move Alice, could probably throw Alice over her shoulder if she really needed to, but Van's polite enough not to mention it and it's important for Alice not to think about such sexy things. "It's literally on the way. And we both know there's not a snowball's chance in hell that I was going to walk past this without getting an explanation." She gestures at the picture on the wall, and Van grimaces.

The whole hallway is filled with family pictures. They're crammed together like jigsaw puzzle pieces, frames large and small, everything from school portraits to embarrassing candids to those posed shots from Sears of all five of them dressed in identical outfits.

The one from the late nineties of the four of them (pre-

Marie, probably) in overalls and denim bucket hats absolutely deserves a long and thorough period of admiration, but the one that has Alice almost delirious is much, much better.

Alice's voice squeaks. "You were a *cheerleader?*"

Van rolls her eyes, pushing at Alice's shoulders again. "I was not."

"Umm," Alice says, grinning and pivoting to face Van, gesturing up at the picture and trying to stifle her laugh so she can demand answers. "Deny it all you want, but the photographic evidence doesn't lie. Admit it. You—the handsome, stone-cold butch standing before me—were once forced into this outfit, and it's been immortalized on this wall ever since."

Van must be only five or six in the picture. Her black hair is curly and wild up in two high pigtails, each secured with an enormous blue sparkly bow. She's wearing an honest-to-goodness cheerleading outfit, blue and silver and glittery as hell, and she's holding matching pom-poms. Her face is still obscured in the baby softness of childhood, but Alice would recognize that scowl anywhere. Little Van is clearly furious, a second away from ripping the bows out of her hair and yelling every bad word she knows, and it's absolutely the best thing Alice has ever seen.

"The whole thing lasted about five minutes," Van admits, yielding to the fact that Alice will absolutely never let this go. "I screamed the entire way there for the first day, and then lay down on the mats and refused to stand up for the whole hour. The teachers asked my mom not to bring me back."

Alice bursts out laughing, belatedly clamping a hand over her mouth. The Van in front of her is making pretty much the same face as the one on the wall, and Alice can't think of anyone less likely to like cheerleading.

"You could have been a cheer prodigy," Alice says, shaking

her head in faux sadness. "What if you've been depriving the world of your brilliance this whole time?"

"Seems likely," Van deadpans. "What with my immense pep and all."

Alice snorts—which is absolutely humiliating—and Van shakes her head again, smiling this time, and even when being mocked, Van is so affectionate that Alice can't help it. She reaches out, resting both palms on the top of Van's chest. Van is so tall and solid, and every time they touch Alice is surprised by how soft she is, by the give of her flesh, the way it feels like her body is trying to let Alice sink down into it, to envelop her.

"I would pay so much money to watch you lead one single solitary cheer."

They're standing very close together now, connected by Alice's hands, but Van leans even closer. "You couldn't afford me," she whispers into Alice's ear, and it's both hilarious and so, so painfully intimate that Alice's fingers flex, curling around Van's collarbones.

"Van?" That's Marie's voice. Alice springs backward, and Van does too, so that by the time Marie comes around the corner they're standing weirdly far apart. "Hey, Mom wants you to get down the box of blankets." Marie looks between the two of them, clearly trying to make sense of what she's seeing. "What are you guys doing?"

"Alice found the cheerleading picture," Van says, and her voice sounds different. Higher, maybe. Tighter.

"I had a lot of questions," Alice adds, trying to pull Marie's focus away from how Van won't look anywhere near Alice.

"Oh," Marie says with a laugh, her shoulders relaxing. "Isn't it amazing? Come down this way, there's one of me on my first day of soccer absolutely sobbing."

Alice isn't sure why Babs needed Van to get a box of blankets, because there are already so many on the couch that Alice can't tell what color the fabric of the couch actually is. She, Van, and Marie—"the kids"—have been banished to clean the already spotless living room while Babs and Aunt Sheila bang around the kitchen. According to Babs they're "not cooking at all," but it kind of sounds like they're preparing for a nuclear launch from the way they're yelling back and forth and opening and closing what seems like every cabinet in the Portland metro area.

"Should we help?" Alice asks after one particularly loud crash, but both Van and Marie immediately shake their heads.

"*This is our process,*" Marie says, in what is clearly an impression of Babs.

"Dad used to complain about how loud it was, until Mom told him that if he wanted a quiet kitchen, he could cook himself," Van says. "That shut him up pretty quick."

"They're literally just supposed to be putting frozen latkes from Trader Joe's in the oven, though," Marie says in her real voice. "No freaking idea what's so complicated in there."

"*Women's secrets,*" Van tells Alice, using air quotes and affecting her own Babs impression. "Which I think is also the name of one of the books about getting my period she gave me when I was eleven."

Alice chokes on a sip of water, and Marie giggles.

"Girls," Babs calls from the kitchen, sounding so like Marie's impression of her that Alice almost chokes again. "I'm hearing a lot of laughing and not a lot of cleaning!"

Half an hour, two extra-loud bangs, and one smoke alarm later, things have settled down somewhat. Alice is leaning against a wall, furtively googling Chanukah facts on her phone, but she quickly clicks it off and shoves it into her pocket when Van approaches her. Van hands her a can of sparkling water, and pulls her back into the hallway, away from everyone else. "I wanted to run something by you," she says, like Alice can focus on anything other than her proximity. "I really want you to feel free to say no, okay? Like, legit no hard feelings."

That makes Alice perk up, her curiosity slicing through her attraction just enough for her to be able to pay attention. "Okay."

"My colleague and I are leaving Total Body PT and starting our own practice," Van says, leaning close, like it's a secret. "We need an office manager slash receptionist, and I was wondering if maybe you'd want to do it."

Alice wouldn't be surprised if her jaw has literally dropped, like a cartoon character. "You . . ." She swallows and tries again. "You'd want me to come work . . . for you? At your new physical therapy practice? To, like, single-handedly run your office?"

Something changes in Van's face. It looks like she's shuttering up all of her expressions, like she's packing herself away. "I'm sorry," she says, "I shouldn't have assumed you'd—"

"No," Alice interrupts, holding up a hand. "Sorry, I'm . . . processing." She's not sure why Van is closing herself off, but she wants to be crystal clear right now. "That honestly sounds fucking amazing."

Van's eyes clear, softening again in that way they always do when she looks at Alice, like she never wants to look at anything else. "Really?"

"Yes," Alice says, for once able to tell the absolute truth. Spending her days with Van and patients, with a complex workload, getting to set up the office and the systems, doing everything from scheduling to ordering to billing, always someone to talk to or a task to accomplish—it would be like the dentist job but without all the wailing toddlers. And hopefully significantly less spit. "I'd love that."

"Okay," Van says, a grin growing on her face despite what looks like her best efforts to keep it under control. It's like she doesn't want to be so joyful in the middle of a business proposition but she can't help it, and god. Alice likes her so much. Van clears her throat, trying to pull down the corners of her lips and failing spectacularly. "I'll, um, circle back with details when we have them?"

"Great," Alice says, not bothering to be cool about it. Alice Rue may be many things, but cool is not one of them.

"Psst," Marie hisses to them from the living room. She's as far from the kitchen as she can get, after having been chastised twice for setting the table wrong. "C'mere."

They walk over, Alice belatedly trying to make her face less lovestruck and quickly checking to make sure Babs and Aunt Sheila are distracted by whatever it is they're doing with the stand mixer.

"Happy Chanukah," Marie says, pulling three cans of beer out of the pocket of her hoodie, and a stack of cookies out from under her sleeve.

Alice decides that little sisters are very underrated.

They all crack open their cans, and Marie holds hers up. "L'chaim," she says, and Van says it back. Alice tries to decide if it's more offensive to gabble the sounds back at them or stay quiet. She settles on staying quiet, partly out of polite religious confusion and partly because she's still trying to get her libido under control. She's literally sneaking a beer with her comatose fake-boyfriend's baby sister—Alice needs to pick a more appropriate time and place to be randy. Jesus.

"Oh my god," Marie says, her mouth full of cookie. She seems to like the cookies more than the beer, which makes Alice want to squeeze her and tell her a bedtime story. She's both so adult and still such a kid, and Alice's affection for her throbs inside her chest, a feeling that's entirely different from what she feels for Van but slots up next to it perfectly, like Alice has always been meant to feel it. "Van, have you showed her the costume closet yet?"

"No," Alice says, looking between the two of them. "Which seems absolutely unacceptable."

"Come on," Marie says, her eyes wide with excitement. She ditches her beer and grabs Alice's wrist, pulling her down the hallway and up the stairs. Alice blows a kiss to little cheerleader Van, which makes the real-life Van behind her grumble in an absolutely adorable way.

Upstairs is carpeted, with two bedrooms connected by an adjoining bathroom. The ceilings are sloped and low like Alice suspected, but it's not cramped. The room on the right must be Babs and her husband's room; Marie leads them into the room on the left, what was probably one of the kids' bedrooms but is now something of a random storage room with a small futon shoved into the corner. Marie walks over to the closet, opens the door, and . . . wow.

For the second time tonight, Alice stops dead in her tracks. "That's . . . a lot of glitter."

"Girl, that's not even the half of it," Marie says with a grin, flicking on the light. "Step inside."

Alice does as she's told, and holy shiitake. It's a walk-in closet, not square like Nolan's but long and narrow. She can take probably ten steps in, and it's positively bursting with costumes. A full-length purple ballgown scratches at her as she walks past, a creepy mask looms down from the top shelf, there seems to be a whole *Wizard of Oz* section, and way too many sequined jumpsuits.

It smells musty and like that cheap polyester that most bargain costumes are made out of, mixed with rubber and face paint.

"Holy god," Alice breathes, her brain honestly refusing to process the input from her eyes. "What the fuck is this?"

"This," Van says, from the doorway, "is Babs's happy place."

"She's obsessed with Halloween," Marie says unnecessarily. That's quite clear, yes. "And she's kept every costume any of us have ever worn. Plus everyone in the neighborhood knows to give them to her or come get one. All of October is, like, a costume swap meet in here." Marie squeezes past Alice to get to the very back of the closet. "Let me try to find my favorite."

Alice runs her fingers over a hippie outfit (long wig, tie-dye shirt, round purple sunglasses), a child's bear costume, and a glow-in-the-dark skeleton onesie.

"I used to sneak up here and try on the suits from the *Men in Black* era," Van says softly, only for Alice. "When I was in high school, before I knew any queer people. They were all enormous and old and, like, awful, but I still loved it."

Alice turns to look at her and tries very hard not to kiss her. "I wish I'd known you then," she settles for saying. "I bet you were a total stud."

Van scoffs, but she's still standing so close, looking at Alice so intensely. "In a cheap suit that some old guy probably died in before Mom found it at Goodwill, yeah. Absolute chick magnet."

Alice shrugs one shoulder, feeling her lips curl up. "Would've worked on me, I bet."

"Guys! Check it out!" Alice turns, and almost screams at

the enormous shark head that has taken Marie's place. "My great white costume!"

Alice jumps backward, her heart rate so high that it takes her almost a full minute to realize that she bounced back into Van, and now Van's hands are on her hips, warm and steady and solid.

Marie runs out of the closet to scare her mother—Alice hopes no one else ends up in the hospital—leaving Alice and Van alone in the dark, claustrophobic costume emporium, Alice's heart still galloping in her chest.

Van touches the sleeve of a poofy white shirt, cinched at the wrists, like a rich old-timey man might wear. "This was my costume last year," Van says. "My ex, Sarah, wanted to be Ariel so I was Prince Eric. And Frank was Sebastian; he has a little crab costume." Alice thinks that's adorable—except for the whole Van ever having kissed or slept with or shared canine custody with anyone else part—but Van is frowning.

"That sounds cute?" Alice offers, making it a question even though it's not. "I bet Frank looked amazing. And you do have that swoopy Prince Eric hair thing happening."

Van self-consciously runs a hand through the thick black hair that, now that Alice thinks about it, is totally Disney prince worthy. "I guess, yeah," she says, but her mouth is twisted up, and Alice can't help but reach out and lay her hand on Van's arm.

"What?" she asks softly.

Van's frown turns wry, like she knows she's being weird. "It's stupid," she says, trying to brush it off, starting to turn to leave the closet, but Alice stands her ground, her grip on Van's strong forearm unwavering.

"It's not," Alice says, and something that looks suspiciously like affection wells up in Van's eyes.

"Sarah's all, like, femme usually, so I thought it would be funny to switch it," Van says, half her mouth quirked up, but not like she's having fun. "For me to be Ariel, and her to be Eric. But she totally flipped out." Her mouth slides back down. "She was always, like . . . I don't know. Wanting me to be the guy? Like, that really mattered to her."

Alice nods, a lot of things clicking into place. Babs wanting Van to be a pink blanket, frilly dress, femme girl and Sarah wanting her to be a mannish prince are two sides of the same coin. Gender essentialist bullshit by any other name would smell as foul.

Van isn't femme, and she's not a man. She should get to put on a long wig and a seashell bra, she should get to bind her chest and draw on facial hair. She should get to be everything, because she is. She's everything.

Right now, though, she's uncomfortable. Alice wonders if she's ever told anyone she feels like that before. Van is a woman of few words—someone who seems to value actions more than declarations—so Alice decides against giving a stern, affirming lecture, and turns away only long enough to find a long, red cape.

"Here," she says, draping it over Van's shoulders, a move that brings her much closer to Van's gorgeous, troubled face than she meant it to. "Next year, you'll be Little Red Riding Hood, and I'll be the woodsman, and Frank can be the wolf dressed up as Granny."

Alice is holding the edges of the cape together under Van's chin, and Van reaches up, trapping Alice's hands under hers. She looks like she's trembling on the knife's edge between smiling and crying, and Alice isn't sure if it's because of the gender-expression swap or Alice's assumption that she'll be around next year, or maybe that Alice wants to be in a group costume with Van and her dog—like a girlfriend would.

"Deal," is all Van says, her body hot and steady against Alice, the scent of her cologne sharp and delicious. "Deal."

An hour of trying on costumes and arranging blankets downstairs later, and the front door opens. One of the men comes in the house, and Babs meets him in the living room. He gives Babs a peck on the lips, so either there is something very weird about this family or that's Van's dad (whose name Alice has learned by stealthily flipping through the mail is Steve). He further cements his identity by announcing that he's left Uncle Joe to keep Nolan company at the hospital.

"He can't eat any of this anyway, not with his cholesterol," Aunt Sheila says from the doorway to the kitchen, two hot pink oven mitts on her hands, brushing off Alice's protestation that she could have sat with Nolan and let the whole family be together. "He's happy with his ESPN app and his deli sandwich."

That sounds like an extremely raw deal to Alice, but hey. She was kidnapped and brought here against her will, so it's not like anyone's dying for her input on their holiday plans.

Van risks her mom's wrath by daring to sit down, and Alice joins her, hoping that Steve's immediate grab for the remote will give them some non-cleaning cover. It seems to work, because Babs, Aunt Sheila, and the oven mitts retreat back into the kitchen for another ten minutes or so until the explosion sounds finally stop. Babs calls them all to come gather at the dining room table to light the candles. Alice hangs back, not sure what to do, but Aunt Sheila pulls her forward, hooking her elbow around Alice's and keeping her close.

"Tonight is the last night of Chanukah," she says in what she probably thinks is a whisper as Marie gets everything set up. "But we missed the first, obviously, so we're going all out tonight instead."

Alice nods, like she knows what that means.

Marie sets the candle holder on a sheet of tinfoil, and carefully places nine candles in it. Alice wonders why it's nine instead of eight. Isn't that the thing, aren't there eight nights? That's what her aborted research session told her, but what the hell does she know. Maybe it's like birthday candles, one to grow on?

"Traditionally, only women light the candles," Aunt Sheila whispers at a volume that is louder than Alice's normal speaking voice. "But everyone says the prayers."

Babs turns off all the lights in the house, and Alice's eyes slowly adjust to the darkness, only the orange glow from a streetlamp down the block filtering in through the window. It's startling and oddly bright when Marie strikes a match and lights the candle in the middle, which is up higher than the others. It glows fiercely in the darkness, just the one little flame. Then Marie picks up that candle, and as she uses it to light the others, everyone sings something in what Alice assumes must be Hebrew. It's pretty, lilting and a little staccato. One part of it repeats a few times, both the words and the melody.

Alice has no idea what it all means, but there's something beautifully reverent about it, about standing in a dark room and watching light bloom, about being with parents and children and siblings, singing the light back into their home.

The house smells delicious—fried potatoes, onions, and what might be dough—and Aunt Sheila's arm is steady around Alice's. It doesn't feel like going to church did, when Alice was little and they used to go. That was intimidating—cavernous and cold and echoing, and you got in trouble if you talked too loudly about how the priest's hat was funny. They never did any religious stuff at home. Alice didn't even really know that was an option, other than having a Christmas tree, which never felt very connected to the Jesus she heard about at church. Lupe was a chaplain, but Alice thought of her more like a friend, more aunt than pastor. Lupe never talked much about religion, opting instead to let Alice demolish her in Go Fish and, later, Texas Hold 'Em.

The idea that your house, your dining room table, could be a site of ritual, of prayer over candles, of something holy—Alice likes that. Being able to invoke God or spirits or whatever, right where you are, without having to go to a place? That feels . . . oddly powerful.

But Alice also understands what Van meant when she said it wasn't going to be very religious, because as soon as the prayers are done—probably less than a minute, all told—Babs flicks the lights back on, Steve carefully moves the candle holder from the table to the windowsill, and everyone sits down at the table like it's any other day.

Alice finds herself next to Aunt Sheila, across from Van and Marie, with Babs and Steve sitting at the head and foot. They pass the food around while Aunt Sheila tells Alice the story of Chanukah. "That's why most of what we eat tonight is fried," she says after a long meandering story full of interruptions from Babs (aggressively distributing food) and Steve (historical commentary), heaping what Alice would have thought were hash browns before her furtive google session onto Alice's plate without asking. "To honor the miracle of the oil," she says. "Latkes, and, for dessert, donuts."

"Dang," Alice says without thinking. "Being Jewish is delicious."

"Damn right," Aunt Sheila says, grinning. "Damn right."

Once everything has been passed around, Steve stands up. "Chanukah is about a miracle. About God giving the Maccabees what they needed to survive. I hope that a similar miracle is coming to our family, and that soon we'll have another chair at this table for our Nolan, returned to us happy and healthy."

It's the most Alice has ever heard him say. She wordlessly raises her glass of red wine a beat after Aunt Sheila does. It's kind of easy to forget what this is really about, here in the house. Away from the hospital, Alice can sort of pretend she's on holiday, getting to playact like she's part of this happy family for a little while. She's been so consumed by not getting caught in her lie that she's sort of lost sight of the central piece of all of this.

Nolan is in a coma.

Their son, brother, and nephew—her supposed boyfriend—is lying in a hospital bed, unresponsive, and possibly brain dead. He should be here. He should be in this chair; he should be the one laughing at the costumes upstairs, sneaking beers with Marie, and eating the truly impossible amount of latkes heaped on this plate.

It's not just that Alice doesn't belong here. It's that Nolan *does*. It's not Alice's fault that he's not here—she did literally everything she could to save his life—but it suddenly all feels so wrong.

She's enjoyed herself, these last eight days. Sure, they've been stressful and hard and confusing, but she's laughed more in the last week than in the last year combined. She's been hugged more, cared about more, touched more. Marie and Babs and Aunt Sheila (except when she's driving) have brought love into Alice's life, and Van has made her feel more than she has since her dad died. Even Frank has brought her so much happiness.

Alice's life is better than it was last week. And that's because their son, their baby, their big brother, is probably going to die. All of her joy turns sour in her mouth.

She stares hard at the candles burning merrily on the windowsill. *Please,* she prays, not sure if she's asking God or the light itself, wishing she had a song to sing. *Please let him wake up.*

THIRTEEN

"Um, everyone, I have an announcement."

Five heads swivel to Van. Steve and Aunt Sheila are done eating, and everyone else has considerably slowed down. Alice wonders if there's a *Strega Nona* pasta pot situation going on, because she could swear the number of latkes on her plate has only increased, despite how heavily a half dozen of them are sitting in her stomach.

Van clears her throat. "Um, I know it's not a great time or anything, but, uh . . ." She spins her fork in her hand. "Stephanie and I are leaving Total Body PT and opening our own practice."

Alice takes a big sip of wine to hide her face. Okay, so she was the first in the family to know about this new adventure for Van. That's fine. That's casual. Most people tell their comatose brother's fake-girlfriend their big life news before they tell their parents or siblings. That doesn't mean anything.

"Oh my god!" Marie says, half a latke still in her mouth. "That's so cool!"

But no one else at the table seems pleased.

"Why?" Steve asks, his forehead suddenly wrinkled with frown lines. "Total Body is going well. Why leave something so stable?"

Van bites her lip, but Alice sees her square her shoulders under her blue sweater. "I've told you all about the new management. We haven't been happy since it started going corporate, and our contracts expire at the end of the year. So now is the best time for a spin-off and we're pretty confident that a lot of clients will come with us." She looks down at her plate, her cheeks pink, and Alice wonders if she's feeling guilty for announcing something so exciting while Nolan's still in the hospital. Van keeps going, her words coming out faster now, like she's apologizing for having to say them. "We signed a lease, and we're hoping to start in February at the latest. I was going to tell you all on the first night of Chanukah, but . . . you know. Uh, anyway, Stephanie didn't want to delay the big launch, so it's being announced next week."

Steve harrumphs, but he doesn't say more. He looks like he wishes he were anywhere else.

"Only you and Stephanie?" Babs asks, and Van nods. Babs looks lost for words, and Alice doesn't miss the helpless look she shoots over to Aunt Sheila, or the way Aunt Sheila nods back at her, like she's encouraging her to say something. "But, sweetie," Babs says, her voice hesitant, "what about your health?"

Alice blinks. Van's . . . health? Van is quite possibly the heartiest-looking person she's ever met. She got down the heavy box of blankets without a single grunt of effort just half an hour ago, and Alice hasn't heard so much as a single sneeze or cough.

Van's face is stormy now, and her voice is clipped. "My health is fine."

"But—"

Van cuts her mother off, sterner and more sharply than Alice has ever heard her. "No buts."

The silence is long and harsh. Alice tries not to breathe.

Something eventually seems to break in Van; her shoulders sag, and she's softer as she says, "I promise, Mom, my health has no bearing on the new practice. Stephanie and I talked about it, and we're good."

Aunt Sheila seems to shrug at Babs, a sort of *what can you do* style surrender, and Alice's mind is going a million miles a minute. What the hell is everyone talking about? What's wrong with Van? What kind of health problem could mean she can be a physical therapist with her own practice, walk up and down stairs, stay up late, breathe deeply, live alone with a dog who needs long daily walks? Maybe, like, Crohn's? High cholesterol, like Uncle Joe? Asthma? A cancer in remission that Babs is still worried about?

Whatever it is, Van clearly doesn't want to talk about it. She avoids eye contact with everyone, staring down at her plate like she regrets ever bringing it up in the first place.

"Well," Marie says a little too loudly, after way too long of a profoundly awkward silence. "How about a movie?"

Everyone helps clear the table, the relief in the dining room palpable, and Alice welcomes the banging sounds of Babs and Aunt Sheila putting leftovers away. Anything is better than that horrible silence.

Once order has been more or less restored and the banging has ceased, they all roll themselves into the living room to collapse on the two couches that make an L shape against the walls, both facing the TV. They end up with a "kids" couch and an "adult" couch, with Frank lying on the floor at Van's feet. Alice isn't sure if that's standard or if Van is avoiding her parents, but either way Alice ends up between Marie and Van, content to slouch in her food coma—or, well, whatever the your-son-is-in-a-real-coma-so-let's-not-make-coma-jokes equivalent term is—while the Altmans good-naturedly bicker over what movie to watch.

"There aren't really Chanukah movies," Van says softly to Alice as Marie seizes control through the simple expedient of being the only one who knows how to use the remotes. "So we usually end up watching a random Adam Sandler movie."

"This one has a bar mitzvah scene," Marie says, still defensive from the bickering even though she won. "It counts."

Steve seems to be the only one still grumbling, but all the women ignore him, and Marie presses play on *The Wedding Singer*.

Alice hasn't seen the movie in years and it's even funnier than she remembered, so she inadvertently takes a large sip of wine right before one particularly funny moment ("Julia Gulia"), which results in her making a relatively horrible noise as she swallows it all at once to keep from spitting it out with laughter.

"Um, what the fuck was that?" Van asks, reaching over like Alice might need the Heimlich. "You alive?"

"I'm fine," Alice chokes, her eyes watering, trying to wave off Van's concern, but she still can't exactly breathe.

All the commotion is too much for Frank, who leaps up onto the couch to personally make sure she's okay, which is very sweet but does involve him standing directly on her legs, all sixty pounds of him boring down into her thighs, and his tongue licking her entire face.

"Oof! Frank, hon—okay, that was *inside* my mouth—ouch, baby, not to body-shame you, but you're heavy as shit."

Marie laughs, helping Alice haul Frank off herself, pulling

him down to sit between the two of them. Alice slides over to make room for him, which means she's now pressed into Van's side.

Van shifts around, and Alice is about to kick Frank off the couch so she can scooch back into the middle and stop making Van uncomfortable, but then suddenly everything feels better. It takes Alice a beat to realize it's because Van has been trying to extract her arm, and now it's draped over the back of the couch, right behind Alice's shoulders. Alice knows it's to make more room on the couch for their bodies, not because she's trying to, like, hold Alice or something ridiculous like that, but still.

Tell that to her stupid brain and her horny body, which are firing off warning signals like she's a tween on a first date.

"Pause it," Babs says after a few more minutes. "It's donut time."

Alice is incredibly full, but Aunt Sheila insists that's part of the holiday, so Alice manages to eat half of a truly delicious jelly donut, covered in a generous helping of powdered sugar that immediately goes everywhere. Apparently much of the kitchen banging was Babs and Aunt Sheila making them from scratch, which Alice didn't even know you could do. It's dicey to eat a jelly donut on a couch without all of the jelly splatting out onto your lap, but somehow Alice manages.

After her donut triumph, Alice's eyelids start to feel heavy, like they're as weighed down by fried food as the rest of her is. The only thing keeping her awake is the slight chill in the room as the temperature outside keeps dropping.

Babs must be feeling the cold too, because as soon as she's brushed the powdered sugar off her shirt she immediately digs through the blankets—the ones that were already out and the others Van got down from the closet earlier—and hands one to each person. Alice wonders if the donuts were slightly hallucinogenic, because no way is everyone being given their own blanket with sleeves?

"Is that . . . are these Snuggies?"

"Yup," Marie says, happily burrowing into the one her mom hands her. "Mom's obsessed."

"You can knit in them!" Babs says, like this is something Alice has been struggling with her entire life. "Oh no, but we brought some to the hospital. So we're short one." She looks up from the box, dismayed. She has one in each hand, a blue and a pink, but she, Van, and Alice are all blanket-less. She looks around the room quickly, clearly taking stock, and before Alice can say anything, Babs walks over and hands the blue one to Van. "You two girls can share," she says, gesturing between her and Alice. "Since that dog is making you sit so close together anyway."

"He has a name," Marie says, tucking part of her blanket over Frank's skinny back, clearly offended by "that dog."

Alice decides to focus on how cute Frank looks all covered up, only his enormous head poking out, instead of what it'll be like to be cuddled up under a blanket with Van. Van takes the blanket with a quiet "Thanks, Mom," and Alice wonders why Babs doesn't want to share one with her literal husband. Wouldn't that make more sense than to encourage Alice to snuggle even closer to her boyfriend's extremely hot sister?

Okay, Babs probably (hopefully?) doesn't know Van's extremely hot, but still! If Van were a dude, Alice would one hundred percent be in her own Snuggie right now. It's not that Alice wants Van to be a dude, or for anyone in the room to be aware of her raging crush or anything, but, come on. The weird forced-asexuality of their gay child is the second most awkward thing to happen tonight, for sure.

But Van clearly isn't going to protest. She shakes out the blanket, sliding her right hand through the armhole and putting her left back behind Alice again, using it to tuck the blanket up over Alice's shoulders. "You don't have to use the arm thingy," Van says softly, "but it's kind of amazing."

Alice wriggles her left arm into it—she'll try anything once—and, dang. Van's right. Alice can pet Frank's head without jostling the entire blanket or losing the heat that she and Van are rapidly generating.

She doesn't know how to knit, but she honestly *could* knit in this thing.

Marie presses play, and Adam Sandler comes back onto the screen, singing some hit from the eighties, and Alice finds herself melting into the couch. Warm, soft, and full, she doesn't even panic when Van's arm slips down from the couch cushion to rest on her shoulders. It's dark in the room, but Alice doesn't want to have to explain to anyone, so she gently reaches up and tucks the corner of the blanket over Van's hand, trapping her in their little navy-blue cocoon.

Van's thumb rubs up and down, hot even over the layers of Alice's shirt and sweater.

Alice can see the last vestiges of the candles still burning in the windowsill. She lets herself sink into Van, her right side pressed into Van's body from shoulder to ankle, the front of her shirt lightly dusted with sugar. When the movie ends, Alice realizes that her hand is on Van's thigh. She doesn't remember putting it there, but she knows that it feels right.

An hour later, after the credits have rolled and the candles have gone cold, Van stands up and reaches toward the ceiling to stretch. "Okay," she says, as Alice pointedly doesn't look to see if there's a strip of stomach visible under her sweater. "Alice, I can take you home. Mom, I'll be back in thirty."

Alice tilts her head, confused. "Wait, you're coming back here?"

"Yeah, I'm gonna crash here tonight," Van says, holding out a hand to help pull Alice out of the comfortable nest of a couch. "Easier to leave Frank here in the morning than to schlep him up north and then come back here before hitting the hospital. And I usually don't like to drive at night, but your place isn't too far."

But Alice is shaking her head. "If you're staying here, why would you drive me home?"

Van looks kind of amused. "Well, Mom's drunk, Dad's asleep, and you definitely don't want to experience Aunt Sheila driving in the dark after two glasses of wine." Alice literally shudders at the thought, and Van laughs. "So you're stuck with either me or Marie, and we're both staying here tonight."

"You should stay too," Marie says from the couch, her head pillowed on Frank's side. "It's late."

"Yes, Alice, honey, please stay," Babs says from where she's shoving the Snuggies back into their box. She's had a lot of wine, so she's more balling them up than folding them. "I'd feel so much better if none of you girls had to venture out tonight. The streets must be frozen by now."

"You haven't lived until you've had leftover latkes for breakfast," Marie says. "Dad always fries ham and eggs—sorry, Moses—and it's like a latke breakfast sandwich. Truly a transcendent experience."

Alice quickly runs a pro/con list about staying in her mind. Pros: She's exhausted, and her tiny, freezing studio holds very little appeal after tonight. It's really late, and the sooner she can get to sleep, the less exhausted she'll be tomorrow at work.

Post-Chanukah breakfast sounds like a wonderful way to develop heart disease. More time with Van and Marie. Not having to pay for an Uber. Not forcing Van to drive her all the way home and back in the freezing rain after midnight, when the streets are probably slick with ice. She can take the bus directly to work from here in the morning, which will be faster than coming from her apartment. Cons: She'll probably have to leave before latke breakfast, actually, because her shift starts so early. No change of clothes. No toothbrush. More time with Van.

The pros have it.

"Sure," Alice says. "I'd love to stay."

Twenty minutes later, Alice bites her lip. *This'll teach me not to make a pro/con list without all the facts,* she thinks, staring down at her bed.

Or, well. Down at the bed she'll be sleeping in.

With Van.

Babs and Steve are upstairs in their bedroom, and Aunt Sheila has already made her way up to the futon in the storage room attached to the costume closet. Marie's childhood room downstairs has only a narrow twin bed, the couches aren't comfortable for a whole night, and Babs would rather die than make her guest or her (possibly unhealthy?) daughter sleep on one. The only viable option is the double bed in the second downstairs bedroom.

It makes sense for Alice to bunk in there with Van. It's the only thing that makes sense, according to Babs and everyone who doesn't know about Alice's raging hormones. The only possible solution for this slumber party Tetris clusterfuck is for Alice to spend the night, in the dark, alone, under the covers with Van fucking Altman. It's the sensible thing for Alice to breathe in the scent of Van's cologne all night, for them to be tucked together in what has to be the world's smallest double bed after touching each other way too much during the movie.

Alice is pretty sure that this is one of the biggest mistakes in human history, slotting in right after "let's try this capitalism thing," but before low-rise jeans.

Marie's loaned her sweatpants and a T-shirt to wear. The shirt is cobalt blue with white writing that says GRANT HIGH SCHOOL VARSITY DRAMA. It had made Alice smile when she first saw it, but now that she's wearing it, it seems a little less funny. She's one hundred percent living a varsity drama right now, and it's much more confusing than it should be.

She's chosen to keep her bra on underneath the shirt, which won't be at all comfortable, but the thought of being braless in bed with Van is several thousand bridges too far. She hates sleeping in pants too—shorts or underwear are the only acceptable bottoms—but lord knows she's not shucking them off. She'll deal with being overly hot and claustrophobic any day over being in her fucking undies in bed with Van.

"Hey," Van says softly from the doorway. "You good?" Alice looks over at her and then immediately regrets it. She absolutely cannot handle the sight of Van in boxers and a soft black shirt. No. Absolutely not. No thank you.

Or, well. *Yes please,* but also, and more urgently, *no thank you.*

"Yeah." Alice's voice is pinched, and she wishes that, for once in her goddamned life, she could play it cool. "Good. Just, um . . ." She crosses her arms over her chest, even though Van's seen her in a T-shirt before. Right? Or has she always been wearing a sweater? Fuck, should she put on a sweater? Are there, like, sleep parkas or something, and if not, why hasn't someone invented them for this specific situation? She clears her throat. "Wasn't sure which side you wanted."

Van blinks, and then pointedly looks over to the right side of the bed. Frank's bed is nestled between that side and the wall, and Van's phone is on that nightstand, already plugged in.

"Right," Alice says, laughing way too nervously. "Sorry, I'm . . ." She trails off, all of the truths swimming to the surface of her mind. *I'm distracted. Confused. Super horny. Lying to you and your entire family. Very aware of the extra pounds around my stomach that I hate. Anxious. Excited. Overwhelmed.*

She says the only thing she can: "Tired."

"One good solution for that," Van says, pulling back the covers. She seems so chill, like she spends many nights cuddled up to her brother's girlfriends after gently caressing their arms under a blanket for an hour. Like contemplating sharing a bed with someone she's been having . . . moments . . . with is no biggie.

And they have been moments, right? Alice is pretty sure they've been moments. Van was so mad at Cherry/Kerry, and told Alice that she would choose her over Cherry/Kerry. Right? At her house, she said Nolan didn't deserve Alice—that meant something, didn't it? The long gazes, the constant heat between them, the way she looked at Alice in her own living room, the confessions out on the balcony at the hospital, those were all moments, right?

Alice isn't alone in this, is she?

Well, she's certainly not alone in this bed anyway.

Van is under the covers now, and the weirdest thing Alice could do is keep standing there, staring, so she forces herself to get in. She lies on her back, looking up at the ceiling, unfortunately reminding herself of the way Nolan is currently lying in his hospital bed. She hears the sounds of Frank's feet clicking on the hardwood as he circles the room a few times before curling up in his bed and settling with a loud, long sigh.

"Good night, Franko. Love you." Van's voice is so impossibly soft and loving that Alice's ribs collapse, her heart flattening and oozing up to the surface to offer itself to Van.

"Good night, Frank," Alice echoes.

"Are you comfortable?"

No. It's too hot with both of them under the covers and these thick-ass sweatpants, and Van smells way too good and this is the first time Alice has seen her bare arms and legs. She's like a randy Victorian man, turned on by a scandalous flash of elbow.

"Yep," Alice lies. "I'm great."

"Cool," Van says. She rolls over and clicks off the light, and the room is plunged into darkness. Alice doesn't move, and slowly her eyes adjust, the dim orange from the streetlights filtering through the closed blinds enough for her to make out the ceiling, the dark dresser in the corner, the contrast between the white sheets and the blood-red comforter.

It's quiet for a long time. Alice assumes Van's asleep. She wants to roll over but she's afraid to wake up Van, to shake the bed, to accidentally get too close. She feels like a prey animal, like if she doesn't move a muscle then maybe everyone will forget that she's here and nothing bad will happen to her.

But after what must be at least half an hour, Van says something from the darkness next to Alice.

"Do you love him?"

Almost against her will, Alice turns her head. Van isn't looking at her. She's flat on her back too, and her eyes are closed. Pinched closed, Alice is pretty sure, like she's screwing them shut, like she can't bear to see Alice answer the question.

Something in the middle of Alice's chest, deep below her sternum, clenches and throbs. She tells the truth into the thick darkness.

"No."

"I should want you to," Van whispers, still not looking.

Alice takes a deep breath, holds it for three, and then lets it out slowly. "Do you want me to?"

Another long pause, and then, "No."

She can't help it. Alice rolls toward her. "Van," she breathes, reaching out to brush the back of her hand down Van's arm.

Van rolls too, and only once she's facing Alice does she open her eyes. Her hand comes up, and Alice doesn't move out of the way, letting Van tuck a piece of her hair back behind her ear. Van's fingers are so gentle, her face so tender in the darkness, that now it's Alice who has to shut her eyes for a few long seconds.

"We can't," Van whispers as Alice finally looks at her again, and Alice nods against her pillow.

"I know."

But Van doesn't take her hand off Alice. She cups Alice's face, running her thumb softly across Alice's cheek. "But I want to."

Alice lets her eyes flutter shut. She can't. They can't. She knows it. But for once in her fucking life, she can be honest about what she wishes was true.

"Me too."

FOURTEEN

Alice groans at a horrific beeping sound in her ear. It takes a while to realize it's her alarm, and longer for her flailing arm to find her blaring phone on an unfamiliar nightstand. It isn't until Van grumbles next to her that Alice remembers where she is, who she's with. She bolts upright as the belated spike of adrenaline hits her nervous system. She's in Van's bed. She spent the night with Van, tucked up under the same comforter, bare ankles rubbing together. She's in bed with Van, and a few hours ago Alice touched her on her perfect face and told her way too many truths.

Jesus fucking Christ, she's the worst fake-girlfriend of all time. Not only a liar, but a cheat at that.

She gets up as quietly as she can, pulling on her clothes with the sinking realization that she's doing a true walk of shame today. She, like everyone else showing up to work in yesterday's clothes, certainly made a questionable romantic decision last night. She just didn't get to enjoy it as much as Delilah will hope.

She leaves the bedroom, intending to tiptoe out the front door without waking anyone—it's only six in the morning and they were up past midnight—but before she's gotten her boots on, Van pads sleepily into the living room, rubbing her eyes. She's pulled on dark blue sweats and a faded OSU sweatshirt, and Alice is immediately tempted to fling herself at Van, to pull them both back into the soft darkness of the bedroom, to do something that would turn this from a sad, relatively chaste walk of shame into an X-rated one.

She's saved from doing something that monumentally stupid only by a heavy tread on the stairs above her head. A breath later, Steve lumbers out of the hallway in a bathrobe.

"Good morning," Van says.

"Morning, Van. Alice."

"Sorry if I woke you," Alice says, but Steve shakes his head.

"Always up this early," he says, and Alice isn't sure if the sentence fragment is because he's tired or if that's just kind of his vibe. "Gotta start on the latke sammies."

Van looks askance at the boots hanging limply from Alice's fingers. "What are you doing?" she asks. "Latkes. Breakfast. Coffee. Warm."

Okay, maybe the sentence fragments in the morning are hereditary, but Alice can't argue with the logic. Cold hungry bus has absolutely no appeal over latkes breakfast coffee warm. And Van.

Alice, completely charmed and utterly overwhelmed by her feelings, can only nod, set her shoes back down, and follow Van into the kitchen. They wordlessly help Steve, and soon the delicious smells of brewing coffee, reheated latkes, and sizzling thick-cut ham have lured all the other Altmans out of their bedrooms, even though it's horrifically early.

Marie gives Alice the sleepiest, warmest hug, and Alice

doesn't hesitate to pull out her phone and text Delilah that she's sorry but she'll be in a little late today. She's simply not ready to leave yet. She can't quite believe she's this lucky; not only to have been invited—or kidnapped, as the case may be—to celebrate Chanukah with the family, but to have these people that would haul themselves out of their comfortable beds to eat breakfast with her at the crack of dawn, simply because they want to be with her one last time before work.

She'd maybe cry about it, if she were the type of person to let herself do that.

The latke, ham, and egg sandwiches turn out to be even better than advertised. Van sits across the breakfast table from Alice, like last night, and her cheeks turn an adorable light pink every time they make eye contact. Alice is finally sent off to work with a full thermos of steaming coffee and sticky cheek kisses from Babs and Aunt Sheila. Alice doesn't hug Van goodbye—they'd barely made it through the night unscathed, and the impulse to accidentally lean in for a makeout might have become overwhelming—but Alice gives her a goodbye arm squeeze during some profoundly meaningful eye contact that feels enough like sex that Alice isn't sure if she needs a cold shower or wants to never wash her hand again.

But the day takes a steep nosedive from there. The streets are so slick with ice that the buses are super delayed, and Alice feels the warmth of breakfast and last night congealing into a cold knot of regret deep in her stomach as she inches across the river. There's going along with a falsehood and then there's taking advantage, and the hard ball of anxiety in her gut is telling Alice that she's tipped into the latter. She doesn't get to work until close to eight, which Delilah is slightly grumpy about, so Alice doesn't take a lunch break, offering Delilah a full hour off. It's only right, and plus, Alice feels like she might be due for some penance, to dig her fingers deep into her bruises, to punish herself for getting so close to blowing everything up last night. She's already doing a horrible thing by (essentially) lying to Nolan's entire family, and last night she pretty much made a move on his fucking sister, god. She doesn't deserve to eat lunch.

She tries to bury her thoughts in work, gritting her teeth and telling herself that this is what being responsible looks like: visitor passes and security logs and smiling at douchebags, not cuddling with hot girls and recklessly endangering their place in their own goddamned families. By the time her shift is over and she's taken the bus to the hospital, she's frozen and cranky. The sugar and carb rush from the latke breakfast wore off hours ago, leaving her jittery and starving underneath her slight nausea, and she feels disgusting in yesterday's clothes. She wants to stop in the cafeteria for food and some chamomile tea, but she figures she didn't come this far to ignore the Altmans. Penance doesn't deserve chamomile tea, a settled stomach, or clean underwear.

She trudges her way through the lobby, leaning her head against the wall of the elevator as it takes her up to the fourth floor. She hadn't slept well, too aware of Van's body next to her, of how close they'd come to slipping up and ruining everything, and she's feeling it in every muscle fiber of her body. She had some deodorant in her purse, but even that, the fresh eyeliner, and staticky side braid she's pulled her hair into aren't doing anything to hide her exhaustion.

The elevator dings, and Alice steps out. She's halfway to Nolan's room when she's intercepted by Van. She's wearing dark brown cords, her scuffed work boots, and a green half-zip sweater, and she looks so beautiful that Alice is momentarily breathless. Her brown eyes are warm and bright, her jaw so square and sharp, her hair tousled from running her fingers through it.

"Hey," Van says, as Alice sways from the concussive force of seeing her after last night. She's holding something out, and it takes Alice a second to realize the paper cup and brown bag in Van's hands are for her. "Thought you might be hungry."

Alice wordlessly takes the cup, which warms her fingers instantly, the smell of mint wafting up through the lid. But it isn't until she takes the bag and opens it that the world tilts under her.

It's bao. Bao, from that food truck Alice had aimlessly pointed out as her favorite the first time Van had driven her home. Van remembered. Van drove from her mom's house down to the food truck this afternoon on the off chance Alice hadn't eaten lunch, on the slim chance that what Alice wanted so many hours after latkes and donuts was bao and mint tea.

Alice is horrified to find tears in her eyes, to have the image of the bao suddenly blurred.

"Hey," Van's voice says, suddenly very, very close by. "Hey, it's okay, you don't have to eat it. I'm sorry—I didn't—"

But Alice shakes her head, cutting Van off without a word. She's not sure why this is the thing, why of all of the times Van has taken care of her, has gone out of her way for her, this is the one to put Alice over the edge, but it is.

It's like Alice was only supplied with a finite number of times she could say no to Van, and, without realizing, she'd used up the final stash last night. In that bed, closing her eyes against Van's face, letting Van caress her cheek but somehow keeping herself from leaning forward and kissing her . . . that was the last one.

She said no yesterday over and over again in the most tempting circumstances of her life—alone in the costume closet, on the couch, in the bed, after breakfast—and today she's absolutely defenseless against even the gentlest feeling of desire. Last night she'd been able to stop herself from kissing Van in the darkness of her bedroom, their hands on each other's bodies, only Frank as their witness, but today a simple bag of street food in the hospital hallway is breaking her.

Alice sets the food and drink down on the windowsill next to her and grabs Van's wrist, pulling her along.

"What are—Alice, where . . ."

But Alice doesn't speak. She can't. She opens the door to a single-occupancy bathroom and nearly throws Van inside. Van is still sputtering, but Alice simply walks in after her, flicks the lock closed, crosses the distance between them, takes Van's face in her hands, and finally, finally fucking kisses her.

Van is motionless under her for only a second. Only one second for Alice to start overthinking before something flips inside of Van, and suddenly it's everything Alice has ever wanted. Van both melts and grows against her, softening to let Alice slide inside the space of her body, and somehow getting so large that Alice is entirely enveloped in her warm, strong arms. Her hands are everywhere, twisting in Alice's hair, fisting the back of her sweater, gripping her neck, sliding up and down Alice's spine, grasping her jaw to hold her close.

Her mouth is overwhelming in the best way, hot and greedy without being messy. Her lips are soft but she's insistent and demanding, leaving no room for doubt about her intentions, her desire. Alice licks inside Van's mouth, and the little sound Van makes against her, the way her fingers dig into Alice's skin—Alice knows she'll remember that for the rest of her life.

They're in a hospital bathroom but all Alice can smell is Van, all she can hear is the sound of their kiss, of Van's breaths puffed against her cheek. Alice dips one hand under Van's sweater, finding the warm, soft flesh of her hip that is better than she could have dreamed. After a moment, she slides her hand around, feeling the muscles of Van's back flexing at the cold shock of her fingers.

Alice pulls her lips away just enough to look at Van, to take in the sharp angles and soft planes of her face, her lips open, her cheeks pink. Her brown gaze flitting between Alice's mouth and her eyes. "You're so fucking gorgeous," Alice hears herself whisper, and she watches as a hot, pleased blush creeps up from Van's neck into her already flushed cheeks.

"So are you," Van says, her hands tight on Alice, and then they're kissing again.

Van is all wet suction and thick lips, and Alice is quickly lost in her. The texture of her tongue, the feeling of her long fingers on Alice's neck, the way breaths seem to keep getting caught in her throat. Van adjusts her stance to pull Alice even closer to herself, to hold both of them up even when Alice almost loses her balance, too distracted by Van's mouth to worry about things like gravity.

Alice feels something like buzzing near her hand under Van's sweater, and it takes her way too long to realize that it's the phone in Van's back pocket. Someone is calling. They both ignore it in favor of continuing to devour each other, but it doesn't stop.

With a groan of frustration, Van pulls back from Alice, just a few inches. "Hold that thought," she breathes, wrapping one arm low around Alice's waist, like she's ready to keep Alice pressed against her no matter what.

Alice finds the very thought of pulling away absurd. She drops her head onto Van's shoulder, pressing a soft kiss to the hinge of the jaw that she's been staring at for so long. She snakes her other hand up under Van's sweater as Van pulls out her phone and stares at it. "It's Marie," she mutters, which is weird, because Alice is pretty sure Marie's a few feet away, in Nolan's room.

Van presses the green button and holds it up to her ear. "Marie?"

It's not on speaker, but Alice can hear it plain as day.

"VAN, WHERE ARE YOU? NOLAN'S AWAKE!"

FIFTEEN

Nolan's room is chaos. The entire family is there, including Aunt Sheila and the guy Alice has finally nailed down as Uncle Joe, plus what looks like every nurse and resident on shift today. People are bustling around, calling things out to each other, Babs is wailing loudly with happiness, and Alice tries to disappear into the background.

Her mind is spinning. She should be figuring out her next step here—she needs to act quickly. He's awake; that means it's time to come clean. To tell the Altmans about the misunderstanding, to plead for their forgiveness that she let this charade get so out of hand. It was always the plan to tell them right when he woke up so that their elation would keep them from realizing how weird her obsession with the family is, how fucked up it is that she (technically never) lied to them.

But now that it's happening, now that "when he wakes up" is the same time as "right now," it feels impossible. It's so busy and frantic in the room; what did she expect? That it would be quiet and soft, only the family there, maybe just Babs and Marie, actually, and she'd say, "Okay, so, fun fact about me . . ." and they'd all say, "Whatever, honey!" and that would be that?

What the fuck kind of plan was this? Why the hell did she convince herself this was going to work?

"Holy shit," she hears one of the young doctors whisper to another. "I'd have bet serious money this guy wasn't waking up."

"Dude, I know," the other whispers back. "Never would've seen this coming."

Oh right. That's why.

Because the good thing has never happened to Alice in this hospital. Every test to "rule something out" always came back positive. Every operation that had a good chance of success failed. Every condition they could have survived, they didn't. Her mom died. Her dad died. At one point or another, both of her parents had better odds than Nolan did after nine days, and they both died.

Alice didn't think he would wake up.

But he did. And it's not that she's upset about it—she's thrilled for him, for the family—but she's quickly realizing that she is well and entirely fucked.

She looks over and sees Van wiping a tear off her cheek, and her heart clenches. The plan was shitty twenty minutes ago, but as of ten minutes ago, this is a full-fledged catastrophe. Ten minutes ago, Alice had her tongue in Van's mouth, her hands under Van's sweater. Alice was literally groping Nolan's sister ten minutes ago, only feet away, and now Van is crying with joy that he's awake and what Alice is about to tell her is going to absolutely ruin everything.

No way can they come back from this enormous lie. No way can Alice see any of the Altmans ever again, nor would they want to see her. The girl who lied to them, who manipulated them during the worst nine days of their lives, the girl who abused their kindness and ended up pitting Van against her comatose brother.

No way will Van ever want to kiss her again.

"Van," Alice says, because she's already losing what nerve she has, but she has to do this before Nolan sees her and asks who she is. "I have to tell you something."

Van is turning to look at her, but at that moment, Nolan says, "Marie, when did you dye your hair back?" and the whole family stills.

Alice looks sharply over at Marie, who has the same jet-black hair as everyone else in the family. Is it dyed? It looks natural, but what does Alice know? She's not a cosmetologist. Although there were those couple of pictures of Marie from high school on the wall when she had bright blue hair, weren't there?

"What?" Marie asks. Maybe they all heard him wrong.

"Your hair," Nolan says, blinking as a resident shines a light into his eye. "It was blue."

"Nolie," Babs says, her voice weirdly high. "Marie got rid of the blue for her sophomore musical. That was . . . years ago, honey."

Nolan blinks, clearly confused. "It . . . was?"

"What the hell," Van whispers. She's not taking her eyes off the bed, but her hand finds Alice's, and she squeezes it so hard that Alice starts to worry about permanent damage. But it's the last time they'll ever hold hands—not to mention the first—so Alice swallows back her wince of pain and returns the pressure as best she can.

"Nolan," his dad says, leaning down over him. "What's the last thing you remember, son?"

Nolan shrugs, still prostrate in the bed. "I don't know. Being at work. Talking to Angela about the Howerman case."

"Angela?" Babs says, looking at her husband with what Alice thinks might be panic. "Wasn't she . . . doesn't she work in L.A.?"

"Yeah," Nolan says slowly. He looks like he's aware there are some puzzle pieces missing, but he has no idea how many or what it means. "She has the office next to mine."

"In L.A.," Steve says, and Nolan nods.

"Obviously, yeah. In L.A. Is that not . . . Aren't we in L.A.?"

Van's grip gets even tighter. Alice can feel the sweat on her palm. "Fuck," she mutters, and Alice figures that's pretty apt.

"Nolie, honey, what year is it?" Babs asks, and Alice doesn't need to hear his wrong answer to know what's going on.

Nolan is missing almost five years of his life. He thinks he still lives in L.A. He doesn't remember moving back to Portland. Doesn't remember Marie graduating from high school.

Doesn't remember ever seeing Alice before, not even the four times he said *hi,* the three times he said *hey,* and the two times he said *how's it going.*

The men and Aunt Sheila try to play it cool while the doctors and nurses spring back into action, but Babs has to step outside to wail, Marie tucked under her arm.

Van looks like a statue. A sweaty, terrified, squeezing statue. "Van," Alice says softly. "Van, honey, look at me."

Van does, slowly, but as soon as her eyes hit Alice, something crumbles in her face. "Oh no, Alice," she breathes, her free hand coming up to grip Alice's arm as hard as she's squeezing her hand. "Oh god. He doesn't remember you. Oh my god."

"No," Alice says quickly. "No, no, I don't care about that. Don't worry about that. I just—are you okay? Do you need to sit down or something?" She looks desperately around the room. Aunt Sheila has pushed both Steve and Uncle Joe down into the chairs the nursing staff have shoved aside, and the room is humid and loud and claustrophobic.

"Let's go outside for a breath," Alice says, and Van wordlessly follows her out of the room. Alice takes her to their balcony, and Van doesn't even let her close the door behind them before she's folded herself into Alice's arms.

Alice takes her weight with a little grunt, adjusting her feet and wrapping her arms low around Van's waist, holding her up the best she can. She tries not to think about how Van had done the same thing to her fifteen minutes ago in the bathroom—shifted her feet to hold Alice up, pressed her hands tight to Alice's back.

Van huffs out loud, harsh breaths into Alice's neck, her fingers digging into Alice's shoulders. She doesn't say anything, and Alice doesn't either, but her mind is racing in panicked circles, back on her hamster wheel of doom.

He's awake, yes, but they're not elated. Van is crying into her shoulder, and Babs is sobbing all over Marie a few feet away. Steve looks like he might have a heart attack, and even Aunt Sheila is in a stunned sort of silence.

Alice has to tell them now, but now is turning out to be worse than ever.

"*Amnesia?*" Isabella's voice is louder and higher pitched than Alice has heard it since they were in kindergarten. "Are you mucking kidding me? He woke up but he has *amnesia?*"

Alice shakes her head, picking at the plate in front of her. She'd texted Isabella something garbled that must have seemed distressing, because Bella had strapped both kids in the car and driven down toward Portland Grace without hesitation, leaving Henry to finish his afternoon mushroom forage alone. They're at a burger restaurant nearby, between the highway and the river, both kids suitably distracted by the unfailing combination of screen time and pre-dinner French fries.

"Girl," Isabella says, her eyes wide. "I'm sorry, but what is your life?"

Alice almost laughs. "I don't know," she admits, picking up a fry and then dropping it back down again. "I can honestly say I didn't see this coming."

Bella shakes her head, like she didn't either. "This is some soap opera shiitake," she says, taking a bite of her burger. "Honestly, I feel like I'm letting you down right now. I should have been prepared for this. I don't think my mom has ever missed an episode of *General Hospital* and those idiots are constantly getting amnesia."

Alice had forgotten about her aunt's soap obsession. Her own mom had said it was stupid, but if they'd all been over at Bella's house when *General Hospital* was on, Alice's mom would end up glued to the TV, enraptured, until the end of the episode, just like her sister.

"Any advice?"

Isabella tilts her head, considering. "Depends. How appealing is killing yourself off and then coming back as your own evil twin?"

Alice does laugh this time. "Honestly, sounds better than some of my other options." But considering those options has her groaning and dropping her head onto her arms, folded on top of the table. "I can't believe this is happening," she moans. "I can't believe I have to come clean while they're dealing with fucking amnesia."

"Do the doctors think it's permanent?"

Alice doesn't pick her head up but she does roll it to the side so she can look at Isabella. "They don't know. I'm starting to think they kind of don't know shit, actually. Or—sorry! Ships. They don't . . . they are totally ignorant about ships."

"Landlubbers," Isabella agrees, nodding seriously, and Alice kicks her under the table but doesn't bother to hide her smile.

God, she likes her.

"Well, okay," Isabella says slowly. "Hear me out. Obviously, if his memories come back, you're mucked and there's no way around it." She squints, though, like she's thinking it through. "I mean, I guess not any more mucked than you were before. The level of mucked you'd planned for, really." She shrugs, almost smiling, like Alice is ridiculous, and Alice can't help but agree. This plan was freaking terrible from the start. Absolutely the worst-thought-out plan in the history of humanity.

Bella keeps going. "But if it's permanent, then does it . . . really matter? If you tell the truth or not?"

Alice picks her head up, indignant. "Yes! Of course it does! I can't keep, you know . . . pretending that we . . ."

"I guess I don't see how it's different from what you were doing yesterday," Isabella says when it's clear that Alice never intended to finish her sentence.

"Yesterday I was lying to *them*," Alice says. "This is lying to *him*. About himself."

"Ah," Isabella says, mindlessly catching Hazel's iPad right before it clatters to the floor with some sort of mom-spidey-sense. "Okay. I get that. But also, like . . ." She purses her lips, and Alice watches as the thoughts flicker over her face. "It kind of still feels like a victimless crime to me."

Alice's face must do something, because Bella holds up a hand. "No, but, listen. If you say, 'Hey, I'm going to step back while you all deal with this recovery, I don't want to make things more confusing for him, and when he's ready we can be together again,' how much does that really hurt him? Or them? You get to eject yourself for a while without blowing up the relationships and making everyone feel like crap; when it comes time you can date him and if it works, then, like, hey, bonus boyfriend! And if it doesn't, it's, like, 'Boy, bye.' You break up—no harm, no foul. You're not gaslighting anyone; it honestly didn't work out."

Alice stops herself from rejecting the idea out of hand just because she didn't have it first, and she really turns it over in her mind. It does . . . it does kind of make sense. Like, *Hey, if he doesn't remember me, that's cool, I won't force it. Y'all focus on him, and I'll be okay. Maybe send me a Christmas card or something.* And then when he's ready—if he's ready—she could date him for a few weeks and if he's as great as she had always imagined, then super. And if he's the douche she's been suspecting him to be for the last nine days, then it would simply be over.

"Yeah," she says slowly. "If it's permanent, if his memories never come back, then that could work. For sure. But . . . one small other problem." She grimaces. "Um, I might have, uhh . . . made out. With Van. This afternoon."

"You *what*?" Isabella's screech is so loud that both kids rip their eyes off their iPads, and every patron in the restaurant turns to stare at them.

Alice hides her face in her hands. "I know."

Isabella drops her voice to a harsh whisper, patting Sebastian on the head reassuringly, but Alice is pretty sure the nearby tables can still hear her. "You made out with Van?"

Alice doesn't take her face out of her hands. "Yes."

"This afternoon?"

"Yes."

"Before or after he woke up?"

"Umm . . . I think, like, during?"

"Oh my god. This *is* a soap opera."

"Bella," Alice whines, dropping her forehead directly onto the table now. "Help me."

Isabella sounds like she's almost laughing when she says, "Speaking as a professional, may I just note that you're a walking PR disaster, Rue Rue?"

Alice moans into the scratched, waxy wood of the table. "I *know.*"

"Okay, pause," Bella says, and Alice picks up her head. "Did you know you liked girls before this, or are we also having an identity crisis right now?"

Alice shakes her head. "No, no. I've known I was bi since high school."

"Okay, whew," Bella says, literally wiping off her forehead in a move that's so corny Alice can't help but smile. "Glad that's one thing handled."

"Only one million to go," Alice says, trying to fake a cheerful, announcer-type voice.

Bella has finished all of her fries, and Alice can see her eyeing the ones on Alice's plate. She pushes the whole plate over, her stomach churning too much even for potatoes.

"So," Bella says around a bite of Alice's fry. "How was it?"

Alice blinks a couple times. "What? The . . . the making out?"

Isabella nods and Alice tries not to think about it, about how Van's lips glided against hers, how her tongue tasted, how she can still feel Van's hands everywhere they touched.

"Oh boy," Bella says, watching her face carefully. "I don't think I'm old enough to hear the thoughts you're having right now." Alice feels her cheeks heating up like she's in front of a blazing fire, and Isabella laughs. "That good, huh?"

"Yeah," Alice says softly. "That good."

Bella considers it all, holding out a French fry and practically forcing Alice to eat it, like Alice is her third child. "So if you do this plan, and say 'Good luck, call me later' to the family, that would leave you and Van where?"

Alice shrugs. "I don't know."

Isabella narrows her eyes. "Where do you want to be?"

Alice thinks about Van's living room, that comfortable big brown couch. She thinks about curling up on it with Van, alone except for Frank, maybe falling asleep during a movie with her head on Van's shoulder, maybe languidly making out with Van on top of her, maybe peeling Van's clothes off and taking her to bed.

"It doesn't matter what I want," she says softly. "We couldn't. Things are already weird between her and her parents. I wouldn't want to make that worse, and stealing her amnesiac brother's girlfriend or whatever would definitely make it worse."

Isabella makes a humming sound, like she's considering it. She picks up another fry and dips it lightly in the ketchup before holding it out to Alice. "Don't you think maybe that's a decision Van should get to make for herself?"

SIXTEEN

Alice gives it a day, returning to the hospital the next evening after work. She's hoping the doctors will have figured out what's going on with Nolan by now, that they'll have a guess about if this is going to be a permanent or temporary loss of five years of memories so that she'll have a better sense of which kind of screwed she is.

If it's permanent, she's ready to do what Isabella suggested, to gently remove herself from the equation for a while, to extricate herself from this enormous lie through the simple expedient of giving them time to get him back on track. Not breaking up with him, exactly, but fading away until she and Nolan can decide together if they want to date or shake hands and say "good game" and mutually back away from each other.

Bowing out of his life without any of the fanfare with which she arrived.

She's not sure how she'll say goodbye to Van, if Van will even let her bow out at all, but she's ready to try. And if she gets out of this fake thing, and then Van wants to start a real thing, if Van is willing to take the risk of pissing off her mom and confusing the rest of her family . . . yeah. Alice would do it.

She would.

If Van wants her after all of that, Alice won't stop it.

She's honestly not sure she could if she wanted to. This thing between them feels almost inevitable, like all they could possibly do is delay it a little. Like they might as well give in and start making out in earnest now, because it's going to happen sooner or later. Which of course they can't do for a million reasons, but Alice is only a weak, weak person and she can't control fate.

She gets to the hospital and finds Nolan sitting up in bed, looking better than he has since he collapsed on her lobby floor. There's more color in his cheeks than she'd expected to see; he almost looks like his old self, but it doesn't feel like it used to when she looked at him. Before all of this, it was like her feelings were screaming at her when she saw his beautiful face, his thick hair, his sharp jawline, but today she doesn't feel any of that. The memories of those feelings come to her, but the little throb in her chest is more from nostalgia than from actively wanting him. He's still beautiful, but . . . yeah, no. It's not the same.

She doesn't need to, but she lets her eyes slide from him to Van anyway, and she feels exactly what she knows she will.

Something hot and wanting erupts inside her, ferocious and insatiable and impossibly melancholy. God, she wants Van so badly, and the fact that she can't have her right now doesn't dull the wanting at all, it just tints it, like a wash of a blue watercolor over a dried painting.

Alice knows, with a painful jolt, that no matter how Nolan acts, what he's like, that she won't want to date him. Not with Van right there, a shining, beautiful, wonderful person that

Alice is so desperate for. That even if Nolan did want to try again to be with her—*again* being a slightly inaccurate term, of course—Alice's real answer would be, as Bella so eloquently put it, *Boy, bye.*

But, okay. One thing at a time. Figure out this amnesia thing, then figure out how to transfer herself from fake-girlfriend-of-Nolan to real-girlfriend-of-Van.

Babs is sitting on the edge of the bed, talking with her son.

Alice sidles up to Marie, who is sitting on top of one of the counters in what must be a breach of hygiene standards. "Any news on his amnesia?" Alice asks softly.

"Kind of," Marie says. "He remembers more today than yesterday." Alice's heart slithers down into her lower intestine. Is this it? Is she found out already? But Marie keeps going, not looking as happy as Alice would expect if it were all better. "But only, like, a few months more. He's still missing the last four years, and the doctors don't know if more will come back or not." She scoffs. "Dad says they're so scared of being sued for guessing wrong that they won't tell us anything."

Yeah, that sounds about right.

"Shit," Alice says, her heart absolutely sinking, and Marie pats her on the shoulder.

"Yup."

Okay.

Well. If the memories are creeping back, month by painstaking month, Alice needs to bail now. She needs to do what she brainstormed with Isabella: get out of this before it gets worse, and create some distance between herself and his family, which will serve her especially well if his recent memories come back and they all realize she's a fraud.

Honestly, not being in the room when they figure that out sounds pretty damn good.

So, even though there aren't updates, it's game time. While things were slow today at work, Alice made Isabella text her a script of what to say to Babs, so now Alice has all of her lines written down and memorized. She's about to ask Marie and Van to step outside with her—she figures doing it all at once would be making too big a deal out of it—when she tunes in to what Babs and Nolan are talking about.

"Why did I leave L.A.?"

"To be closer to the family," Babs says, her face proud. "With everything going on with Van and all."

Alice is confused—what was going on with Van?—but she's not the only one who seems to be objecting.

"Mom, no," Van says, stepping forward, her arms crossed over her chest. "That's absolutely not why he moved back."

"Yes, it is," Babs says, smoothing down the sheet and studiously not looking at her daughter. "He wanted to be here to support you."

Van doesn't look at her mom either, staring at Nolan with hollow eyes. Her voice is shaking, and Alice wants nothing more than to reach out to her, to run her hands down Van's arms, to curl up against her back and let Van lean into her. "You moved here because you wanted to be a bigger fish in a smaller pond at work," she says flatly. "And because it made Mom happy. It had nothing to do with me."

"You wanted to be here to help Van with the MS!" Babs's voice is shrill now, and then there's a ringing silence.

Or maybe it's just Alice's ears that are ringing.

To help Van with the MS? As in multiple sclerosis, MS? As in the degenerative disease that killed Michelle Obama's dad, as in the one that Selma Blair from *Legally Blonde* has? As in the one that lands people in wheelchairs and hospitals? That MS?

To help Van with the . . .

Van . . . Van has MS?

Alice blinks, rewinding and replaying every interaction she's had with Van. She remembers the first time Van seemed tired, the day they went up to Nolan's office and she walked slowly and leaned against things with big circles under her eyes. She kept opening and closing her hands that day, like she was trying to increase circulation to them. She remembers Babs's concern about Van's health, about if she should be opening her own PT clinic. She thinks about how Van has been translating what the neurologists have been saying this whole time, how she knew all about the MRI; Alice thought it was because of her professional training, but maybe it was because of this.

Because there's something wrong with her brain too.

"Well, if that's why you moved here, then you might as well go right back to L.A.," Van snarls, and even Alice can tell she's furious with her mom, not her brother, but she's saying it to Nolan anyway. "Since you've done fuck all for me and the fucking MS."

"Vanessa!" Babs is standing now, her cheeks pink, her hands balled up into fists at her sides, but Van is pushing through everyone and stomping out of the room, like maybe if her boots are loud enough on the floor, no one will see the tears in her eyes.

There's a long, horribly loud silence, eventually broken by Marie's sarcastic, "Nice one, Mom." She hops off the counter and grabs Alice's arm. "Come on," she says, pulling Alice out of the room with her. "Let's go find her."

But, no. Alice can't go find her. She needs—she needs a minute. Or ten.

She begs off, telling Marie she has to make a phone call and she'll find them in a few, then takes the elevator up to a random floor and curls up in a chair in the farthest waiting room she can find, pulling out her phone and typing *multiple sclerosis* into her search bar with shaking fingers.

Words jump out at her, each one worse than the last. *Autoimmune disease. Nervous system, brain, spine. Chronic, disabling. Unpredictable relapses. Permanent damage. Progressive.*

Incurable.

She claps a hand over her mouth, trying to stifle her sob. God, poor Van. Strong, beautiful, stoic Van, whose own body is eating itself up from the inside. Van, who works with her hands, who stands all day, who fixes other people's bodies and their problems, who holds her entire family together.

No. It doesn't matter what Alice feels, what she wants, how looking at Van takes her breath away, what it felt like in the bed with her and in the bathroom, to be pressed against her, to be wanted by her. No.

She can't be with her. She can't.

Van is sick. Van has a progressive, permanent, horrible disease and Alice cannot—she absolutely cannot—watch someone else she loves waste away and die in front of her.

She can't.

She won't.

SEVENTEEN

Three days later, on Monday after work, Alice stands tall in Babs's living room and clears her throat loudly to get everyone's attention so she can make the speech she and Isabella incessantly rehearsed over the weekend. Even poor little Sebastian could probably recite the entire speech from memory at this point, and he still hasn't even nailed the alphabet song.

She practiced it twice in front of Delilah at work today, and now she's here. Standing in front of all of the Altmans, except for Nolan who is still at Portland Grace, saying it exactly like she practiced. "Listen, there's a lot going on right now. With the amnesia and everything. So I'm going to, um . . ." She takes a deep breath in and out, summoning courage from the memory of Hazel's (likely unrelated) applause yesterday. "I'm going to step back for a while. I know Nolan doesn't remember me right now, and I don't want to add that pressure onto him. He needs to focus on his recovery, so I'm going to back off for a while, and whenever he's ready, we can start dating again, if he wants to. But if not, that's okay too. In the meantime, though, I really hope he gets better quickly, and that you know how much I've loved getting to know you all."

No one says anything, and Alice immediately starts to sweat. She's never seen the Altmans silent before. Especially not Aunt Sheila. Even Hazel had said something when she'd finished, although she's guessing "Where Daddy" was less a compliment and more a plea to be rescued from Alice's company.

It's Marie finally who squeaks, "What?"

"You're . . ." Van clears her throat. "You're, what? Just . . . leaving? Us?"

Alice tries not to look at her. She can't look at her. She can't be in love with her and she can't look at her and she can't think about her slowly decaying in that hospital without crying and she's trying to pretend to be fine.

"He has enough to deal with right now," Alice says, digging deep for a line that was cut from a prior draft. "Really, it's okay."

"But you're his girlfriend," Babs says, and Alice shakes her head.

"I don't need to be right now," she says. God, but she's gotten good at evading the truth, hasn't she? "He doesn't need to feel guilty or awkward about not remembering me when so much else is going on."

And the thing is, she knows she's right. He doesn't remember moving from L.A. to Portland, doesn't remember his coworkers or his clients. Doesn't remember Cherry/Kerry or any of the other girls he's actually been with. He thinks Marie is still in high school, that Uncle Joe's cholesterol is fine. That he's thirty-one, instead of his true thirty-six. If she really had been a casual girlfriend, that's too much to deal with. She'd probably be bailing even if it were real. Honestly, if it were real, she might have bailed way before now. If she weren't desperate for a family, if Babs's hugs didn't fuck her up beyond belief, if she weren't in love with Van—which she's not, for the record—she'd probably have bounced after the first day or so. Faded into the background and ghosted everyone, retreating to the safety of her shitty apartment and her new day-shift life.

She stayed for all the wrong reasons, but she's fixing it now.

"Alice," Van says, stepping forward. What she wants and what they did is practically written all over her face, and Alice has to wrench her gaze away.

"Thank you for everything," she manages to say to the room at large, proud that her voice isn't shaking the way her hands are. "I mean it."

Alice turns to go, but somehow Aunt Sheila has slipped around behind her, and is leaning against the closed front door, blocking her only exit. "Well," she says as Alice stops dumbly in her tracks. "When you're quite finished with that."

Alice blinks at her. Not only is she confused, but that was a sentence fragment. When she's quite finished with what? She can't help but look over her shoulder for reinforcement from the rest of the family, but they all seem quite used to this sort of thing, because none of them are batting an eye. Marie's flopping down on the couch with Frank, like the show is over.

"Alice," Aunt Sheila finally says, pushing herself off the door and crossing her arms over her chest. "Honey, you've got to stop thinking of yourself as a burden on this family. So Nolan doesn't remember you yet. Okay, who cares? Start over. Here, now."

Alice knows she should say something, but her brain is stuck. She *is* a burden on this family. She's lying to them. She's directly responsible for them believing things about Nolan's life that aren't true. She doesn't belong here; they don't owe her anything and she owes them so much, beginning with the truth and ending with a lot of gas money.

Aunt Sheila seems to take her silence for confusion, because she spells it out. "You're his girlfriend. You supported him. He cared about you. So be here. That'll help him with his recovery much more than if you leave now, and even if he doesn't remember falling for you, he'll do it all over again."

That's absurd. Life isn't some kind of romance novel, where he'll fall in love with her in any universe, in any permutation, some kind of soulmate bullshit. He didn't give a rat's ass about her in real life when he had all of his marbles. He liked girls like Cherry, tall and polished and skinny. So there's absolutely not a prayer of a chance of him wanting her—dowdy and overweight, undereducated and horribly in debt, no professional skills to speak of—especially now that his brains have been addled and he's missing the memories from the years of living near his family that might have actually made him more open and compassionate.

Yeah, no. Not going to happen, Aunt Sheila. Sorry. He's never going to pick Alice, and the one person who might pick her, who could feasibly pick her, well.

Alice can't pick her back.

"I don't think that's a good idea," she starts, but Aunt Sheila shakes her head, walking right into Alice's space and wrapping an arm around her shoulders, steering her toward the dining room table with an unrelenting grip.

"Sit," Aunt Sheila says, and it's not a request. "Eat something. You look hungry."

Alice casts a desperate look over to Marie, but the traitor shrugs, a little smile on her lips.

Fuck.

Alice comes back to the hospital two days later, on Wednesday, after work. She stops in the doorway of Nolan's room but doesn't step all the way inside because it's the worst possible scenario: It's only Nolan and Van inside. He's sitting up with his legs hanging over the side of his bed, and she's sitting on one of those low wheeling stools doctors use. Neither of them seem to notice her.

She has one hand on his arm, like she's bracing him in case he falls, and the other on top of his knee. "Press up into my hand," she says. "Press, press, press."

Alice can't see much movement, but Van nods. "Good," she says. Alice lingers in the doorway as Van gives him what looks like a full workup, testing his knees, his ankles, his wrists and arms, his ability to open and close his fingers, touch his nose, track her finger. Alice has never seen her work before, and it's kind of mesmerizing. Her voice is low and even, encouraging without giving anything away. She reacts the same when something happens as when something doesn't, and she gives off a steady energy that Alice envies.

She can't help but remember how chaotic and frantic she'd been trying to give Nolan CPR. Van would have been so much better at it, so much calmer and more effective. There's a reason Van's a doctor and Alice is a receptionist, apparently, and it's not only that Van got to go to college.

Alice is maybe not super great in a crisis.

"When do I get to go home?" Nolan asks as Van brushes her fingers across his cheeks and asks if it feels the same on both sides.

"Probably soon," Van says, most of her concentration shifting to hitting his knees with a little hammer to test his reflexes. "There's not much more they can do for you here." She looks up at him then, and her eyes narrow. "But it's not recommended for anyone with a traumatic brain injury to live alone. They'll probably send you to stay with Mom and Dad for a while, see if more of your memories come back there."

Nolan shakes his head, but that was clearly a bad thing to do because he abruptly sways and Van has to catch him with both hands. She eases him back onto his pillows, moving his legs for him, and Nolan grimaces. Alice isn't sure if he's reacting to the idea of staying with his parents or at how his body isn't working right, and either way, watching it hurts.

How many times did she watch a nurse swing her dad's legs around for him, hear a doctor use that same tone Van did for his lung capacity tests, even after Alice knew enough to know he was failing them, one after another? How many times did her dad ask to be sent home, did the nurses look over at her like they were trying to evaluate if she was old enough for the responsibility of taking care of him?

How many times did she bring him home, spending money they didn't have on cabs until she was old enough to drive, with him promising her this was the last time? He was going to get better, and they'd never need to go back to that hospital again.

She can't help but picture the roles reversed, now, with Van lying in the bed, being asked to lift her knee and open her fingers and touch her nose. Van in a hospital gown, Van staggering up the walkway to her duplex, Van insisting that she's fine when she's clearly not. Van being smothered by her mother's anxious affection, Van gritting her teeth and pretending she's not in agony.

"I refuse to live with them," Nolan says, relaxing back onto his pillows. "That would be awful. Mom wouldn't let me take a piss without her supervision."

Although Alice can't think of a nicer place to recuperate, he's probably not wrong about how Babs would hover. Van seems to agree, nodding at Nolan. "I know," she says. "You could . . ." She pauses, busying herself with tucking the stool back where it goes under the little sink in the corner of the room. She takes a breath, and then says, "You could stay with me instead."

Nolan blinks. Alice tries to picture him in Van's house, on her worn brown couch that's covered in a thick layer of Frank's hair. No sweeping views of the city, no balcony, no garage for what is surely a fancy car. Just a cozy two-bedroom unit on the ground floor with succulents on every surface and dog toys scattered across the rug.

"Maybe you could stay with me at my condo?" he offers. "Apparently it's very nice."

"It is very nice," Van says, her voice steady and calm like she's still in doctor mode. "But I have a dog, and it would be absolute ass to take him down nineteen stories every time he has to pee. Plus, he'd destroy all your nice shit."

It isn't until Nolan says, "Well, maybe someone else could take care of him," that Alice remembers her suspicions that maybe he's not a very nice person, that maybe he's kind of selfish. The rest of the family is so kind and loving that it's easy to forget, but right. Yeah. Sometimes wonderful families happen to spawn jerks, she guesses. Alice thinks about the venom in Van's voice when she'd said *Since you've done fuck all for me and the fucking MS,* about the drawer in his apartment with hair ties in every color for what must be his parade of one-night stands. About how, from the couple of snide comments Van's made, Alice is pretty sure he's not contributing to Marie's tuition or his parents' mortgage, even though he's living in one of the most expensive pieces of real estate in Portland.

Van seems to be remembering all of this too, because her face is tightening up and her voice is harder when she says, "No, they couldn't. You're welcome with me at my house with my dog, Nolan, or you can stay with Mom and Dad. Let us know what you decide."

She finally catches sight of Alice in the doorway and nods at her.

"Nolan, you remember Alice from the other day?"

He looks over at her, and there's nothing at all in his face when he says, "Yeah, sure. Hello."

Alice wonders if that counts, if it should be five times he's said *hello* now, or if she should start over. New brain, clean slate.

"Hi," she says. "How are you feeling?"

He shrugs, and she can see him wiggling his toes under the sheet Van's pulled up to his waist. "A little better, I guess." He takes a moment then and really stares at her, and Alice feels entirely naked. He's looking her up and down, clearly trying to find what he must have seen in her, and coming up empty. "They said . . ." He pauses for a beat. "They said you were my girlfriend?" Alice tries not to grimace at the confusion in his voice, the disappointment. The way there's nothing even close to resembling happiness at the idea of having been with her.

"Don't worry about that," Alice says quickly. Too quickly. "It doesn't matter." Van makes a sound, and Alice tries to reel it in, to act even the tiniest bit like their relationship mattered to her. "You don't remember it, and I don't want you to feel like you have to fake it."

One of them shouldn't have to anyway.

"So . . . you're not my girlfriend anymore? If more memories don't come back?"

"Let's not push it right now, while you're still recovering," Alice says, seizing the easy out while Aunt Sheila isn't around to yell at her about it. "You can think of me as, I don't know . . . a weird new family friend who happens to be around a lot." Or, maybe, not around a lot, if Alice can manage to extract herself. He clearly doesn't want her, she doesn't particularly want him, being around Van is the kind of torture the Geneva Conventions tend to frown upon, and Alice truly isn't sure what she's still doing here, other than basking in the care of Babs, Aunt Sheila, and Marie. Why did his family have to be so fucking wonderful? Why couldn't he have come from a normal family that begrudgingly sees one another on holidays and pretends like they have stuff in common? Alice could have bounced out of that scenario on day one.

"Okay," Nolan says slowly. "Um, sure. Fine. Good." There's a quiet beat and then, "Could you get me some coffee?"

Alice blinks. He doesn't know about her job, but damn. Dude can spot a receptionist at twenty paces even with a traumatic brain injury. "Uh, sure. I'll be, um, right back. I guess."

"Tea," Van says quickly, her eyes full of the apology Nolan doesn't realize is warranted. "He's only allowed decaf tea."

Nolan grumbles, but Alice nods. "Want anything?" she asks the wall behind Van's head. It's too hard to look at Van right now, to see the hurt and confusion in her eyes. As far as Van knows, Alice threw her into a bathroom and kissed her senseless nearly a week ago and has done everything in her power to avoid looking at her or speaking to her since. Van has to be horribly confused, whiplashed by Alice's abrupt one-eighty from *Fuck it, I want you* to *It would be easier for me if you didn't exist,* and it's not like Alice can explain it. Not like she can say, *Hey, so the problem isn't that your brother is awake, exactly; it's that I'm a piece of shit who is refusing to even entertain the notion of being with you because you're sick and that freaks me out.*

Those are thoughts better left unsaid, better left buried with all of the potential they'll never fulfill, all of the love and care that Alice refuses to acknowledge.

"No," Van says softly. "Nothing from the cafeteria."

Right. Because she does want something and they both know it, and it's not a cup of fucking decaf tea. Alice almost laughs at how obvious Van is, how brave. How truly horrible Alice is for hurting her like this.

Alice wishes she could set it all aside and wrap herself around Van again, that she could fix the scars in Van's brain, could make her as healthy and strong as she seems. Or maybe that she could make herself brave enough and kind enough for it not to matter, to be able to say—and mean—that she's willing to risk it, that she wants Van more than she's afraid of the MS.

But she can't. She's not.

Nolan isn't the only selfish person in this hospital.

She leaves the room, but doesn't walk away quite yet. She leans against the wall outside, trying to breathe through how hard it is to be near Van, how painful it is to see what has quickly become her favorite face in the world and only be able to think about her slowly and painfully disintegrating, shrinking down to nothing under a hospital gown.

"I don't get it," she hears Nolan say. "I really dated her?"

"Yup," Van says, a little gruffly, like maybe she's trying to swallow down a big feeling.

"She's not . . . my type," Nolan says slowly. "Like, at all. Is she?"

Alice hears what he doesn't say, and she knows it's true—

has known it for her whole life and for the last two weeks especially—but it still hurts.

"No." Van's voice is soft now, and for some reason Alice wants to cry. "She's not." There's a beat, and then Alice can almost hear the smile in her voice. "And that, brother, is proof that you've always had fucking terrible taste in women."

EIGHTEEN

Three days later, Alice looks around her apartment, dismayed. She's holding her little plastic tabletop Christmas tree in her hands because somehow it's Christmas Eve, and she hasn't done a single thing to decorate. The dishes piled up in the sink aren't exactly getting her in a festive mood, and she's been spending so much time with Isabella and the Altmans—and trying not to think about Van or Nolan or the lie or anything at all, really—that she hasn't so much as opened her box of ornaments yet. It looks like the dreary short days of February in here: gray, depressing, cold, morbid. Lonely.

She went to Target yesterday, which was, as to be expected on Friday, December 23, an absolute nightmare. She'd gone a wee bit overboard on toys for Sebastian and Hazel and managed to find a decent cookbook and novelty oven mitts for Isabella and Henry on sale that she hopes are okay.

She'd thought about trying to find things for all of the Altmans, but the gifts for Isabella's family already put a dent in her January budget, and there are *seven* freaking Altmans. It was out of the question, so Alice stopped herself from touching a warm umber sweater that would look beautiful on Van, from picking up a necklace she could perfectly picture on Marie or grabbing a wacky purse that would probably suit Aunt Sheila. The Snuggies in aisle twelve gave her pause, but she forced herself to keep walking, loading up on baking supplies to make her favorite cinnamon cookies for them instead.

Even the presents for Sebastian and Hazel aren't brightening up the apartment much, since Alice wrapped them in old newspaper that she swiped from work. Usually she sets up the tree weeks in advance, hangs little fairy lights around, and uses electric candles, binging stupid heterosexual Christmas movies and listening to the *NSYNC Christmas album on repeat. But this year it all snuck up on her, and she's feeling more like a grinch than she has since her first Christmas without her dad when she was nineteen.

A knock on her front door startles her so thoroughly that she almost drops the plastic tree. No one ever knocks on her door. The last time must have been months ago, and it was someone high out of their mind looking for her next-door neighbor, who Alice is pretty sure is the weed dealer for the entire building. Weed is legal and everything in Oregon, but she guesses some people still like the personal touch.

She opens the door and it's not someone looking for some fresh flower—or, well, it could be, she supposes. She doesn't know Babs's life.

Marie and Babs are standing there grinning at her, their cheeks pink from the cold.

"Merry Christmas," Marie says, pulling Alice into a hug before Alice has truly processed what's happening. Marie's jacket is wet, but Alice doesn't care. She smells like gingersnaps and rain, and she's safe so Alice lets herself love her.

Babs hugs her too, and like always, it makes Alice's chest want to cave in. It's worse here, in her dim apartment—the brightness of their smiles, the warmth of their hugs making her life seem even bleaker in comparison.

They both bustle inside, shucking off their coats and making themselves comfortable as only Altman women seem to be able to do. "Well, get to it," Babs says, reaching out a finger to touch Alice's little mini plastic tree with something that looks like disapproval. "Gather up your things."

"My . . . things?"

"It's Christmas Eve," Marie says, like that explains it. At Alice's blank stare, Marie rolls her eyes but deigns to fill her in. "We kidnapped you for Chanukah, Alice, did you really think we weren't going to do the same for Christmas? Come on, you're staying with us tonight."

No. Alice absolutely cannot stay with them tonight. She can't sleep in a bed with Van again. She can't. Not after what happened in the bathroom, not after she's been avoiding her, not after learning about her MS. Absolutely not.

But just like for Chanukah, it doesn't really seem to be a request. Alice definitely hasn't said yes, but she finds herself being shoved into the area of her studio that serves as the bedroom to grab clothes and a toothbrush. She says something about needing to bake cookies, but Babs simply waves a hand, declaring that she has every ingredient known to womankind in her kitchen already, and won't it be more fun to bake them at home with everyone there?

"No." Alice tries one more time. "I couldn't—"

But Babs is shaking her head before Alice can get any of the words out. "Van told us your parents aren't with us anymore," she says, her tone somehow both kind and bossy. "So you're ours now. Come on, chop-chop. We've got cookies to decorate, and we've left the menfolk alone with the icing for too long already."

She says it so quickly, like it's obvious. *Van told us your parents aren't with us anymore, so you're ours now.*

Not *Nolan's,* not *Van's,* but *ours.* Like maybe they want her around even if she and Nolan don't successfully rekindle their fake romance, like maybe she gets to have Babs and Marie and Aunt Sheila even if she doesn't get to have Van or Nolan.

It's a terrible idea, because Nolan's memories could keep marching toward the present, Van could have a relapse, everything could still come crumbling down. But Alice has been alone for a really long time, and Babs's grip is firm and warm on her arm.

"Okay," Alice says. "Let's go rescue some cookies."

Marie spends the entire drive to Laurelhurst chattering to Alice about all of her favorite Christmas traditions. Cookies, tree decorating, hanging outdoor lights, caroling around the neighborhood, watching movies all Christmas Day in matching pajamas, Babs making a mulled wine so strong one time one of the neighbors fell asleep in their driveway. "This year we had to cram all of December into, like, two days, so it's gonna be wild," Marie advises from the front seat, an almost manic happiness in her eyes now that Nolan is awake. "Get ready."

"I'll do my best," Alice promises. This honestly sounds amazing, way more cheerful and celebratory than any Christmas she's had since she was a kid. Or maybe ever. Back when her mom was alive they'd done the full-on Christmas thing, but they'd never had much money. No place for outdoor lights in their apartment, and they usually had a fake tree—ironically for fire safety in such a small space. Even after her mom died there were still presents and ornaments and stockings, but Alice had to do as much work as her dad did, if not more, and their budget for presents got smaller and smaller until it was trinkets only.

And then there was nothing.

They arrive at the house, and it's exactly as chaotic as Alice expects it to be. Nolan is parked on one of the couches, and he looks almost healthy in a soft gray sweater, his lap covered, of course, with a Snuggie. Uncle Joe is with him, and while there's a football game on TV, they're both staring intently at their phones, barely even glancing up to nod hello.

The sounds coming from the kitchen seem to be even louder than they were on Chanukah, so Alice assumes that's where Aunt Sheila is. There's an enormous Christmas tree in the corner now, already wrapped in lights and tinsel but surrounded by boxes of ornaments that have yet to be placed. It smells like evergreen and roasting sugar, and it's so warm that Alice can't shuck off her layers quickly enough.

She's ushered into the kitchen, where Aunt Sheila is surrounded by what looks like every mixing bowl in the state of Oregon. Babs jumps immediately into the fray, and Marie crosses the kitchen to the far wall, where two aprons are hanging on hooks. She picks them up and holds them out to Alice. "'Kiss the Chef' or 'I Like Big Buns'?"

Alice blinks. Well, she definitely can't do "Kiss the Chef," not with Van around. "'Buns,' please," she says, reaching out for the hideously pink apron with a drawing of some kind of cinnamon bun on it.

"Nice," Marie says with a sly smile, and Alice wants to die. She puts it on anyway, and Marie forces her mom and Aunt Sheila to stop banging around for long enough to take a selfie of all four of them in their aprons (Babs's reads "Queen of the Kitchen" and Aunt Sheila's is hard to make out but Alice thinks it says something about the Latke Flippers' Guild).

Alice can't help but notice the gender dynamics and wonder where Van is. There isn't another apron on the hook—so either Alice is wearing Van's, or Van isn't expected in the kitchen with the rest of the women.

After satisfying herself with the picture, Marie heads over to the pantry. "Alice, you said you wanted to make cinnamon cookies?"

Alice joins her, immediately overwhelmed at how well stocked it is. She always has only the bare minimum ingredients she needs for whatever she's making, but Babs's pantry is overflowing with multiple different types of flours and sugars, three different kinds of chocolate chips, several jars of sprinkles, countless ziplocks of things Alice doesn't even recognize.

Alice tentatively takes what she needs, letting Marie's happy chatter wash over her as she tries to stay out of the way of the dual boomer tornados. It isn't until her dough has come together and she's starting to roll it out that she hears the front door open and feels a gust of cold air.

"Whew!" That's Steve's voice from the living room. "It's a cold one out there!"

"How are the lights?" Babs yells toward the living room, and it's only a moment before Van appears in the doorway, and she takes Alice's breath away. She looks taller and broader than usual, her cheeks flushed pink with exertion, her thick blue jacket zipped up to her sternum. Her eyes are dancing, and there are water droplets on her black hair.

"Great," she says, sounding a little breathless. Alice tries not to focus on how this is exactly what she'd sounded like after kissing Alice to within an inch of her life in the hospital bathroom. "It was pretty slippery up there, but we managed to get it all nailed down hard."

Is it just Alice, or does that sound impossibly dirty? Probably her mind is in the gutter because Van is so hot and Alice is such a mess, but, like, really? Nailing something down? Being slippery? Come on, Vanessa Altman, cut out the porn talk in front of your mother!

"Van, taste this," Marie says, holding out the bowl of chocolate icing she's mixing up. "Does it need more vanilla?"

Alice turns away in an act of self-preservation, resolutely not watching Van lick chocolate off her finger. But this means that she doesn't realize Van is coming toward her until she feels a warm, looming presence behind her, smells rain and wet grass and the familiar spice of her cologne.

"Nice apron," Van says, soft and low, right into Alice's ear, and Alice takes in a big breath through her nose, trying to keep herself from leaning back and melting into Van's body, letting Van pick her up and abscond with her into a bedroom.

"Thank you," she manages to murmur. She's wedged in the corner, a wall on her right, and on her left, Marie, who is currently turned away, arguing animatedly with Babs about cookie cutters. Van slides her right hand forward to rest on Alice's hip, and Alice sucks in another breath, this time clearly loud enough for Van to hear it.

All Alice can think about is how Van's hands felt on her body for those blissful five minutes before Nolan woke up—warm and strong and demanding in all the best ways.

"I do too, for the record," Van whispers, and it takes Alice a second to come back to the present enough to figure out what she means. They'd been talking about the apron, and oh. It says

"I Like Big Buns," and Van said, *I do too,* and she's extremely close to Alice's quite sizable buns at the moment, and fuck.

God, Alice is going to hell for this, but she lets herself press backward, just for a second. The merest brush of the back of her pants against the front of Van's, but it's enough.

It's Van who makes a sound this time, a sharp breath, and Van's fingers that twitch against Alice's hip, like she's barely able to stop herself from grabbing hold and pulling Alice fully into herself.

But that little twitch is enough for Alice to remember the other thing about Van's hands, how she opens and closes them when she's tired, how Alice read in one of her anxious fits of research that having pins and needles in your hands is a common MS symptom.

That's enough for the horny filter in her brain to dissipate, and for her to remember why she's not allowed to give in to this. Right. Van has MS, and Alice simply cannot sign herself up for another decade or two or four of caretaking, of watching the one person she loves slowly die in front of her.

She presses her hips forward until the counter is digging into the flesh of her stomach. "I, um, I have to roll these out before the dough gets too warm," she says, and Van backs off.

"Can't have that," she says, but her voice sounds tight, and Alice knows she clocked the rejection. She hates herself for being so inconsistent, so unable to keep her hands—and ass, apparently—to herself. She knows she's giving mixed signals, that Van doesn't deserve any of this.

Alice needs to get it together, stat. That's easier said than done, though, because she's under constant scrutiny here. Babs keeps checking in on her cookies, giving her unsolicited but helpful advice, Marie keeps leaning into her shoulder—Alice's heart certainly isn't exploding, she's fine—even the men are popping in and out of the kitchen to grab more snacks or high-five everyone about football-related things Alice doesn't care to understand.

Even worse, it turns out that Aunt Sheila is not only one of the chefs, she's apparently also the official photographer. All afternoon, she snaps picture after picture on her iPad, and Alice is sure most of them must be horribly unflattering. Sideways shots from below of Alice frowning down at an icing bag, Alice and Marie mid-bite, Van halfway through clipping Frank's leash on. Alice just hopes she isn't getting any of Van staring sadly at Alice, of Alice looking like she desperately wants to wrap herself around Van like an octopus and never let go.

But it's sweet, honestly, that Aunt Sheila wants to capture the mundane moments with her family. And if Nolan happens to be in more than his fair share, well, who can blame her, really? He's home, he's alive, and you can't tell from the pictures that he has amnesia.

"Alice," Aunt Sheila says after taking a whole series of the three men on the couch that Alice has silently named *The Patriarchy Is Alive and Well,* "go sit with Nolie."

"Uh, sorry?" Alice pretends she didn't hear, that she's absorbed in her work piping white icing onto cookies with Marie at the dining room table, but Aunt Sheila is, of course, unperturbed.

"Go sit with your boyfriend, honey," she says, grabbing Alice's arm and practically throwing her at the couch.

Alice manages to get her apron off but it gets caught in her hair, and she can see the way Nolan's eyes linger on her frizzy tangles. She tosses the apron to Marie to hold for her, and she tries not to wonder if Nolan likes big buns the way Van does.

She tries not to think about how she has a great view of Van's buns right now, because Van is turning away from her, hurt clear in the set of her head, the way her shoulders are creeping up to her chin.

Alice sits next to Nolan, who pushes the blanket off his legs.

"Nolan, put your arm around her," Aunt Sheila directs. "Isn't this lovely, your first official portrait as a couple!"

Alice hopes her smile doesn't look like a grimace as Nolan obediently drapes his arm around her shoulders. He seems to be touching her as little as possible, but his arm is still heavy. Alice tilts toward him so the picture doesn't look tremendously awkward, but she's pretty sure whatever Aunt Sheila manages to get will look more like a hostage photo than a happy couple celebrating their first Christmas together.

Although she's honestly not sure which of them will look like the hostage and which like the hostage taker.

"Now how about a kiss?"

Alice blanches. "Oh no, no, no."

"Just on the cheek, dear," Aunt Sheila says, flapping her hands at them in a *get on with it* motion.

Alice looks desperately around for backup, but Babs is standing next to Aunt Sheila, her hands clasped under her chin, beaming at Nolan like watching him kiss Alice is all she's ever wanted for Christmas. Even Marie is grinning, holding her own phone up now. Steve and Uncle Joe seem unmoved, largely fixated on the football game, and Alice can't see Van but she can feel her presence—distressed, disapproving. Disappointed.

She turns to look at Nolan. She's never been this close to him before. She tries to call up her feelings from three weeks ago, when she'd have given anything for the chance to be here under his arm, to get this close to his face, to have a picture of them together that she could stare at for the rest of her life.

She'd been in love with him, as much as it's possible to be in love with someone who barely knows that you exist. She'd written *Alice Altman* in the margins of more than one piece of paper, and she may have even practiced a signature.

This whole fucked-up situation is because she thought he was pretty and then she wanted to make his family happy. He's still pretty, and right now his family is nearly crying tears of joy at the thought of him pressing his chapped lips to her cheek for half a second. And she did give him mouth-to-mouth, so it's not like they haven't almost made out before, right?

She nods at him, and he doesn't look thrilled about it but he leans in too, and Alice turns her face, closes her eyes.

It's a barely-there press of lips to skin, and it's over in a second. She hopes the Altmans all think she kept it chaste—her hands in her own lap, her failure to kiss his cheek back, no coy smiles or flirtatious whispers—because making out with him in front of his mom and aunt and baby sister and their Instagram audiences is weird, instead of the truth, which is that the idea of his tongue in her mouth is kind of turning her stomach. She decides not to dwell on why he gave it so little energy and enthusiasm himself; her self-esteem probably can't take the hit of knowing precisely how revolting he finds her.

She tries so hard not to think about how she'd have kissed Van in this situation, how she'd have turned her head back at the last second to find Van's lips with her own, how her body would have sunk into Van's without a thought, how Marie would've had to smack them with a spatula to get them to stop kissing. How Van would have leaned in, smiled into Alice's lips, grasped her waist like she never wanted to let go.

She hates that she thinks about how Babs might have turned away, her face tinged with discomfort at the sight of her daughter kissing a woman, instead of the rapt bliss she has right now watching her son do it.

It's less than half an hour later that Alice's phone buzzes in her pocket during a quick breather before caroling. The boomer men are napping, Marie and the boomer women are digging through the costume closet for "special bobbles," whatever that means, and Van is tucked in the corner of the living room, as far away from both Nolan and Alice as she can possibly be without raising suspicion.

Alice pulls her phone out and sees a text from Isabella. She quickly tilts her phone, making sure Van and Nolan can't see her screen.

Um, what the heck is this? the message reads. Alice clicks on it and sees that Isabella has sent her a screenshot from Marie's Instagram account. It's two pictures of her and Nolan—one where they're both smiling awkwardly at the camera, and the other of him kissing her cheek. Alice zooms in. The kiss looks about as uncomfortable as it felt, not particularly warm or intimate, and you can see Steve's knee in the corner. But the caption is what really makes Alice's heart sink: *My Christmas miracle of a big brother and my brand-new almost-sister.* There are a couple emojis, both of the Christmas and joyful variety, and Alice simultaneously wants to die and to scoop Marie up in her arms and hug her for a hundred years.

Shit, Alice writes back.

He kissed you?

His aunt made us for the picture, Alice types quickly. It was awkward.

Yeah I can tell. But still. What about the plan?

Funny story about that. Alice presses her lips together, trying not to laugh at the absolute mess she's made of her life. I gave them the whole speech, and they were like, lol no.

Isabella sends three question marks before she writes, What does that mean?

Alice sends a shrugging emoji. They basically rejected my rejection of them. Literally came to my apartment today and kidnapped me to spend Christmas with them.

Oh, Alice adds, remind me that I have presents for you guys!

Isabella's quick reply, DO NOT TRY TO DISTRACT ME, makes Alice laugh, and Van looks over at her. They're all ostensibly watching football but mostly trying not to touch each other.

"Isabella," Alice offers, lifting her phone a little bit. "Being her usual ridiculous self."

"I liked her," Van says, almost smiling.

"She liked you," Alice says without thinking. "She asks about you, like, every day."

Van swallows, and Alice wishes she could take it back. She really doesn't need Van knowing how much Alice and Isabella talk about her, what Alice says. Who Isabella is rooting for, in all of this.

"Tell her 'Merry Christmas' for me," Van says after a long beat, and Alice nods, grateful for the excuse to duck her eyes back to her phone and read the messages that have piled up.

So are you back together with him?

Well I guess not "back"

Are you with him?

What about Van?

Are you smooching both of them?

RUE RUE WHAT IS GOING ON IN YOUR LIFE RIGHT NOW

Ksdskdhfo!*!^#*)($o

Okay that was Hazel but honestly I agree with her
DUDE

Alice laughs. Sorry. I had to have a human conversation for a second.

I don't know what I'm doing
I don't know if I'm with him or not
Like neither of us really want that I don't think
But his entire family wants us together and we both seem to be playing along with that?
I mean, except for Van
Obviously

Isabella doesn't write back immediately. It's almost two minutes before the next text comes through. Alice wonders if Hazel grabbed her phone again, or if Bella was carefully deciding how to phrase what she wanted to say.

Just make sure you're doing whatever you do for the right reasons, Bella sends. And I think we both know that making his mom and aunt happy aren't it.

Okay, The Bachelor, Alice types, but she knows Bella is right. I promise I'll be here for the right reasons.

Isabella sends her a GIF of a rose ceremony, and Alice tucks her phone back into her pocket.

Bella's right, but it's more complicated than she knows.

"Alice, Van, it's time to get the cookies out of the oven!" Babs shouts down the stairs, and Alice gratefully stands up, scurrying into the kitchen.

It's Christmas Eve. That means cookies now, existential dread later.

NINETEEN

The existential dread comes more quickly than Alice would have hoped. It's after the delicious roast ham dinner, after Alice shamefully confesses that she doesn't have presents for anyone and is resolutely shushed by Babs for worrying about it, and midway through a double-feature viewing of *Elf* and *Home Alone*. They've all changed into brand-new matching pajamas, Alice included—they're red and flannel and warm and they make Alice want to cry.

Babs and Van had to help Nolan into his, and Uncle Joe and Steve are both covering theirs up with giant bathrobes, but it's still fucking delightful and so picture perfect that Alice sort of can't believe this is her life.

Well, of course, it's not, really. It's a life she's borrowing until Nolan dumps her or his recent memories come back or Alice kisses Van again and everything falls apart.

But even so, she can't stop feeling like she's on the verge of tears, like the rub of the soft fabric against her skin is unraveling every piece of armor she's made for herself since she was eight years old. They're not her parents, her aunt, her siblings, but god. She wants them so badly anyway.

At the intermission between films, Babs brings out the box of Snuggies, and, like a Chanukah-themed déjà vu, starts handing them out to everyone. Somehow, despite no one being at the hospital anymore, there's still one too few Snuggies. Alice has read a lot of romance novels where there's only one bed, and she is rapidly becoming suspicious that Babs has hid a blanket or two in order to manufacture the manic joy in her eyes when she announces that Alice and Nolan can share one.

Alice would rather share a Snuggie with Uncle Joe, who she's spoken to less than Nolan despite him never having been in a coma, but she's not sure how to say no. *We didn't actually date and have no history of intimacy* wouldn't cut it even if she were willing to hop right up and say it, because she hadn't made a single peep of complaint before she cuddled right into Van during the other winter festival of lights. She considers turning the blanket down altogether, but the old heater in the house can't keep up with the freeze outside. Plus, Alice has a sneaking suspicion rejecting the Snuggie might make Babs cry, which is theoretically the whole reason she's here anyway, isn't it? To keep Babs from being sad?

So Alice simply gives a meek smile and accepts the half Snuggie Babs lovingly drapes over her lap. She doesn't put her arm through the hole, and she tries not to look over at Van, who is sitting in a straight-backed chair she dragged in from the living room. Alice can see from the corner of her eye that Van is sitting with impeccable posture, her gaze boring holes in the TV, which hasn't started playing the second movie yet. She looks like a statue, a monument to rejection, and it hurts so fucking much. She wants to be on Van's lap, under her

Snuggie. She wants to be as far away from this house and these people as she can. She wants everything to be different.

She forces herself to stop staring so obviously at Van—there would be no heterosexual explanation for the mournful expression on her face, she's sure of it—so Van's sharp intake of breath is Alice's only indication she, sitting all the way across the room, hears Babs's loud whisper to Aunt Sheila.

"Maybe next Christmas we'll have a grandchild cooking under there!"

That's so preposterous that Alice almost laughs, almost stands up, sloughing off the Snuggie and dropping a few truth bombs before calling the world's most expensive Uber. Alice pregnant? Alice and Nolan, baking a grandbaby? Alice and Nolan making a genetic stew that's congealing inside of her body? Alice thinks the fuck not. But as the slightly hysterical urge to laugh begins to fade, the thought of having Nolan's baby starts to make her want to claw her uterus out with her bare hands. She settles for clenching her teeth and unobtrusively scooching her hip away from his.

Marie snickers at her mom, the boomer men honestly probably didn't hear Babs, and Van aggressively presses play on *Home Alone.* Nolan seems to be pretending he didn't hear what his mom said, so Alice does too, her discomfort sitting hot and heavy right in what Babs hopes is her baby oven.

After *Home Alone* ends, robbers suitably foiled and child somewhat supervised, the party breaks up. Everyone starts cleaning up before bed, Babs and Aunt Sheila already making plans for breakfast. Alice has mainlined more cookies and icing than ever before in her life, and the thought of another morsel of food makes her a little nauseous, but she's learned that's basically a constant condition in this house, and she can't say she minds.

Steve, Aunt Sheila, and Uncle Joe head upstairs, leaving Babs downstairs to wedge the four "kids" into the two remaining beds. Since Marie has her own room, Alice assumes she's spending the night in bed with either Van or Nolan, and she can't decide which is worse. She's pretty sure she'd end up having sex with Van or enduring the literal most awkward night of her life with Nolan, and both of those seem like significantly bad options.

She opens her phone, and as she expects, an Uber would be approximately five bajillion dollars, seeing that it's after midnight on what is now Christmas morning, and she remembers that Van doesn't like to drive at night, which seems very octogenarian of her, but whatever. Who is Alice to judge? She basically lives like an old lonely widow who isn't on Social Security herself.

"I'll take the couch," she offers.

"Nonsense," Babs says, flapping her hands at Alice as if to dispel the very idea. "You can share with Nolan, sweetie. Steve and I don't mind; we're not old-fashioned like that. It's not like you haven't done it before, and lord knows we didn't wait until marriage!"

Oh yes, it's just Alice's luck that her fake-boyfriend's parents are so modern that they don't mind the idea of her having sex with him under their roof! They've done it so many times before! What twenty-first-century parenting! And how fun for Alice to know about Babs's sex life! This is delightful on each and every level!

Alice waits until Babs finally troops upstairs before she turns to Nolan. "I don't want you to be uncomfortable," she says quickly. "I'll sleep on the couch. Honestly, I'd prefer it."

"No," Van says, and Alice almost has a heart attack before she realizes Van is saying no to Alice taking the couch, not to

Alice refusing to curl up with her brother. "You and Marie take the guest room. Nolan, take Marie's room. I'll sleep on the couch."

"No," Alice starts to object, but Van glares at her, that chiseled face drawn with disappointment and confusion, and Alice swallows back what she was going to say, some thoughtless drivel about Van being sick and needing the rest.

Alice expects that Nolan might object to spending the night in his baby sister's twin bed, but apparently the thought of bunking with her is enough to send him running toward the small room with the pastel pink walls and the enormous RED, WHITE & ROYAL BLUE poster. "Thanks," he says as Marie helps him to his room, not even looking back over his shoulder as he says, "Good night."

Two hours later, Alice is exhausted and awake. She's tried everything—counting, practicing her apology for when this all goes to shit, running the list of inventory she remembers from when she worked at the pediatric dentist's office, a full-body-scan meditation, doing her multiplication tables, remembering every embarrassing thing she's ever done in excruciating detail, but nothing works. Eventually she slips out of bed, deciding that doomscrolling in the freezing dining room sounds much better than holding herself stiffly so she doesn't wake Marie, who is a surprisingly loud snorer.

Hell, maybe she should have just taken a Snuggie into the costume closet and died tonight like a man.

She's grateful for the warmth of her new pajamas as she tiptoes across the room, opening and closing the bedroom door as quietly as she can. It's dark in the living room, but she picks her way through it, avoiding the coffee table like a pro until her foot catches on the dining room chair Van had been sitting in earlier. Alice hadn't factored that into her mental map of the dark space, and she tumbles forward, luckily landing face-first on a couch instead of smashing her head open on the floor.

One small problem, though.

There's something hard on the couch, and it grabs her.

She almost screams, swallowing it down at the very last instant as her brain catches up to her racing heart.

"Oh my god," she says at the same time a voice from under the blanket says, "What the hell?"

"Van?"

". . . Alice?"

Shit. Alice tries to scramble off her, but it's confusing in the dark. She's somehow tangled all of her limbs in the various Snuggies Van has layered on top of herself—it's like the arms of each blanket have grown sentient and are lashing her down.

"Okay, hold on," Van mutters, and Alice feels Van's hands come up to her waist. "Let me—okay." She shifts and Alice sinks down, now tucked neatly between the solid warmth of Van's body and the back of the couch. She's on her side, one arm tossed over Van's stomach, and both of Van's arms around her. "Better?" Van asks, and Alice doesn't know what to say. Like, yes, she's infinitely more comfortable, and god, if this isn't almost everything she's ever wanted, but also, no! This is now much worse!

Why does Van smell so fucking good in the middle of the night, after eating her weight in sugar cookies and cuddling with her dog?

"Couldn't sleep?" Van asks, her voice rough, and Alice wants to kiss her so badly that it hurts.

"No," she says, but right now she can't figure out why. She's exhausted, suddenly. She can feel her head dropping, sinking down onto Van's shoulder, can feel the little designs Van is aimlessly drawing on her back lulling her to sleep.

"What, um . . . what does this mean?" Van asks, and Alice blinks a couple times, as confused now as she is tired.

"What?" she asks, eloquent as always.

"You coming out here to me," Van says. "After today, with him and the Snuggie and, you know. Your pregnancy."

Alice scoffs—the pregnancy is ridiculous—but Van isn't laughing.

"Are you really getting back with him?" Van asks, a bite in her voice now. "After everything?"

Alice figures she doesn't mean the coma and the hospital and the amnesia. Not that kind of everything. Van means this everything, the gayer, more confusing everything that has Alice's hand clenching the Snuggie over Van's chest, her nose buried in the warmth of Van's neck.

"It's all more complicated now," Alice says, too emotionally and physically exhausted to do a good job at walking the tightrope between evading the truth and outright lying. "I didn't think he'd wake up."

Van tenses under her. Alice wants to sleep but she can't—she's just said something wrong and she doesn't know what it is.

"So, you're saying, what? You hoped he would die?"

"No! Never." That's the truth. She never wanted him to die, but she had simply thought he would. Not a desired outcome, but a fact.

"But you're saying if he'd died, we'd be together? The only way I'd get to be happy is if my brother was dead? And now that he's alive—that I don't have to mourn him—I have to lose you?"

Fuck.

Alice squeezes her eyes closed, presses herself tightly to Van. She wishes the layers of Snuggies weren't there, that she could dig herself into Van so tightly that they'd never be pulled apart. "No," she breathes. "No, that's not—I didn't mean . . ." She trails off. She doesn't know what she means. In a way, Van's right.

If Nolan died, Alice could be with her.

If it weren't for the MS.

Or, no.

If it weren't for Alice's absolute, abject, shameful cowardice related to the MS.

"So that's it," Van spits when Alice can't find the words to defend herself, her voice almost loud enough to carry to the bedrooms. She shifts, pushing them both into more of a sitting position, still tangled up in each other and the Snuggies. "He's not dead, so now you're going to, like, shack up with him and make his babies?"

"No!" Alice is the one who is too loud now, and she tries to pull it back to a hoarse whisper. "God, of course not, Van. That's *insane*."

"That's not the song you were singing earlier." Alice has never heard Van's voice sound like this before, the harsh scrape of sandpaper under her words, the tremble of pain she's trying so hard to conceal.

"Your mom said it," Alice snaps. "Not me."

"Well, why didn't you say no?"

"Because it didn't matter!" Alice hisses, her throat clenching like she's yelling. "None of this fucking matters!"

It isn't until Van's eyes fill with tears that Alice realizes what she's actually said, what Van thinks she meant. Not that things with Nolan don't matter because they'll never become anything, but that none of *this* matters. That Van doesn't matter.

"No," Alice says as quickly as she can, reaching out both

hands for Van. "Van, no. That's not what I meant. I don't think that. You matter."

But Van is shaking her head.

"Look," Van says, her body moving in earnest now, like she's trying to get out from under Alice. "I can't do this, okay? You know what I want, and I thought you wanted it too, but I'm not going to do this. I'm not going to stand here and let you—whatever. Have his babies and then crawl into my bed. That doesn't work for me."

She gets free, sliding off the couch and out from under the Snuggies. She stands, and it's so dark but Alice can still see the pain in her eyes, the exhausted lines on her face.

Alice struggles to sit up, feeling like all of her limbs are submerged in quicksand.

"Van, no," she says, not quietly enough. "That's not it."

"That is it, though," Van says, and she's walking across the room to her shoes. She puts them on and whistles softly, and Frank hops off the other couch, stopping to stretch halfway across the living room.

"I'm going home," Van says, not looking at Alice. "Tell everyone . . . I don't know. Tell them whatever you want." There's a long beat, and then, "I'm sure you'll be fine lying to them. You're pretty good at it."

The door closes behind her, firm but not loud, and it takes Alice what feels like ages to pull the Snuggies up around her, to curl into the spot that's still warm from Van's body, to cry.

TWENTY

Alice spends Christmas Day at Isabella's house. Taking the earliest morning bus from the Altmans was a pretty depressing experience—anyone on a bus at six in the morning on Christmas Sunday is not having a great day—but Isabella's house is a riot of color and squealing children and wrapping paper and good food and sugar crashes. Being there eases the pinch in her chest; it doesn't erase the way Van's eyes had looked, the way she'd slid out from under Alice like she never wanted to touch her again, but it makes that all easier to live with. Here, in this warm house, filled with a family she isn't lying to, a family she belongs with, a family she loves in a not-totally-fucked way, she can breathe a little better.

She hasn't forgotten how she hurt Van—she'll never forget that. She'll regret that and be responsible for it forever, but being with Isabella, Henry, and the kids helps her remember that there's some stuff in the world that's okay too. Hazel dances like a toddler Beyoncé when Henry plays ukulele, Alice and Sebastian make the tallest Lego tower in history, Bella loans Alice the softest sweater in the world, Henry makes a sizzling Korean tofu soup for dinner that's full of mushrooms he foraged himself and he swears won't kill them. Things worth living for.

Alice texts Marie and Babs a thank-you for having her yesterday, makes up some lie about needing to get to Isabella's early. She's tempted to say she'll see them in a few days, but she doesn't.

She's done.

Nolan's rampant disinterest means that Alice can't keep being the embodiment of Babs's hopes for him; he's alive now, walking and talking, so it's okay if Babs goes back to hating his taste in women. Alice's part in this charade is well and truly finished. And of course, much more important, Van was right. It's not fair for Alice to still be coming around, making everything confusing and gray, pitting Van against her recently comatose brother. Even if Alice isn't kissing him or fake-dating him—and certainly not having his babies, fucking gross—Van's right that Alice can't flirt with her. Can't lead her on if she's not willing to be with Van, and she's not.

As her text whooshes out her phone and into theirs, it feels like part of her heart is being twisted and pulled until it rips out. She silently says goodbye to Babs, to Aunt Sheila, to sweet, perfect Marie.

To Van.

It hurts like hell, but it's finally over.

Daycare and preschool are closed between Christmas and New Year's, and Isabella and Henry are going crazy with the kids in the house all day, so on December 30, they pack up the double stroller and enough luggage to travel to France, and prepare to venture to the big park a few blocks away even though it's as cold and rainy as ever.

"If they're going to be true Portlanders, they need to become amphibious," Isabella says, shoving Hazel's fat little arm into her puffy waterproof coat. "Like we were."

Alice nods. "Gotta purge that weak Texan blood right out of 'em," she says, and Isabella laughs.

"Exactly."

Isabella's right—when they were kids, recess always took place outside in the rain, and they spent a lot of time at the park, learning how to navigate wet, slippery monkey bars and wearing rain pants so they could go down the slide without looking like they peed themselves.

"Where are we going?" Sebastian asks as Alice pulls the Velcro on his little boots as tightly as she can.

"To play outside," Isabella says.

"Why?"

Alice looks down at him, putting on a purposely goofy look. "How old are you now? Three?" He nods, quite proudly. "Well, then," she says, rubbing her hands together to warm them before she plunges them, without warning, under his jacket to tickle his belly. "It's time to harden you up! Go play out in the rain where you belong!"

He screams and squeals, and Alice gets kicked very hard in the stomach, but it's worth it.

The park is huge, grassy and dotted with big trees that have lost their leaves. There's a tennis court and baseball diamonds, and even a pool that's closed for the winter, but they head directly to the playground tucked into the corner. Hazel is too young to do much other than toddle around and have Henry hold her up to the monkey bars so she can feel like she's doing something, but Sebastian is big enough to run amok, to shout for them to watch him every five seconds as he climbs, balances, and slides.

Alice wishes she were as proud of anything as Sebastian is of his ability to let gravity pull him down a smooth piece of plastic.

After an hour or so, though, Alice wishes he were a little less enthusiastic. "Nice one, buddy!" she calls for the fifty millionth time. Turns out there's a reason adults like to stay inside in the winter; her hands are freezing inside her gloves, her butt is numb, and her ears may have fallen off. Hazel has crashed out and is napping in her stroller under twelve thousand blankets and her parents seem to have nodded off on the bench next to her, but Sebastian is still fired up. Alice has pushed him on the swings until her arms almost fell off, and then spotted him as he climbed some very tall, very slippery things, her heart in her mouth the whole time. Now he's going down the slide over and over, which is nice because Alice doesn't have to do as much, but if she doesn't stand there and compliment him each time, he gets adorably mad about it, and she's still trying to earn her Auntie Points.

So there she stands, doling out compliments and letting Isabella and Henry get some much needed rest. Being a parent seems hard. Alice is glad that at the end of the day, she'll go home to her quiet apartment and do only what she personally wants to do, not responsible for any living thing except herself and that succulent she keeps almost killing.

Although of course, when she's home alone, there will be nothing to distract her from the unread texts from Marie that are piling up, the six missed calls from Babs and two from Aunt Sheila. When she's fully immersed in the kids, the hot, anxious feeling in her stomach that urges her to respond to them is less noticeable, but whenever she takes her focus off Sebastian, it overwhelms her and makes her feel nauseous. They don't deserve to be ghosted, not any of them, but Alice can't respond. What would she say? She's pretty sure texting, *Sorry, I lied to you, and it turns out I'm very much into your unfortunately disabled daughter, not your son, and your daughter hates me now! Happy New Year!* wouldn't go over great. Ghosting seems to be the kindest thing she can do, but that logic doesn't have any impact on the constant guilty twisting in her gut.

Deciding to refocus on Sebastian to drag her thoughts out of the Altman house, Alice puts on her fake-excited voice. "You going up again?"

"Yeah!" Sebastian cries. "Watch me!"

"I'm watching," she says, like she has the last trillion times. "I'm watching!"

But right then, a blur of white and green bounds into her peripheral vision, and Alice barely has time to register it as a dog before it's jumping up on her, muddy paws landing with a thud on the top of her chest.

She doesn't need the tongue deep inside her ear canal to know it's Frank. She'd recognize that enormous, perfect, pointy face anywhere, those long legs, that skinny body high above the ground like a graceless giraffe. He's wearing a green vest she hasn't seen before, and he's ecstatic.

"Hi, Frankie! Hi, buddy!"

Frank is wiggling all over her, trying to lick her entire face and hug her entire body. His tail is going like a propeller, hitting the side of the slide with a dull thunk on every rotation.

Sebastian starts wailing, and Alice isn't sure if it's because Frank is so big or because she's stopped watching his impressive slide performance.

"Oh, buddy," she says, Frank's tongue on her eyeballs keeping her from looking over at Sebastian. "It's okay." She has to close her mouth for a second, lest she and Frank accidentally French kiss. "This is—oof, down, boy, get off, that's a good boy—this is Frank the dog."

Sebastian, safe on the top of the slide, looks at Frank, considering, his little lip still trembling.

"You're okay, Sebby," Isabella says from behind Alice, clearly woken up by all of the commotion. "He can't get to you all the way up there."

Frank has all four feet on the ground now, wriggling around in joy, and Alice scratches his face with one hand and his butt with the other. She's missed him so much. Missed his bony ass and his dopey smile, the warmth of him tucked up next to her on the couch, his hugs and easy affection.

No one else—not even Sebastian and Hazel—gets as excited to see her as Frank does. It's not that she hadn't known she missed him, but seeing him again makes her realize just how much, what a big role he played in her life for those beautiful few weeks when she was around him so often.

"Hi, sweet boy," she whispers to him. "Hi, my love."

"Frank! Come!"

Oh shit.

Right.

Where there's Frank, there's going to be . . .

"Frank! Come! Come he— Oh."

Van is striding toward them, a leash in her hand, her face sliding from frustrated to shocked as she sees who exactly is holding on to her dog's collar.

"Alice."

Alice swallows, her throat suddenly rough and scratchy like she's on day five of a nasty cold. Van is so fucking beautiful. She's bundled up, like they all are, hair wet and cheeks pink, and she looks so damned good that Alice's body feels like it's suddenly vibrating.

Alice wants to kiss her. She wants to duck behind the slide and pretend she's not here. She wants to sink into Van's arms and be held for the next seven to ten business days. She wants to apologize. She wants to throw up.

"Hey, Van," Isabella says, way too loudly, from behind Alice. "Wow, long time no see! I forgot you live right around here." She's overly cheery, and also walking over to the slide and plucking Sebastian off the top of it and into her arms. "Sebastian, do you remember Van?"

"No," he says, still sniffling, mostly preoccupied with making sure his little legs aren't anywhere near Frank's mouth. Alice wants to tell him that the worst thing Frank would do to his legs is lick them until they were gummed up and sticky, but she can't quite find a single word right now, so she doesn't.

"That's okay," Van says, resolutely looking at the kid and not at Alice. "We only met one time. You showed me your trucks."

Sebastian blinks at her. "I have lots of trucks."

"You sure do," Isabella says, hauling him away. "Let's tell Daddy about them."

And then it's Alice and Van, standing alone together in the middle of an empty playground. It's not actively raining at the moment, but the air is so wet it sort of doesn't matter if it's drizzling or not. Alice's face is damp and she hasn't even started crying yet. She has the absurd thought that it's probably great weather for Henry's mushrooms.

"Hi," she finally manages to say. "Uh, how's . . ." She trails off, not sure what she wants to ask. *How are you?* Stupid question. *How have you been since I obliquely agreed to have your brother's baby and broke your heart?* Yeah, no.

"Fine," Van says, which is simultaneously vague, unhelpful, and probably untrue. "Nolan's remembering more. He's gotten another year or two back."

"Great," Alice lies faintly. Nolan's memories are like a doomsday clock, counting down the seconds until her lie is laid bare. Until Van hates her even more than she does now.

Van clears her throat. "Sorry about Frank."

"Oh no," Alice says, petting his head again. "Always happy to see Frank."

"No," Van says, something strangled in her tone now. "I mean . . ." She gestures to her chest, and it takes Alice quite a long time to drag her eyes away from Van's body, but when she finally does and looks down at her own chest, it looks like she was mauled by a mud monster.

"Oh boy," Alice says, and out of the corner of her eye she sees Van's mouth twitch.

"Sorry," Van says again, but Alice shakes her head.

"It's only dirt; it'll come out," she says. "Besides . . ." She scratches behind Frank's ears, knowing this is maybe the last time. The silky feeling of his big, floppy ears trailing through her fingers makes a sob catch in her throat. She doesn't want to think about a life that he's not in, about going through every fucking day and night without him. About never getting to hold his big, dumb face in her hands, rub his soft coat, get slapped by his happy tail and licked by his enormous tongue ever again. "I missed him."

It's quiet for a moment, so Alice can hear Sebastian say to Isabella, "But I wanna slide again!" and Isabella's very unsubtle shushing.

"Looks like he missed you too," Van says, but she's still not meeting Alice's gaze.

Van has bags under her eyes, and she's opening and closing

her hands like they're bothering her. She hasn't been sleeping well.

Standing here, talking to Alice—maybe it's hurting Van just as much as it's hurting Alice. And Alice can't do that to her. Not anymore. She lets go of Frank, and he prances over to Van, who clips the leash onto his collar without a word. She finally looks up at Alice, and she opens her mouth like she's going to say something, but then she closes it again.

She turns, and something in Alice's chest is screaming and crying and shouting for her to move, to throw herself at Van, to beg for mercy and forgiveness and for that blinky thingy from *Men in Black* to erase the last month of their lives and start over. Maybe Babs has a working model in her costume closet they could use? Two queers meeting in a park because of a dog—what a cute rom-com that would be! If only that could be their story, instead of this fucking mess Alice made.

"I'm sorry," Alice chokes out. Van is already a few steps away, but she pauses and then, very slowly, turns back.

"For what?" She sounds hoarse, and Alice wonders if she's as close to crying as Alice is.

Alice almost shrugs, almost smiles. "For everything," she says, quiet as the rain starts to fall in earnest again. It's not the apology Van deserves, not even close, but it's honest and Van clearly wants to go, and Alice can give her that. Alice will let her go.

Van nods. Not like she forgives Alice, but like she heard her. Like she accepts that Alice apologized, not like she accepts her apology.

Van doesn't say anything else as she turns and walks across the muddy grass. Frank is the only one who looks back, his eyes a little sad, his tongue lolling out of his mouth.

TWENTY-ONE

A week later, on Thursday morning, Alice dresses more carefully than usual for work. All of her clothes are relatively crappy; almost all bought from Goodwill, and her size has fluctuated over the years, so everything is either a little too loose or too tight. Well, mostly too tight. She's happiest in her oversize black turtleneck sweater and thick leggings, but she can't exactly wear that to work. Her coworker Delilah is one of those people who goes vintage shopping not because she has to but because she thinks it's fun, and Alice is pretty sure she ends up paying more for her "great finds" than she would if she went to Target, but it means she always looks trendy and put together.

Tonight Alice is going to happy hour with Delilah and her friends, who Alice assumes are all equally as fashionable and pretty as Delilah, and Alice knows she won't be able to measure up. She knows it, but she stares into her closet with dismay anyway, wishing that somehow everything inside would have gotten a fairy godmother makeover while she slept.

"Knew I should have been nicer to that mouse family last year," she mutters as she pushes aside lumpy sweater after frumpy shirt. Maybe if she hadn't put out traps, and instead had coaxed the family out and taught them how to sew, she wouldn't be in this predicament right now. Well, hindsight is twenty-twenty.

She eventually settles on a black button-down shirt, black dress pants, and her least appalling shoes. Maybe she can pretend she's edgy. She puts on some eyeliner—three times because she messes it up twice—and makes sure to pack her deodorant in her purse because a long bus commute has never made anyone smell their best.

She wishes she weren't so nervous. It's just happy hour, drinks with people who, worst case, she'll never see again. Delilah has personally experienced Alice being a hot mess, and she invited her out anyway. Alice knows she's an uncool, dowdy disaster, so there's nothing they could think about her that she doesn't already think about herself. Alice has nine regular hours to go before one becomes happy, but her heart is racing anyway, her palms sweaty. Damn, she hasn't left the apartment yet but she already needs another hit of that deodorant.

Trying to make friends shouldn't be this scary—but Alice hasn't tried to make friends in . . . ever? No, that's not true. She's tried to make friends a lot, but it hasn't quite worked. When she was a kid she had Bella, and then after Bella moved away when they were eleven, Alice's dad was already getting worse and worse. Alice was never willing to have anyone over to her house for a playdate or sleepover, not wanting them to see the oxygen tanks or hear his wet, rattling coughs in the night. He didn't have the energy to drive her around much, so she wasn't on any teams, and she never had the money to hang out at the mall or go to the movies like other kids did.

By high school she was lumped in with the burnouts, the kids who had already fried their brains on drugs, who didn't give a shit, and she didn't fit in with them at all. She gave a shit! She gave so many shits, in fact, but it wasn't like she had a quiet, stable place to do her homework, or like the biggest stress in her life was her chem final. She was busy after school, working to supplement their paltry disability payments, taking her dad to medical appointments—guiding him on and off the bus, sometimes skipping school to make it to appointments with specialists—and by the end he was in and out of the hospital so much that sometimes she didn't bother to go to school at all. She didn't get great grades and she wasn't in any clubs, so she found herself alone at lunch and after school, isolated in her small apartment with her dad who, despite all of her best efforts, kept getting sicker and sicker.

Some weeks, the only people she spoke to were her customers at work, her dad, his doctors, and Lupe.

And then she graduated, and a few months later, he died.

She should have tried to make friends after that. After she cleared out their small two-bedroom apartment and moved into her cramped studio on Division, she had so much time on her hands—no more Dad meant no more caretaking, no more waking up five times a night to check on him, which meant no more midday exhaustion naps. She should have spent her twenties partying, meeting people, having a delayed adolescence, doing all the irresponsible shit she didn't get to do in high school.

But instead she grieved. For him, for herself, for her mom. For her life. She spent her twenties grinding, feeling the weight of the world on her shoulders. All she did was work, put her head down and try not to think about anything but making rent, paying down her dad's medical bills, surviving.

She dated, sometimes, but it never went anywhere. A couple guys from work over the years, a girl in her building for a while, some meaningless hookups from apps that she'd hoped would take the edge off her loneliness, but never really did.

She's never done happy hour with a group of friends. Never sat around and ordered a pitcher without being on a mediocre date with some forgettable person and their equally forgettable friends. Alice isn't trying to date any of Delilah's friends, she's not looking for a hookup; she literally just wants a friend.

It shouldn't be a big deal—Delilah certainly didn't mean it to be anything but nice and low-key—but Alice is on the verge of hyperventilating for her entire bus ride to work.

After their shift is over, Alice follows Delilah for a couple of blocks like a pathetic little duckling. They step inside a dark bar, and Delilah leads Alice to a table filled with some of the trendiest people Alice has seen in real life. They're all tall and thin and interesting-looking, although one has a truly horrible mustache and Alice wonders if anyone has ever told them it makes them look like a real creep. They all seem kind of queer in the way so many Gen Z people do, the way that's maybe just fashion Alice doesn't understand but maybe is also a much more highly evolved sense of self and gender than she's used to.

She likes them.

They don't pressure her to talk much; not as if she isn't there, but more like she's not any different from them. Instead, they fold her into their conversation like she's always been there, and even though she can't follow some of it, it's thrilling.

It's like how Babs and Aunt Sheila and Marie brought her into their lives, but without all the lying and comatose people and sexy, confusing butches.

"So, Alice," one of them says, a gender-ambiguous person with a mullet whose name is some nature word Alice was told and then immediately forgot. Maybe Raisin? That can't be right—who would be named Raisin?—but it's Portland, so. It could be Raisin. "You're the one who saved that guy, right? Delilah told us about it."

Alice nods, taking a sip of her beer to hide her face. She ordered a PBR because it's cheap and some of the others ordered them too. It's more like a beer-flavored LaCroix than a beer, but hey. If it means she fits in and can still pay her rent, all the better.

"And isn't he, like, your boyfriend or something?"

Fucking Raisin. Alice was enjoying not lying for one stupid minute—was that too much to ask?

"Well, not exactly," Alice says, slipping back into her mental gymnastics with a silent groan. She feels like a forty-year-old woman trying to put on her teenage leotard again, suiting up for a competition she's long since gotten too old for. "And not . . . it's over now."

"Oh shit," Raisin says. "I'm sorry."

"That sucks," the person next to Raisin says, who Alice is pretty sure is named Juniper. Or Maple? There are so many nice kinds of trees to name Portland children after! Alice isn't immune; she doesn't want kids anymore, but when she was younger she'd always wanted to name a kid Cedar.

Alice hums, and then realizes she's kind of sounding like a closed-off bitch right now, and she's trying to make a good impression, damn it. "He has amnesia," she volunteers, and the table goes silent for a second.

"What?" That's the third friend, Jessica, which feels like the weird name after Raisin and Maple.

"Amnesia?" Raisin says, their eyebrows so high it's like they've melded with the mullet. "For real?"

"Yup," Alice says, taking another sip of her watery beer. "Lost five years of his life, although it's started slowly creeping back. He had no idea who I was." That's technically true; she's careful to make that second sentence a separate one rather than a dependent clause.

The beauty of omission.

"You were pretty tight with his family, right?" Delilah says, her big eyes warm and sympathetic. "They came by the office."

"Yeah. They're . . . they're great. Definitely the hardest part of the breakup."

Delilah gives her a bit of a considering look, then seems like she's steeling herself before she says, "His sister stopped by a lot."

Alice blinks at her. The words are casual, but Delilah's tone is making Alice nervous. She nods slowly, and Delilah keeps going.

"She's hot."

Alice almost spits out her beer. Instead she chokes it down, and creepy mustache dude slaps her on the back, trying to keep her alive.

"Um," Alice wheezes. "Sorry, you surprised—" She finally swallows and takes in a few big breaths. "Yeah," she says, able to be honest now. Hopefully none of them know Van—she knows queer communities can be small, but these people can't be over twenty-five and Alice is going to hope that the Gen Z/Millennial social divide is working in her favor right now. "She's very hot."

"Did, um . . ." Delilah scrunches up a napkin in her hands

and then looks sideways over at Alice. "Did anything happen? Between you and her?"

Alice looks around the table. Raisin, Maple, and Jessica are looking at her, eyes blown wide open, and mustache dude is muttering *Oh shit,* and fuck it but Delilah asked.

"It . . . did," she says, and she's pretty sure everyone at the table screams.

Alice drops her face into her hands, but Delilah and Raisin are quickly reaching out, pulling her arms down.

"Spill," Raisin says, surprisingly invested for someone who has never met Van, Nolan, or even Alice before an hour ago.

Alice shrugs, like the memory of it isn't setting her guts on fire. "We kissed," she says.

"And?" Maple asks, breathless.

"Look at her," Raisin says, grinning. "It was clearly life changing."

"It . . ." Alice lets out a breath, and then she tells the truth. "It was."

Jessica, Maple, and mustache dude scream again, and Delilah has her hands cupped over her mouth, either in excitement or horror.

"So what happened?"

Alice shrugs again. "I was supposed to be with her brother," she says, trying to keep it simple. "And I couldn't . . . I don't know." She twists her lips, trying to smile instead of cry. "I lost them both."

"River!" Raisin yells, and Alice wonders if that's a code word for something until the server comes hurrying over, and Alice realizes her name must be River. "We need heartbreak shots! Immediately!"

River brings over a tray of shot glasses filled with what

Alice is sure is an incredibly cheap whiskey. Delilah distributes them, and Raisin says, "To gay awakenings!"

"Wait," Alice says, and everyone pauses, their shot glasses held up to their lips but not tilted back yet. "I mean, sure, gay awakenings are great, but this wasn't one. I've been bi forever."

Raisin blinks at her, setting their shot down on the table. "Wait, for real?"

Alice nods slowly. Aren't the kids all supposed to be somewhat gay these days? Why is this weird?

"Okay," Raisin says slowly. "No offense, but if you're a, like, relatively young, absolutely chaotic bisexual, why are you dressed like a middle-aged suburban housewife going back to work after catching her husband sleeping with the nanny?"

Jessica and mustache dude both do spit takes. Maple hits Raisin on the arm, and Delilah hisses, "Oh my god, you did not just say that!" but Alice laughs. They're not wrong.

"Poor?" she offers, still laughing, and Raisin picks their shot glass back up.

"Okay," Raisin says. "First, we get you drunk enough to forget about this hot-sister situation, and then next week I'm taking you shopping." They gesture at Alice, and Alice should be offended by how cheerfully critical this brand-new person is, but she's not. "I think you're probably hot under there, so poor or not, I can fix this."

Three hours and one long bus ride later, Alice is still smiling. She did it. She made a friend. A very weird, aggressive friend whose name she honestly doesn't know, but, whatever. She has Delilah, and the-person-who-is-possibly-named-Raisin, and Isabella and Henry and the kids and the mushrooms, so even without Marie and Babs and Van, she's going to be okay. Maybe.

TWENTY-TWO

Almost a week later, on a frigid Wednesday, Alice puts herself to bed at the ripe hour of seven. The high from happy hour had buoyed Alice for a few days, but today sucked. There's no other way for Alice to describe it. The streets had been slick and icy this morning, and Alice fell on her ass, hard, on her way to the bus stop. Then the bus was late and impossibly slow, so when she got to work at seven-twenty instead of seven A.M., her butt still smarting painfully, she wasn't really in the mood to get reamed out by the ubiquitous Mr. Brown. But of course, that didn't matter, and she had to stand there, shivering, her pants still wet from the ice, while he yelled at her for a good five minutes.

Babs called and Marie texted again, which made her feel so guilty and anxious that she cried in the bathroom for six of her ten allotted minutes of break. She forgot her lunch at home and it was too icy to walk down to the coffee shop, so she just starved and tried not to think about bao and mint tea and stolen kisses, and then her bus home slid down a hill and Alice found herself honestly saying the rosary while the lady behind her screamed and the person across the aisle threw up all over himself.

And of course she fell again, twice, on her walk back to her apartment, and the chicken breast she'd splurged on last time she went grocery shopping had gone bad even though it was supposed to be fine until tomorrow. It was the kind of night where she wanted to give up, to order a pizza and climb into bed with her laptop and fuzzy socks and watch *Parks and Rec* again from the beginning until she fell asleep to the soothing sounds of Leslie Knope, but she couldn't. She couldn't ask some poor kid working for a pizza place to risk their life to drive food to her, not now that it was dark—god, it gets dark so fucking early in the winter—so she found a depressing old can of chicken soup to heat up. Too messy to eat in bed, somehow both flavorless and too salty, and *Parks and Rec* is behind a new paywall, and her fuzzy socks are in the laundry.

So now Alice is in bed at seven, sans pizza or socks or Leslie Knope, and she's doing what she's not supposed to.

She's put on her Altman Christmas pajamas and is scrolling through Marie's social media. She knows she has absolutely no right to be doing this with all of Marie's unanswered texts piling up, but hey. What's a little self-inflicted torture when you're already feeling like complete and utter shit?

She misses Marie with a deep throbbing ache, and it only gets worse with each picture and video she sees. Alice isn't sure when the semester starts down in Corvallis, but Marie's still posting a lot of the family. A picture of her and Frank makes Alice's heart seize up, and she lets out a wet laugh that's almost a sob at the video of Marie trying to teach Aunt Sheila some choreography. There's a time lapse of them making a pie, and when Alice catches sight of someone wearing the pink "I Like Big Buns" apron, the tears start rolling down her face.

Great. Crying over a novelty apron. This isn't a new low or anything.

Videos of Marie with Nolan hurt in a different way, and then there's a whole series of Marie with other kids her age, probably her high school friends. They're singing and dancing and joking around, and Alice watches them over and over and lets herself be miserable.

Alice has always thought of herself as a good person beset by bad circumstances. She would have been a good student if she hadn't been so busy taking care of her dad. She would donate to charity if she had enough money, she'd return a wallet if she found one on the bus. She would be a generous partner if she met the right someone. But this whole thing with Nolan and Van—lying to the family, but especially lying to Nolan about himself—it's making her wonder if she's actually a bad person, a person who, at her core, is terribly selfish. A person her parents would be ashamed of.

She tried to steal a man's life, to take his mom and aunt and little sister for her own. She fell for his other sister and kissed her before curling up under his Snuggie. She took advantage of the family's care and hospitality, ate their food and wore their pajamas and soaked up their affection, gave nothing back but lies, and for what? A couple hugs and some Christmas cookies? A hot boyfriend and the love of a parent?

And that's not even the worst of it. Alice might excel at evading the truth with the Altmans, but even she can't lie to herself. The pure and unvarnished truth—no omissions, no technicalities, just blinding honesty—is that Alice ruined everything she could have had with Van. Not out of some misplaced sense of nobility, the self-sacrifice of saying, *I can't get between you and your mother.* No. It was pure selfishness. Alice's desire to protect herself, and only herself, rearing up and smashing all the other options to dust.

And yes, maybe Babs would have freaked out about Alice flitting from her son to her daughter. Maybe they'd have needed to spend time with Marie separately while things with Babs were bad—and that would be horrible.

But Babs and Nolan aren't the reason Alice is alone and miserable in her cold, Knope-less studio tonight. What it comes down to is that if she weren't such an ableist asshole that she refuses to watch Van wither away and die, then she could be tucked up in bed next to her right now, warming her freezing toes on Van's shins, scrolling through Marie's social media together, a strong arm under her head, her chest pressed against Van's.

Alice misses all of them horribly, but she can't think about them—Van, Babs, Nolan, Aunt Sheila—without hating herself. Without being disgusted by what a terrible person she is. But with Marie, it's different. She can miss Marie without feeling like a manipulative asshole, because whether she was with Nolan or Van, or neither, she loved Marie like a little sister. The cookies, the costume closet, laughing at Aunt Sheila together . . . it's exactly what Alice would have wanted from a sister if she'd ever had one. Marie was never filling in for anyone, not standing in for Alice's dead parents or absent aunt or missing cousin or comatose fake-boyfriend. She was the only little sister Alice has ever had, and Alice misses her so fucking badly.

She wants a future where she can drive down to Corvallis to see Marie in some weird experimental play. She wants to help her move out of her dorm and into an apartment with her friends over the summer. She wants to text her memes, to hear about Marie's crushes and classes and roommate drama. She wants to be the cool big sister who buys her hair dye or takes her to pierce her eyebrow or get her first tattoo even though Babs will flip.

But Alice can't have any of that. She can't be Marie's big sister anymore, and she lets herself cry about it.

By ten, Alice is all cried out. She doesn't feel lighter, though. She feels heavy, like she's a soggy piece of bread. She should get out of bed, brush her teeth, turn off the lights. She should put down her phone.

But she doesn't.

And then, while she's robotically refreshing Marie's page, a new post appears.

And, fuck.

She should have stopped. She should have gone to sleep. She should have blocked Marie. She should never have come to this page, to have tortured herself like this, because she's pretty sure there would never have been a good time to see this post, but right now is definitely not it. Not after a terrible day, after hours of misery and hating herself. Now isn't the time to process this, but it's too late.

She's already seen it.

It's a video of Van working with Nolan, helping him use those enormous stretchy bands to improve his balance. "My sister is the best physical therapist in Portland," Marie's voice says over the footage, the captions big and bold across the bottom. "She's opening her own practice and she needs an office manager. Link to the job posting in the comments. You could not possibly have a better boss! Click it!!!"

Alice almost throws up her tasteless, salty soup.

It's not like Alice thought she could still have the job, not after everything. Not after Christmas Eve, not after Van couldn't even look at her at the park. She hadn't thought about the job much, that loss minuscule compared to the rest. But . . . shit.

She still wants it. She still wants Van, still wants out of her boring job, to get away from Nolan and all of the finance bros and lawyers who don't think she exists. She doesn't want to spend every day staring at the spot on the floor where all this started, where Nolan's legs gave out and his head hit the black marble floor with a sickening thud.

She still wants the life she almost had, the life that was never actually a possibility. A life where she goes to work at Van's practice, where she's busy and helpful and happy, and then goes home to Van, who is strong and healthy and okay, and they have mind-blowing sex before getting the best sleep of their lives, on repeat, ad infinitum.

That was never real, but the job was. The job was real, and it was Alice's, and now it's gone. It's not the worst thing she's seen tonight, not the worst thing that's happened today, but it's the last straw. She wants the job less than she wants Van, but she's still not sure she'll ever fully get over it.

She throws her phone across the bed, and sobs into her pillow until she falls asleep a long, long time later.

TWENTY-THREE

It's been three weeks since Christmas and four days since Alice's no good, very bad day, and she's alone in Isabella's house. It was too expensive to fly four people to Texas over Christmas, so Isabella's family is making the trek out to see the grandparents this week instead. Alice wonders why her aunt and uncle didn't simply come to Portland themselves—two adults flying would be both cheaper and easier than flying with a preschooler and a toddler—but, whatever. Since when has Alice agreed with any decision her aunt has made in the past twenty or so years?

Isabella had asked Alice if she would be willing to house-sit for them. She'd claimed that Henry was always anxious about leaving their house empty for more than a night or two. Alice was pretty sure it was simply kindness—would Alice like to stay in a big house with an actual TV and full-sized kitchen instead of her cramped, loud, probably moldy apartment?

Yes, in fact, Alice would.

Or, well, she'd thought she would. But now that she's here, it's painfully quiet. Alice hadn't realized how much the sounds of her neighbors keep her company. How the loud Russian soap operas in 301 drown out the silence of her own life, how the baby crying in 203 reminds her of how happy she is to not have her own children. It never feels like she's entirely alone in her apartment, because she never is. There's always someone pulling up to buy weed from the dealer in 302, someone moving in or out, the endless parade of one-night stands from the girls who live in 304.

Up here in North Portland, on this quiet street of large, single-family homes, Alice can't hide from her loneliness. She has so many rooms she can be alone in. A kitchen to cook in by herself, a dining room to silently eat in like a sad widow in Victorian England, a living room for solitary sitting, a den for solo TV watching. Even a finished basement, in case she wants to watch sports alone in a man cave or build something truly enormous out of Legos. Then upstairs, she can be alone in the bed that Isabella and Henry share because they're fucking married and pledged to never be alone again, or in Sebastian's or Hazel's room, where they're only one loud wail away from having company at any time of day or night.

Alice feels like the walls are closing in around her. She texts with Delilah a little on Saturday, setting up a time to go shopping with her and Raisin in a couple weeks, but Delilah stops responding after a while and Alice isn't desperate enough to endure the shame of double texting. Isabella's busy with her parents—who Alice is quite sure she'll never forgive for abandoning her and her dad—so Alice is well and truly alone. On Sunday afternoon, Alice briefly considers chopping off her own finger to have a reason to scream, to fill the house with noise and the bustle of paramedics. But an ambulance ride would literally bankrupt her, so she decides to put on her coat and boots and go for a walk instead.

She doesn't want to go back to the same park in case Van is there again, so she heads for a different one that her phone tells her is about half an hour's walk away, which seems far enough to make her feel accomplished, while close enough that she probably won't die of frostbite.

It's cold outside, windy and bracing, but she ducks her head down into her collar, one of Henry's beanies on her head and Isabella's warmest gloves on her hands. The beanie says ASK ME ABOUT SHROOMS! on it, so she's wearing it inside out. She does not, in fact, want to be asked about mushrooms of the magical or culinary variety. She's sure she wouldn't be able to do Henry proud.

It's a straight shot down Isabella's street to the park and the neighborhood is so cute that she almost hates it. It's nothing like where she lives, no businesses or dumpsters or billboards or trash. It's just cute house after cute house, big wet lawns and bare trees. There's a Prius or Subaru in every driveway, and she can hear kids playing in several of the backyards. Some have smoke curling out of their chimneys, which makes Alice want to have a childhood-style panic attack but she knows is probably nice for people without fire-related trauma.

She finally makes it to the park and begins to walk across it, grimacing in the sharp cold. The park isn't too big, only a couple square blocks, and something about the misery is kind of working for her. It's nice to feel like shit for a good reason—she's exhausted, her toes have turned to ice in her cheap boots, the skin of her cheeks feels like it's filleting off her face in the wind—instead of because she has irrevocably fucked up her life. It's a good change of pace.

There's only one other couple braving the windchill halfway across the park, and their presence makes her feel less alone than she has in Isabella's house—until she sees that they're holding hands, and her heart clenches.

What would that be like, to have someone next to you, their hand outstretched to you? Someone you want to touch so badly that you'd reach for them even if it meant leaving your hand exposed to the brutal wind, only a thin glove protecting it from the elements? Alice knows painfully well what it's like to want that with someone; she just doesn't know what it's like to have it.

Maybe it's because she's thinking about Van, wishing she could let herself want and be wanted in that overwhelming, simple, entwined-fingers kind of way, that she can almost see Van's broad shoulders in the taller person's frame, in the way they're bowing their head to escape the wind. But a moment later, the couple comes into focus, and her heart stops. It *is* Van. And she's with Sarah.

Sarah, the ex who wouldn't let Van dress up as Ariel the mermaid for Halloween, the ex who made Marie say *ugh* and made Van feel like she had to only ever be one thing. Sarah, who is prettier than Alice, who dogsits Frank and has a whole house in a cute, well-off neighborhood.

Sarah, who was Van's ex two weeks ago, but is now holding on to one of Van's hands. Those hands are sensitive, tender, the first parts of Van's body to show her MS symptoms, and one of them is hanging out in the freezing cold air of the park, unprotected by her pocket, just to touch fucking *Sarah*. *Ugh* is right.

Alice wonders if she's going to throw up, if it's cold enough for her vomit to freeze solid before it hits the ground. She wonders if Van will say anything, or if the love of her life will walk right by her with a blank face, like she's a stranger.

They finally pass each other, and Van pointedly looks down at the path, like maybe it's icy (it's not) and she has to carefully navigate it (she doesn't). Sarah nods at Alice without recognition, and Alice nods back like it isn't killing her.

Sarah isn't the reason Alice isn't with Van—Alice is the reason. Alice and her fucking lie and the fucking MS, or rather, her reaction to the fucking MS. She doesn't deserve Van. She rejected Van. She can't be with Van. None of that has changed.

Alice is just as single as she was yesterday, Van is just as much not her girlfriend as she was this morning, but still. Alice takes the long way back to Isabella's, vowing to never set foot in a park in this cursed neighborhood again.

When she gets back to the house, she strips off her layers and finds the liquor cabinet. She descends down into the man cave, covers herself with a pile of blankets to hide from the judgmental Lego men hard at work on their forklifts, and drinks herself into a stupor.

"Rue!"

Alice stops talking midsentence, her head snapping over to where Mr. Brown is stalking across the lobby. She isn't doing anything wrong—she and Delilah are quietly chatting, and there's no one in the lobby who needs anything. It's getting close to the end of her shift, and most of the people who bothered to come into work on such an icy mid-January day are streaming out without a backward glance before the sun goes down and all the streets turn fully into a slip-and-slide of doom.

"Yes, sir?"

Mr. Brown rucks up his truly hideous gray corduroys and says without preamble, "You're back on the night shift."

It feels like Alice's body splits fully in two, like she can hear the wet splat of her intestines hitting the floor. She's cold all over, and her voice doesn't work until her third attempt. "I . . . what? No! Why?"

He gives her a look like she's stupid, and she suddenly understands. She *is* stupid. He put her on the day shift while Nolan was in the news, while he thought a heroic receptionist would benefit his building, bring him heaps of new, shiny lease applications. But it's been six weeks. The news moved on, the new tenants have either dried up or never arrived, and apparently her being on the day shift has done nothing but keep a prettier receptionist stuck, invisible, on the overnight shift.

"Chloe's starting back," he says. "She'll be on days with Delilah."

Of course. Of course it's Chloe. She used to be on days back when Alice first started, and she left to be a full-time yoga teacher or essential oil saleslady or whatever it is hot twenty-four-year-old white girls with a safety net do in Portland. She'll look much better sitting behind this desk than Alice does. She has cute clothes to go with her pretty face, and when men say condescending shit to her, she smiles and laughs like she doesn't want to murder them—a skill Alice never cared to master.

If someone had asked Alice ten minutes ago if her life was going in a good direction, she'd have laughed in their face. The gaping losses of the Altmans as her family and Van as her love have sent her into what she would have thought were the darkest depths of despair. But as she thinks about going back to the night shift, she realizes that she was wrong. She has things in her life. Good things. Things she wants. Things that, even without the Altmans and Van, could make her happy.

Seeing the sunshine and sleeping at night, like everyone

else. Becoming real friends with Delilah and Raisin and the others. Raisin hasn't transformed her from a fugly straight-passing caterpillar to a (still sort of) young, perceptibly bisexual butterfly yet—lord knows that's something worth looking forward to.

And what about Isabella and the kids? If she's back on nights, she'll never be able to see them. She'll go back to how she was before, so alone that it hurts, but this will be worse because she'll know what she's missing. She'll know that her cousin slash best friend is right there, only a few miles away, wishing Alice could come over. Her little niece and nephew will learn how to use the magnetic tiles and forage mushrooms and traverse the monkey bars without her, will get bigger and say more words and be adorable away from her.

It'll be torture.

Alice straightens her spine. She's not going to simply roll over and take this. She has things to fight for—a life—and she'll be damned if Mr. Fucking Brown, with his nasty clothes and preferential treatment of hot girls, is going to take them away from her.

"Please," she says quickly. "Please, let me stay on days. Please."

He shakes his head, and Delilah grabs Alice's hand under the desk. "Sorry," Mr. Brown says, and he does sound a little contrite somewhere underneath his usual gruff tone, and Alice is horrified to realize it's probably because she's crying. There are actual tears coming down her cheeks, and she drops Delilah's hand to wipe her face.

She's never been much of a fighter, she guesses. Makes sense that her first time standing up for herself is a brutal failure. "Starting when?" she whispers, looking down at the awful big black desk she hates.

"Tomorrow night," he says, and Alice had thought things couldn't get worse, but she was wrong. That's so soon. She won't even have time to mourn.

He turns and walks away, and Alice can't breathe. Everything she almost had—daylight, a family, friends, the Altmans, Van—it's all gone.

Well. She'll be damned.

After a week of night shifts, Alice knows she needs a different job. She knows that. This isn't the only office in the entire city—someone must need a receptionist during the day. But the transition to vampirism has entirely jacked up her sleep cycle and she's so exhausted—body, mind, soul, wallet—that searching for one feels impossible.

Since the sun sets around four-thirty in the afternoon, Alice's commute home after her shift is literally the only time she sees daylight now. She's pretty sure that would be enough to throw anyone into a depression, but that's honestly the least terrible part of being back on nights. It's only been a week, but Alice misses people so desperately. Her people, yes, but also customers and the baristas at Fresh Grounds, visitors and tenants at work, her neighbors on the stairs or doing laundry, the regular commuters on the bus she exchanges friendly nods with.

Alice is alone all the time now, and the silence is almost physically painful. All her limp, exhausted brain can do is taunt her with memories of Van: the scent of her cologne, the way rain looks on her black hair, the sound of her laugh, the comfort of being tucked in the car with her, the feel of her hands sliding under Alice's sweater. There's nothing to distract Alice from her agonizing longing for everything she doesn't have, and the texts from Isabella with videos of the kids or pictures of the drawings they've done for her only make it worse.

Alice could survive losing Van and the Altmans because she had Isabella and the kids and daylight and the promise of a better, non-nocturnal life. And now she has nothing, and every single loss is cutting deeply enough to maim her, and there's no reprieve in sight.

Just an endless stream of nights.

TWENTY-FOUR

Alice is trying her hardest to sleep, even though it's early afternoon, but someone won't stop knocking on her front door. It's the middle of the night for her, and while she hasn't totally reacclimated to her new night-shift schedule, her body desperately wants to be turned off right now.

"I don't have weed," she yells from bed, her eye mask still firmly in place. She can't afford blackout curtains, so the eye mask is a godsend. "He's next door."

"I'm not looking for weed," says a voice that makes Alice sit straight up in bed, ripping off the eye mask. She's groggy, and the voice was coming through the door, but still. That sounded like . . .

"Alice?"

Alice skids across the studio, hardly noticing the way the floor is freezing under her bare feet. She opens the door, and her heart stops beating.

It's Van.

She's standing right there, tall and sturdy like an oak tree, a frown on her face and water dripping from her jacket.

Alice opens and closes her mouth a few times, but the words don't come. The sun is up but it's the middle of the night, and she's so lonely that she's been nauseous for the last week, and now Van is here. At her apartment. Looking serious and focused and a little disappointed.

"Can I come in?" Van finally says when it's clear Alice isn't quite capable of forming words yet.

"I—sorry, yes. Of course." Alice nods too many times, belatedly backing up and making space for Van to come in. Alice is wearing only her sleep shirt and a pair of soft shorts, no bra, and she wonders how weird it would be to go get dressed before another word is said.

Van seems to be opting for bulldozing through the awkwardness. She takes off her jacket and steps out of her boots like she's expecting to stay, and Alice blinks a few times, trying to wake herself up. She's had more than one dirty daydream that started this way, but she's pretty sure this is real life and Alice is not in fact a character in a low-budget porno who is about to pay for a pizza by dropping to her knees.

Van comes to stand in the middle of the apartment, one hand on the breakfast bar that also serves as kitchen counter and dining room table. Alice goes to the other side of it, planting herself firmly in the kitchen like eighteen inches of peeling laminate countertop will protect her from whatever is coming.

"What . . ." It comes out as a bit of a croak, so Alice clears her throat and tries again. "What are you doing here?" Van swallows heavily, and Alice realizes how that sounded. "No," Alice says as quickly as she can, reaching her hands out. "I didn't mean . . ." She takes another breath, tries to reset herself. To be slow and measured and careful, like Van always is. "It's always good to see you."

The side of Van's mouth twitches up, and Alice knows they're both thinking about the last two times they saw each other, in those two parks, when it was distinctly not good at all.

"I just mean . . . hi, I guess," Alice says, feeling like an idiot.

Van dips her head but doesn't take her eyes off Alice's face for several beats too long. "Hi."

Alice doesn't know what to say, or do with her hands. Her floor feels like an ice rink against her bare feet, and she only slept for, like, three hours. She decides to make some coffee to have a task to accomplish, something to do with her hands. She wishes her mind were racing, trying to figure out what's going on here, but it feels like every one of her thoughts keeps getting caught in a tangled cobweb of exhaustion.

"I want to apologize," Van finally says. Alice freezes, her back to Van while she measures the coffee grounds. "For how I acted at Christmas."

Well, that's not right. If anyone should be apologizing here, it's Alice. Van hasn't done anything except be perfect and irresistible and have morals. Alice is the lying asshole here. She turns to Van, a full scoop of coffee in her hand. "You have nothing to apologize for," she says as vehemently as she can muster in her exhausted state, but Van shakes her head.

"I knew the situation," Van says, and Alice sets the scoop down on the counter, sure her hand is going to start shaking and not at all in the mood to clean coffee grounds off her floor. "I knew you were with my brother, and I pushed it anyway. I shouldn't have—I shouldn't have gotten mad at you for being in the position I knew you were in."

Alice shakes her head. "I shouldn't have done that kiss with him." It's nearly a whisper, her voice almost hoarse. "I shouldn't have gotten under his blanket. It wasn't . . ." She lets out a puff of air. She's so tired and lonely and Van is right here. Standing in her kitchen/dining/living room, looking beautiful and strong and sad.

"I think the only person who wanted any of that to happen was your mom," Alice adds. "I shouldn't have done it."

Van holds Alice's gaze as she moves around the counter in the deliberate and careful way she so often does, stepping into the narrow kitchen with Alice, close enough to touch, her strong body blocking Alice in.

"I don't understand what changed," Van says. The air between them becomes thick, every breath humid inside Alice's lungs. Alice watches as Van blinks, the way her long, delicate eyelashes sweep against her cheeks. The constant want inside Alice's body starts to change from a tug she can resist into something that will sweep her off her feet and directly into Van's chest. "You—you kissed me at the hospital. Why?"

Alice isn't quite sure what to say. Her brain isn't moving quickly enough; she can't think right. "I don't know," she finally says, her eyes slipping closed. "I just . . . I couldn't not, anymore."

"You . . . couldn't not?" Van asks, and Alice opens her eyes, almost laughing at the look on Van's face. Something hopeful but confused, still torn. "I—help me out with that double negative."

"I had to," Alice whispers into the electric, crackling space between them, and she sees the way Van almost shudders. "I couldn't go another second without having kissed you."

Van is so close now. Almost looming over Alice, and Alice can smell her hair and her skin and she remembers with perfect clarity what it was like to kiss her, to press her body into Van's, to feel Van's hands slide up her back. Alice feels mesmerized, like her body and mind are out of her control, and all she can do is stare, unblinking, and move closer and closer until the space between them would have to be measured in atoms instead of inches.

"And now?" Van asks, her voice a whisper too. "What about now?"

Alice swallows. She's never wanted a person this badly in her life, never felt this desperate need for someone else's body and affection before, but there's something sticky between them. Well, several dozen sticky things. An entire syrup factory of complications and lies, but their chests are almost touching now, and all Alice can think to say is, "Aren't you with Sarah?"

Van blinks. "Not any more than you're with Nolan."

Alice huffs out a breath. It's a point well taken. Van is scarred from Alice being with Nolan, even though it wasn't ever real, and now Alice will never heal from how deeply the image of Van holding on to Sarah is gouged in her brain. Regardless of what's happening between Van and Sarah—if that was one weak moment, or if Van is seriously considering trying again with her—neither of their hands are clean here. Although Van's hands are lightly dusted and Alice's are caked with mud, so it's not the same.

It's all so entirely messed up, she knows that, but Van doesn't step back, and neither does Alice. She's fully wrapped up in the hypnotic haze of Van's presence now, what Van so clearly wants, and it looks like she may have hypnotized Van herself. It's all both of them can do to stand here in this tiny, molding kitchen, only electrons between them, and breathe the same air. Want the same thing, which they still absolutely cannot have.

"It won't change anything," Alice manages to say, because it won't. Throwing herself at Van now, sleeping together, letting Van devour her, doing everything Alice wants and more . . . it won't change a thing. Van is still sick, and Alice is still a coward, and Babs is still a homophobe, and Nolan is still awake. Nothing is different, except Alice is back on the night shift and her life is over. "It'll still be . . . this."

"And what is this?" Van asks, but she's almost smiling.

"Fucked," Alice says, and Van laughs.

"So," Van says after a beat, taking another step closer, even though Alice would have sworn there already wasn't any space left. "If we don't do this, it'll all be fucked. And if we do, also, still fucked."

Alice sucks in a deep breath, which is a huge mistake because all she smells is Van—it's like she's buried her nose in Van's neck and inhaled. Maybe it's the cologne in the air, maybe the electricity jumping between them, but it almost sounds like Van is making a good point. If her life is going to suck either way, why not give herself this?

Some part of her knows that this is incredibly shaky logic, that sleeping with the person you're desperately pining for but can't have has literally never made a situation better, but it's surprisingly easy to squash that part down underneath the weight of how badly she wants this.

"Tell me to go," Van finally says, and Alice should. The fact that Van's devastatingly sexy and smells delicious doesn't change the lie or the MS or Alice's trauma. Literally nothing is different now from when Van walked out on Christmas, except this time Van is saying, "Tell me to go and I will," and Alice can't.

She won't.

She reaches out instead, grabbing the cuff of Van's sleeve.

The part of her that knows this is a terrible idea is getting quieter and quieter under the ringing in her ears, the thundering sound of her heartbeat, the rushing whoosh of everything she wants rising up from her toes to overwhelm her. It's like Van's very presence has pressed the mute button on all of Alice's higher-level thinking—or maybe just her anxiety—and all she can do now is exist. Is do what she so desperately wants to.

"Don't go," she says, and Van steps into her.

Van doesn't kiss her like she's drowning, or like she's oxygen. She doesn't kiss her like she's dying, or like this is the last kiss before the world explodes. That's how they had kissed in the hospital bathroom, like it was their only chance, like they knew it was a moment snatched out of a different life. Fleeting, temporary, secret and furtive and desperate.

But today, in this small kitchen, Van kisses Alice like she has time. Like she has hours and years to spend exploring Alice's mouth, like this is the first of countless millions of moments they'll spend pressed together like this. She kisses Alice not like she needs her to survive but like she's going to savor her forever.

One arm wraps low around Alice's back, and the other cups her head so gently and tenderly that Alice has to bite down on Van's lip to keep from crying. Van's mouth is working smoothly against Alice's, full and warm and caring, and when she sucks on Alice's tongue, Alice feels her knees buckle. Every shuddering breath Alice takes smells like Van, tastes like her, and she doesn't realize her own hands are moving until Van's shirt is halfway unbuttoned and her fingers find the warm, impossibly smooth skin of her chest. Van gasps into Alice's mouth, and Alice immediately digs her fingers in to make Van do it again and again.

She's not sure how long they stay there, kissing and trying

to fuse together next to the coffeemaker, but eventually Van starts to take steps backward, pulling Alice along with her. They back out of the kitchen, still attached in every possible way, and then Alice takes the lead.

This is the worst idea anyone has ever had, but also already the best thing that's ever happened. She walks backward, pulling Van along with lips and grasping fingers, both of Van's hands hot and gentle on her cheeks, not stopping until the backs of her legs hit her bed, grateful for once for her tiny studio apartment, for how few steps it requires to go from the kitchen to the comforter. Alice wordlessly lays herself down, trusting Van to follow her.

She opens her eyes enough to see the look on Van's face as she plants her knees on the bed, crawling slowly up to where Alice is. It's the hottest thing Alice has ever seen, and she's reaching out to pull Van down on top of her before Van's even made it all the way.

"Please," she hears herself say, and she's not sure what she's asking for until she has it. Until Van's lips are back on hers, Van's tongue brushing against hers, Van's body coming to rest, heavy and perfect, on top of hers.

Alice feels like all of her skin is too small, too hot. She needs to get all of her clothes off, and all of Van's, but she also needs both of them to never, ever move from this perfect position, this perfect moment. She licks into Van's mouth, and Van makes a moaning sound that has Alice curling her toes and clenching her thighs.

She probably should have assumed Van would be a slow, careful, thoughtful, incredibly generous lover, but she'd been trying so hard not to think about Van in this context that every movement of Van's feels like a surprise. How long Van kisses her before sitting up enough to pull Alice's shirt off, how meticulously her hands map out Alice's chest and stomach and back before even reaching for her breasts. How deeply she kisses Alice while Alice is trying to unbutton the rest of Van's shirt, how she finally shrugs it off her shoulders like they have all the time in the world, like building Alice's pleasure one tiny movement at a time is all that matters.

Alice tries to be patient, she really does. She tries to distract herself, but every centimeter of exposed skin, every breath and blink and kiss only spirals her need up higher and higher. She scratches lightly at the red marks on Van's back where her sports bra has dug into her skin, and then Van sits up, pulling Alice to straddle her lap and kissing her for what feels like hours, wet and a little messy and so devastatingly hot that Alice thinks she might die.

Sitting topless on Van fucking Altman's lap, in nothing but her sleep shorts, Van's hands grasping at her back and hips, Van's mouth hot under hers—this is the pinnacle of Alice's short, relatively shitty life. She's never been so happy to be alive, to have a body, to be a person, than she is here, right now, holding on to Van's jaw, licking into her mouth and grinding down on her.

Although, of course, the summit keeps getting higher and higher, every second replacing the last as the best Alice has ever experienced. Because now Van's peeling off her own bra, then wrapping her arms around Alice and toppling her gently onto her back, pulling off Alice's shorts and Alice is unbuttoning Van's jeans, and then Van is lying back down on top of her, naked this time, and that's better than anything that's happened before.

Finally Van touches her, easing first her fingers and then her mouth down between Alice's legs, and Alice has clearly transcended to a higher plane of existence. She comes twice before

Van crawls back up, and a third time along with her, Alice's fingers deep inside Van and Van's lips hot against hers, her hands insistent but so, so gentle on Alice's cheeks.

Van somehow manages to pull a blanket up over them, and Alice drifts off, more than halfway on top of her, their sweaty skin sticking together, warmer and happier than she's ever been in her life.

Alice has always woken up pretty quickly. Even the few times she'd woken up in someone else's apartment, she'd always known right where she was. Probably from all of those years of waking up in a hospital room, or listening to her dad coughing and making sure he was still breathing. So tonight, she wakes up, and she knows exactly whose head is on her chest, whose arm is heavy across her stomach, whose leg is thrown over hers.

She cranes her neck to look at her clock. It's almost seven in the evening, and it's dark as sin outside. She has two hours before she has to clock in at work. She needs to shower and eat something before she heads to the bus stop.

And she has to deal with the fact that she just slept with Van.

That she just had the best sex of her life with Van, and then fell asleep with her. That she's woken up feeling better than she has in recent memory, if not ever.

She looks down at Van, at her perfect, handsome face. She looks younger in sleep, some of her worry lines eased, her lips open, each of her breaths warm and soft against the naked skin of Alice's chest. Alice feels a rush of tenderness, so strong and fierce that it brings tears to her eyes. This woman, this gorgeous, incredible, strong person, sleeping so bonelessly on top of Alice—god. Alice loves her.

Alice loves her.

But in the harsh, stark-naked reality of the evening, Alice knows her choice isn't a lifetime of this—of mind-blowing, tender, loving sex—or a lifetime of emptiness. "This" doesn't exist: a life where the lie doesn't matter, where Van isn't sick, where no one cares how Alice ended up in the family in the first place. No, the choice is a lifetime of wanting Van and watching her slip away as she gets sicker and sicker—cut off from her family because of Alice's lie—or a lifetime of not having her at all.

Alice wants to grab onto Van with both hands and keep her close forever, but she can't. That's not a real option. The only options are to lose her slowly or lose her quickly, and Alice has never found herself to be particularly brave.

She eases herself out from underneath Van. She gets dressed as quickly as she can, and she leaves her apartment two hours early. She can shower at the gym in the basement of the office building. She can buy herself something to eat from one of the fast-food places off the bus line.

She sends Van a text from the bus, something bland about being sorry for leaving, something that says absolutely nothing about how Alice feels, about what it meant to her, about how stupid and beautiful it was, and then she lets herself cry all the way across the river.

TWENTY-FIVE

It's almost dinnertime on Saturday—the only time Alice's schedule overlaps with the kids'—and the kids are in what Isabella calls their "witching hour." Hazel has already had two meltdowns and Sebastian is on the cusp of one himself, one small Lego-related indignity away from losing it completely. Henry is out of town for a conference, so Isabella is more frazzled than usual, and she and Alice haven't gotten to talk much yet.

"Isn't this so fun," Isabella says as she mops up the milk Hazel has spilled all over the table for the fourth time. "Don't you want kids so badly?"

"So badly," Alice says, matching her sarcastic tone. She absolutely doesn't want kids—she feels like she still hasn't started her own life yet and has zero desire to put herself on the back burner to wipe someone else's butt, even if they are very cute and snuggly—but she's missed these two. Being an auntie is exactly the amount of kid time she wants, thank you very much.

"So what's going on with you?" Bella asks as Hazel shoves a literal fistful of cheese into her mouth, like the icon she is. "You seem sad . . . der than usual."

Alice bites her lip. It's weird to talk about this in front of the kids, but they live here, so beggars can't be choosers, etc. "I did a very, uh, adult activity on Wednesday." She lifts her eyebrows, and Isabella makes a truly delighted sound.

"Oh *really*!" Isabella says, and Hazel uses her moment of distraction to grab way more shredded mozzarella out of the bag than Isabella would have given her. "With whom?"

Alice grimaces, bracing for the backlash she knows she well and truly deserves. "With, um . . . Van?"

"WHAT?" Isabella's squawk is so loud that Hazel starts crying and Sebastian throws his hot dog onto the floor. There's some bustling around as Bella hauls Hazel out of her high chair, plops her on Alice's lap, and rescues the hot dog, telling Sebastian she's getting him a new one from the kitchen but really just holding the old one out of sight for ten seconds and then making it magically reappear.

He enthusiastically tucks into the "new" hot dog, Hazel goes back to eating cheese by the fistful, and Alice fiercely wishes all of her problems could be solved so easily.

"With Van?" Isabella says, almost whispering now, clearly trying to overcompensate. "How? Why? When? How was it?"

"It was . . ." Alice pauses, trying not to think about it, but instead remembering it in vibrant Technicolor. The way Van's mouth felt on her, the gentle way she'd brushed Alice's hair out of her face, the tender encouragement she'd whispered into Alice's skin, how strong and sturdy she was, how gorgeous. "It was better than I could've imagined," she finally says, proud that her voice only shakes a little.

"Alice, honey . . ." Isabella pauses for a second, like she's not sure if she should say what she's thinking. Hazel swipes at her milk, and Alice catches it before it topples over.

"Say it," Alice tells the milk.

"Why aren't you with her? You clearly love her."

Alice flinches away from the word *love*, but she knows she's not fooling anyone. Even Sebastian would call bullshit on her, if he were paying attention and knew those words, and that kid is remarkably easy to fool. The new hot dog had the same number of bites missing as his old one and the dude was not at all suspicious. This is possibly a new low for Alice.

She swallows and remembers that she and Isabella have pledged to be honest with each other and love each other no matter what, so she might as well go ahead and admit that she's a terrible person. "She's sick, Bella. She has MS."

"Oh," Bella says, her face falling, and Alice feels it deep in her guts. "Shiitake."

"Yeah."

But Bella's expression turns suddenly businesslike. "This has officially become an after-bedtime conversation," she says, putting some cut-up blueberries in front of Hazel that the toddler immediately smacks across the table.

"Mo chiss!" Hazel demands, her hands balled into pudgy little fists, and Alice can't help but agree with her. She could use a lot more cheese herself.

Alice would have preferred to talk about this with the distraction of Sebastian loudly telling a story to his hot dog. That would make it seem like less of a big deal—any conversation interrupted by trips to the potty and fake curse words can't be that serious, right? Alice can't have totally fucked up her life if it's more pressing to pry cheese out of Hazel's fat, clenched fingers. But stupid Isabella is out here ruining all of Alice's plans to be avoidant. Alice considers bailing for a half second, but she came over to unload all of this on Bella, and she resigns herself to doing it on Bella's terms. She wants to talk it through like a big girl, but she can't help feeling, as Hazel wriggles off her lap and knocks the milk over again, like she's in trouble.

After an eventful playtime, bath time, and bedtime, Isabella collapses onto the living room couch with two glasses of wine. Alice is wearing one of Bella's shirts now because Sebastian splashed so much in the bath that she got soaking wet, and Hazel fell asleep on top of Alice halfway through her first book, her chubby thumb in her cute little mouth, so even this shirt has a big drool spot.

"So," Isabella says. "Van has MS."

Alice takes one of the glasses from her. "Yeah."

Isabella looks like she's trying to see through Alice, to x-ray her feelings. "I see how that could trigger some stuff for you," she says, and Alice gets the impression she's choosing her words carefully.

"That's a nice way of putting it," Alice mumbles, and Bella almost smiles.

"But are you, um . . ." Isabella bites her lip and takes a sip of her wine, and Alice's chest is so tight that she can't breathe easily. "Are you sure that's enough of a reason to not be with her?"

Alice blinks a couple times. "I—yes? I mean, I can't . . . I know it makes me the worst person in the world but I . . ." She's talking too fast. The words are flying out of her mouth and her heart is racing and her tongue feels dry. She takes a gulp of wine, which helps with literally none of those problems. "I can't watch someone else I love wither away and die, Bella. I just can't."

It's the most true thing in her life. Watching her mom die was agony, sharp and blindingly painful. And then her dad died for her entire childhood and adolescence. The most formative eleven years of her life were buried under blood oxygen levels and white blood cell counts and a deep, hacking, wet cough she still hears in her nightmares. Losing her mom over that long, terrifying month would have scarred her for the rest of her life, but the way her dad died, slowly losing piece after piece of himself until there was nothing left but a skeleton covered with ashen gray skin wearing a gruesome approximation of her dad's face—no. There's no coming back from that.

It's a miracle she survived the first time, the second. She absolutely cannot do that again.

"I don't think there's a lot of . . . withering . . . with MS," Bella says, almost like she's apologizing for having to push back against this most tender of spots. "One of Henry's uncles has it, and he's, like, mostly okay."

Alice shrugs. "For now."

"Yeah," Bella says quickly, almost like she's trying to pacify Alice. "For now. But . . . for a long time now. He's in his sixties, and he uses a cane and one of his eyes doesn't work great, but he's not . . . you know." She shrugs. "He's not dying, Rue Rue."

That should feel heartening, but Alice shakes her head, swallowing hard. "But there's no guarantee Van would be like that," she says. "Something bad could happen to her literally any day." The furtive, middle-of-the-night googling has been clear on that.

Isabella doesn't say anything right away, and Alice realizes this feels kind of like being in therapy with her third therapist, who would pause after Alice offhandedly said something super fucked up and quietly wait for Alice to hear it herself.

Finally, Isabella speaks. "Something bad could happen to me tomorrow," she says, soft and gentle like Alice is a skittish animal. "I could be hit by a truck, instantly paraplegic. Would you . . ." She hesitates for a second, and then she says, "Would you still love me?"

"Of course I would," Alice says, almost snapping. "But that's different."

"Why?"

"Because it is!" Alice realizes she's raised her voice, and she takes a few deep breaths to calm herself down. Just because she's triggered right now doesn't mean she needs to be, like, so loud about it. "Because you're my cousin. My family."

"What if it were Nolan?" Isabella asks quietly. "What if you got with him for real, and then in a couple years he ended up having another brain injury. Would you leave him?"

"I—" The idea of being with Nolan feels so foreign to her now, like trying to put on a jacket she'd loved in high school and now realizes is hideous and several sizes too small. "I don't know."

"Or if Van were healthy—no MS—and then fifteen years down the line she gets breast cancer and needs chemo? What then?"

"I don't know," Alice says again, loud enough that Isabella winces, probably worried that Alice is going to wake up the kids. Alice drops her voice, apologetic but still frustrated. "I just don't know, okay?"

"Look," Isabella says after another long pause. "What you decide is up to you, and you know I love and support you no matter what. But I think you need to consider, like . . . okay, you know Van comes with this . . . complication. You know she's never going to be completely healthy. And that's real. But everyone else—me, you, the kids—we're all one diagnosis or accident away from being the same or possibly much worse. So with Van it's a guarantee, right, and with everyone else it's a risk. I know you're super risk averse, and with everything you've been through, that makes so much sense. But, honey . . ." She reaches out and takes Alice's empty hand in hers. "I don't want you to throw away this beautiful, precious love you've finally found because you're scared."

Alice feels like she's going to throw up.

"I don't think your parents would want you to miss out on Van just because they were in an accident," Bella says. "I think they'd want you to be loved the way Van loves you. Even if it means you have some stuff to work through."

That might be the understatement of the century, Alice thinks, but she can't say it because she's too distracted by the way she's started to cry. She knows that Bella's right. Her parents were strong and healthy until one day they weren't, and Van seems okay. She gets tired sometimes, and she opens and closes her hands a lot, and she doesn't like to drive at night, but she seems okay.

Alice realizes with a little jolt that she doesn't even know what Van was like before the MS. Maybe she was exactly the same except a little less tired, a true nighttime-driving machine. Maybe she was wildly high energy, always buzzing, always darting from place to place, but Alice kind of doubts it. She thinks about some of the things she loves most about Van—her steadiness, her careful, deliberate movements, her quiet energy, the intense way she cares—maybe those have always been part of Van, or maybe they're new. But either way, Alice realizes, the only Van she's ever known is Van with MS, and that's the one she fell in love with. That's the person who is so damned compelling and desirable that Alice is repeatedly blowing up her entire life for the possibility of one more hug, ten more minutes with her.

Van has already been hit by the truck. Alice has never known her any other way, and Alice is obsessed with her.

Alice lets her eyes flutter closed, Isabella's hand still warm in hers. She thinks about the things she wants most with Van—those nights on the couch, the feeling of Van's hands on her skin, burying her face in Van's neck, Van's soft caring voice in her ear, Van making her laugh even when she's at her lowest. Making cookies together and having sex and spending all of the holidays tucked under the same Snuggie.

She could do all of those things even if Van's MS progresses, even if she's using a wheelchair or her eyesight gets worse or her balance gets wonky or she's more tired. The thought of Van getting worse, being sicker, is honestly terrifying, but for the first time ever, Alice realizes that she'd much prefer learning to live alongside the MS than to never see Van again, not be with her at all.

Maybe she doesn't need Van to be physically perfect to be exactly the person she wants, the person she needs. The person she loves so desperately that it actually hurts.

Alice thinks about being the one to drive at night, and an unexpected wave of tenderness washes over her as she imagines steering Van's station wagon through the wet, dark Portland streets, Van sturdy and almost falling asleep in the passenger seat. Maybe they'd keep a blanket in the car and Alice would drape it over Van at a red light, Frank curled up in the backseat on top of his gangly legs. There would be soft music playing, and Van might mumble that she loves Alice as Alice drives them home from Babs's house, and Alice would say it back, clear and gentle and true. They'd get home—their home—and Alice would help Van into the house, easing her into the bed and curling up on her chest, Van's arms around her, Van's heartbeat under her ear.

She wants that, she realizes. She wants that with Van. She wants the good days and the bad nights and even holding her hand at the scary doctor's appointments. She wants to be Marie's sister and Babs's kid and Aunt Sheila's niece, and most of all she wants to be Van's.

MS or no fucking MS, she wants to be Van's.

She opens her eyes, looking over at Isabella and taking in the worry in her face, the pinch of her eyebrows, the firm grip of her hand. She would love the shit out of her cousin if she got sick, and it's no different for Van.

Hell, she'd loved the shit out of her dad, even when she was thirteen and crying on the phone to the doctor.

"Bella," Alice whispers. "I'm so fucking stupid."

TWENTY-SIX

Unfortunately it turns out that it's easier to realize you're fucking stupid than to figure out what to do about it. Obviously some kind of admission to Van is required, some kind of prostrating at the altar of "I'm Sorry I've Been Such an Ableist Asshole and in My Defense I Have Some Trauma but Also I Love You, Might You Please Ever Be Able to Forgive Me?" but Alice isn't quite sure how to pull that off.

It's been a week since they had sex and Van hasn't responded to the text Alice sent after cravenly sneaking out of her own apartment. Marie and Babs haven't reached out since then either, and Alice wonders what Van told them, why they erased themselves from her life in a way they'd refused to do for the previous eight weeks.

God, has it only been eight weeks? Everything before Nolan collapsed in her lobby feels like a lifetime ago. Alice can barely remember who she was before the Altmans and Van and Isabella. It's like all of that was a long, dreary, mundane dream, and now that she's awake she can't believe she'd thought that repetitive nightmare was her real life.

The only problem is that she's not sure how to fix any of it, how to beg Van to fall into her arms again. She's not sure how to confess her feelings for Van without revealing the entire lie, because she'd need to say something like, *Oh yeah, LOL, don't worry, I'm not actually into Nolan at all,* which kind of leads right into *I promise sleeping with Van isn't weird because I never actually slept with Nolan.* But that pretty much requires a dip into *Oh yeah, we were never dating, ha ha,* and then, although she'd like to linger on the *technically I never actually said we were,* she's pretty sure she'd have to jump right to *Yup, I straight-up lied to you during your darkest days, please accept me into your close-knit and loving family,* which seems . . . rough.

It's been a few days since her epiphany, and she's still working with a very early draft of her speech, which would be okay except for the fact that the three Altman siblings are walking into the lobby of the office building right now.

Alice can't help but flash back to the first time a group of Altmans descended on the lobby, mere hours after Nolan collapsed. Alice had still been in shock from what had happened—his fall to the ground, her desperate attempt at CPR, the paramedics sweeping him away without a backward glance—and a troop of agitated, excitable people had come rushing in, dressed like aliens who were approximating human clothing for the first time. They'd been loud and chaotic and wrong about everything and Alice had loved them immediately.

Today the three of them are dressed normally even though it's not even seven in the morning, and, more important, Nolan is there, standing and walking on his own, looking so much more like the man Alice had pined after for so long. His black hair is combed, his sharp jaw clean-shaven, the sweater covering his chest clearly expensive. Nolan Altman, Fourteenth Floor, is back.

Van and Fourteenth-Floor Nolan must have switched lives; she looks like the one who has been recovering. There are bags under her eyes, her cheeks are pale, and she won't make eye contact with Alice. She's standing behind her siblings, her usually long, rapid strides diminished into a shuffle, like she hopes Alice won't notice she's there.

It's Alice's first sight of Van since she left her—naked, asleep, sated—curled up in Alice's sheets. Her first sight since her revelation at Isabella's house, since she started drafting the speech.

Alice wants to run to her, to kiss her, to have some brilliant and thoughtful apology spill out of her mouth on cue, but instead she slides off her stool and squares her shoulders. She's not sure what's coming right now, but she's going to try to be ready for it.

"Hi, Alice," Nolan says as they reach her enormous black desk.

"Hi," she says, wary. None of them look happy, and Marie looks particularly upset. Alice wonders why she isn't back at school in Corvallis—surely her semester has started by now?

"Guess what?" Nolan says, and Alice realizes she still hasn't talked to him enough to have a baseline for his tone, his speech patterns. She can't tell if he's pissed right now, or pleased, or simply going to ask her for a key to his office.

"What?"

"I remember this place," Nolan says, and Alice's heart sinks. It's doomsday. She's officially run out of time.

He keeps going. "I remember this building. I remember moving back to Portland. I remember Marie's high school graduation and Van's diagnosis. I remember everything from the last five years. From the last five months. But you know what's funny?" His voice is cruel now, a little taunting, and Alice knows that she deserves it.

It feels like everything in her body is frozen, like she's a rabbit crouching in place hoping against hope that the hawk in the sky doesn't see her, even as it's diving right at her, talons outstretched and a hungry look in its eye. She can't quite breathe, and even though she imagined this happening a million times in the last eight weeks, none of those nightmares came close to how quickly her heart is pounding now, how horribly sad she is to be breaking their hearts. Well, Marie's and Van's hearts, at least. Nolan probably didn't give a shit about her last week, and he certainly won't now that he knows the truth, now that he can place her as the receptionist and not as his girlfriend.

She doesn't respond, but Nolan doesn't need her to. "I don't remember you," he says. "I've never seen you before in my goddamned life."

Okay, that one stings. There had been those little smiles, those four *hi*s, three *hey*s, and two *how's it going*s, and those had meant so much to Alice, back when they were all she had. She'd clung to those, developed a rich and satisfying fantasy life around them, and he'd never even really *looked* at her. Never took in her face at all, despite seeing her every time he walked through the lobby at night.

"I can explain," she says, swallowing down the way his words hurt more than she thought they would, and sounding meek even to herself.

"I'm all ears," Nolan says, spreading out his arms in that aggressive way men sometimes do when they're sort of daring you to talk but you know they aren't planning on listening.

Alice looks around the lobby, taking in all the people that

are starting to show up to work. It's six-thirty now, and the lobby isn't the empty, echoing cavern it was even thirty minutes ago. "Not here," she says quickly, making up her mind. "My shift is over in half an hour. I can meet you at Fresh Grounds, down the street? You deserve . . ." She can't help but dart her eyes over to Marie, to Van. "I owe you an uninterrupted explanation."

Two big groups of frowning men in suits come up to the desk, obviously writing off a group that includes a teenager and a lesbian as a waste of space. "Helloooo!" one of them says, waving a hand like he's been waiting for twenty minutes and is the most important man in the world. "We need elevator passes over here!"

Alice nods at him like he isn't the worst. "Right away, sir. If I could have you come over this way, I can get those for you right now."

The Altmans seem to be huddling up to discuss like they're on *Family Feud,* and then Nolan says, "Fine. We'll see you at the house. Half an hour."

Alice doesn't bother to say that it'll take a while to get to the house on the bus, which is why she originally suggested the coffee shop down the street. They're smart people; they'll figure it out, and the guys in front of her are rude as hell. She nods at him, and lets her eyes linger on Van as they walk away until the asshole in front of her impatiently clicks his tongue.

Alice walks out the front doors at seven, looking down at her phone to double-check that she's right about what bus she needs to take to get to the Altman house.

"Alice."

Her head snaps over, and she's pretty sure her eyes must

bug out of her head, because there's Van. And Marie. And Frank, bless his wiggly little heart.

"Thought you might need a ride," Van says, and she's clearly trying to sound gruff but Alice knows her too well for that. Van's upset and confused and hanging on to the smallest possible thread of hope that maybe this was a huge misunderstanding, that somehow Alice is going to pull out an explanation that will make sense, and everyone will heartily laugh, and then she and Alice can sleep together again.

God, Alice wishes that were true.

"We got you breakfast," Marie says, holding out what is clearly a breakfast burrito wrapped in foil. "Or, dinner? I don't know. But Van said you'd be hungry."

Alice is horrified to feel tears coming to her eyes. God, she hasn't even done this yet, hasn't revealed herself to be a monster yet, and she's already a fucking mess.

This is going to massively suck.

"Thank you," she says, walking closer and taking the burrito from Marie. It's still warm. "Thank you both."

Van leads them to her car, and even though she looks exhausted she's walking quickly, so Alice figures she's probably feeling okay today. Marie gets into the passenger seat, so Alice slides into the back with Frank, which involves a lot of getting stepped on and being licked in the face, all of which she tries to savor even while it's very unpleasant.

They don't say much in the car. It's probably hard to make small talk with someone who might have been lying to your entire family for two months, and they all seem equally averse to breaking the seal on the tough conversation until they're at the house. Alice kind of hopes it's only Nolan waiting there for them, but she's pretty sure if that were true they'd be heading north to his condo instead of across the Burnside Bridge.

Van fiddles with the stereo, and Alice hears a sound she'd almost forgotten, the changing of a CD inside a car radio. The first song is one Alice doesn't know, but the second perks her up. "I love this song," she says over the familiar staccato guitar opening. "I love Ani DiFranco."

"So does Van," Marie says. But then she adds, "Obviously," with a look over to Frank, and it takes Alice a second to figure it out.

"Wait," she says, and despite everything, she can see Van trying not to laugh. "Frank, like DiFranco? You named your dog after Ani DiFranco?"

Van smiles at her in the rearview mirror, and Alice wants to kiss her. "Hell yeah I did," Van says, and Alice grins.

"God," she says, reaching out to scratch Ani DiFranco behind his ears. "You're *such* a lesbian."

Van does laugh at that, and Alice vows to remember that sound forever.

Ten minutes later, Frank bounds out of the car and up the stairs to the house and Alice trails behind him, Van, and Marie, feeling like she's going to the gallows. Marie opens the front door and they all file in, Frank exuberantly and Alice with dread tight and low in her gut.

It's a familiar sight, one that hurts Alice's heart. They're all there. They've clearly just finished breakfast—all three of the men on the couches, and Babs and Aunt Sheila gathering up the dishes from the dining room table. They stop cleaning the minute they realize Alice is there, coming to hover in the living room, and Alice finds herself standing in front of all of them with no idea what to say. "Hi," she says, which is not a great start, but she's hoping she'll improve as this goes on.

"Explain," Nolan says, curt and clearly mad, and Alice gets it. She lied to all of them about a lot of stuff, but she lied to

Nolan about himself. Made him doubt his choices, his taste, his own fucking life. She owes all of them an apology, but she messed with him the most.

Alice opens and closes her mouth a few times, not sure where to begin. She really should have spent more time drafting the speech these past few days.

"Maybe let me start," Marie says, stepping forward out of the group of women. Alice blinks at her. Why would Marie . . . whatever. Sure. How much worse could this get, really?

"Okay," Alice says.

"So Nolan's memories kept slowly coming back, but he still didn't remember you. He wasn't sure when you were supposed to pop up, right, so he asked me the other day when you guys started dating," Marie says, crossing her arms over her chest and forcibly reminding Alice of a lady on a lawyer show, pacing around the courtroom and getting ready to absolutely eviscerate someone on the witness stand. "It's a pretty simple question," she continues, for all the world like she has brand-new DNA evidence from the lab. "When did you and Nolan start dating? But the more I thought about it, the more I realized, I didn't know. And that's weird. Don't you think?"

Marie should get booked on *Law & Order* immediately, that's what Alice thinks.

"You see," Marie says, her mask slipping a little, showing Alice the vulnerable kid underneath the act. "We certainly thought that was weird, Nolan and I. So I started digging."

Alice swallows. She knows what Marie concluded, obviously, but she's not sure if she should jump ahead to the confession or let Marie go through with her monologue. She takes a second, really looking at Marie. She looks tired, sad, and kind of betrayed, but not angry. It feels like she wants an excuse to forgive Alice, to be able to put this very upsetting idea to rest. Alice hates that she won't be able to give it to her.

"Nolan never used social media much, but girls were always posting pictures of him. And last week he went out with this girl who totally sucked, and I remembered that every girl who ever posted him kind of sucked. They were always, like, hot and tall and superficial. None of them were at all like you."

"Ouch," Alice says, but without any heat. She knows what Marie means. She knows Marie's only telling it like it is.

Marie blushes, but she keeps going. "So I went deep. Stalked all the girls I remembered, and I found some posts that were . . . curious. Timeline-wise. This one girl, Kerry, she had a picture of herself on his lap like a week before the accident."

Fucking Cherry/Kerry! No wonder she'd looked so panicked up on the fourteenth floor; she hadn't just slept with Nolan, she'd slept with Nolan *that week,* and then he almost died, and his mom showed up with his frumpy girlfriend. Alice would feel horribly bad for putting her through that if Cherry hadn't been so weird to Van.

"She's the receptionist at his firm," Alice says softly, because Marie wasn't there for that delightful exchange, and she doesn't miss the way Van's eyes narrow, clearly remembering how Cherry had looked at her, how Van had risen to Alice's defense without hesitation when it had become clear that Cherry had slept with Nolan.

"So I started thinking. He wasn't remembering you. You're not his type, and you didn't . . . you didn't seem to know much about him. You got lost trying to find his bedroom."

Alice grimaces. Yeah, okay, she hadn't played that one off successfully. "Not my finest hour," she mutters, and Marie almost smiles.

"And then I remembered it was the EMT at the hospital who first told us you were his girlfriend, not you."

Alice nods. She'll curse Corey J. the EMT for the rest of her life, but yeah. This girl is good. She should consider a career in true crime podcasting or something. She's a masterful sleuth.

Alice takes her in, takes all of them in. She wonders what her life would be like if she'd done it all differently. She looks at Van, and she loves her so much that it hurts.

Marie stands tall, presents her closing argument. "Did you ever actually date my brother?"

Alice loves them, not just Van but Marie and Babs and Aunt Sheila and even the interchangeable Steve and Uncle Joe. She doesn't want to lie to them anymore.

"No," she says, very softly. "I never dated your brother."

There's a loud silence, broken only by Alice's harsh, fast breathing and the sound of Frank nibbling at his own leg.

"Why?" Babs finally asks, holding on to Aunt Sheila as Marie deflates against them, all of her hope that somehow Alice was going to explain this visibly leaving her body. "Why did you lie to us?"

Before she can stop herself, Alice says, "I mean, *technically* . . ." but she shuts her mouth on the next words. They don't matter, and the Altmans deserve much better than a technicality. They deserve so much better than Alice has ever given them. Alice girds herself, and tells the truth, the whole truth, and nothing but the truth, so help her Olivia Benson.

"It was a misunderstanding," she says, and at everyone's incredulous looks, she hastily adds, "at first." She tries to talk mostly to Nolan, but she can't help but be more focused on what Van and Marie think, how they're reacting, because at the end of the day she doesn't love Nolan.

She never did.

"I'd seen you," she says to him, "coming through the lobby some nights, and you were, you know . . ." She gestures at him. She knows he knows this about himself, but she's blushing anyway. "You were cute, and I was lonely so I had this, like, massive crush on you, but we'd never, like, talked." She huffs out a breath, dropping her head for a second. God, this is embarrassing as shit. Pathetic, that's what she was. Pining after someone she'd never really talked to, someone who noticed her so little that they'd swear they'd never seen her before.

She looks back up to see that Marie looks curious, Nolan slightly disgusted, and Van's face is so closed up that Alice can't make heads or tails of what she's thinking.

She forces herself to keep going. "And then everything happened, and I guess wires got crossed—the dispatcher I think heard me say something about caring about you, and told the EMT we were together—and you all thought it was true, and I tried to tell you the truth, I really did, but . . ." She shrugs. "Right out of the gate, literally within five minutes of meeting you all, Babs and Aunt Sheila, you told me that knowing he had a girlfriend who cared about him and was with him during his last moments was so comforting to you, and made you feel so much better."

Marie sucks in a loud breath, and Alice shrugs again. "I thought . . . I didn't want to take that away from you, this one thing that was making it easier to cope," she says, looking imploringly at the women standing to the side of the couches now. "And I really didn't . . . I mean, I'm obviously so glad I was wrong, but I really didn't think he'd wake up."

Everyone flinches, and Alice gives it a second. She'd probably make the same assumption again, based on what she'd known at the time, but it sucks to hear. She gets it.

Alice goes on once Babs's face seems to be ready to hear

more. "And I thought, if this little white lie could make you all feel better, grieve easier, why wouldn't I do it? It felt . . . easy. Selfless, you know. Kind, or something. Plus I—I guess that's not totally all of it. I told myself it was selfless, but I was getting stuff too. Babs, you especially just . . . you kept hugging me and I hadn't . . . it had been so long, and I . . ." She lets out a breath, trying to center herself enough to finish a single sentence. "I didn't want to walk away from you. Any of you." She gives Marie a small, sad smile before she says, "And then it . . . spiraled out of control."

She wonders if she sounds like as much of an asshole as she did on Christmas, when she told Van that she hadn't thought Nolan would wake up, and Van had pushed Alice off her body and walked away.

Marie is tucked under Babs's arm now but is narrowing her eyes at Alice again, like she's trying to poke holes in Alice's story. "But why stick around? Why keep lying to us?"

Alice is horrified to feel something tight rising in her throat, something wet welling up behind her eyes. "Van told you all about my parents?"

Aunt Sheila blinks at the abrupt change of topic. "Yes," she says, something kinder in her tone than Alice deserves. "She said they died."

"Yeah," Alice says. "I haven't had a family for a really long time." She takes a beat, and when she speaks she says it to Aunt Sheila, to Babs, to Van and Marie, and even to Steve and Uncle Joe. "I was never in love with Nolan. Not really. But I—I fell in love with you all, with this family, so quickly. I didn't—it was so selfish, but I didn't want to lose you."

She shakes her head, because when they descended on her for the first time she was lonely and naïve and shortsighted and stupid and so, so fucking sad.

"I told myself that if he woke up, I'd come clean," she says, blinking back her tears. "Right then and there. But then . . . he did wake up, and it was so . . ." She tries to push down the memory of how her first thought when she heard the news, when Marie's voice came through the tinny speaker of Van's phone, was *oh no*. "It was so good you were awake," she says to him, "but everything wasn't okay, and I didn't want to, like, I don't know. Make it about me when the amnesia was such a shock, you know. And the next few days, I tried to leave, I really did, but that didn't, um . . . take, I guess."

She looks over at Aunt Sheila, who seems a bit surprised, like she's—for the first time—remembering how she had literally body-blocked Alice from leaving the house when Alice had tried to bow out.

"So you thought it was better to lie to me?" Nolan spits at her. "Better to make up shit about my own life?"

"It got out of hand," Alice says quickly, holding her hands up in surrender, talking only to him now. *Please, Your Honor,* she thinks. *I'm pleading guilty here.* "I never meant for it to go so far, to hurt you like this. The fact that I lied to you about yourself, made you doubt your own memories and your own sense of who you are, I regret that so much. I always will. I'm so sorry, Nolan. Really."

He shakes his head, but Marie's narrowing her eyes. She can tell there's something else that Alice isn't saying, and Alice decides if she's going to go out in a blaze of honesty, she might as well do the thing.

"I know I should have left earlier," she admits, finally brave enough to look Van right in the eye. "But I—"

Van sucks in a breath, but she doesn't break the eye contact.

"All of this started because I had this stupid crush on Nolan, even though I'd never talked to him," Alice says to

Van, pretending they're the only people in the room. "I thought maybe I even loved him, but, I . . ." She feels the tears falling now, but that's okay. She lets it happen as she says, "I had no fucking idea what love felt like until you."

It's quiet again. She's never heard the Altmans quiet—not Babs or Aunt Sheila or Marie individually, and certainly not as a group—but it's deeply, profoundly quiet as everyone slowly turns to stare at Van, eyes wide, mouths agape.

"I—what?" Babs finally says. "What?"

"Oh my god," Marie whispers, suddenly sounding excited. "Oh my *god*!"

Alice tries to ignore everyone that isn't Van, everyone that isn't the woman she loves so much that it feels like claws are slicing through her skin to shred her organs, like every part of her is torn, tattered, mangled.

"I didn't know how to tell you the truth," Alice says. "At first I tried not to feel it, and then I tried not to act on it, but . . ." She gives Van a wry smile, and Marie makes some kind of triumphant sound, but Alice isn't looking anywhere but at Van, who is still perfectly impassive. "I know it's all too fucked and complicated for it to work, you and me. The history, this lie." She doesn't know how to mention the MS in the middle of all the rest of this, so she gestures vaguely at it instead, saying, "And everything else," while waving her hand around like a dead fish.

Her chest feels too small and her head too hot. Her voice is cracking now, and she knows she only has one or two sentences left before she absolutely loses it. "I need you to know," Alice says, using up the last of her words, hoping that beneath Van's blank, vaguely surprised face, she's listening. "Everything started from this lie, these fake feelings, but this . . . you and me, Van, this is the realest thing in the world to me. I love you so much, and I'm so sorry."

Her voice breaks, and Van doesn't do anything but blink at her, her hands slowly opening and closing at her sides.

"Okay," Alice says, forcing herself to take one last look at everyone in the room. There's a bit of a burden off her shoulders already—the lie is over, and that will feel good later—but the new weight of Van's blank face might be even heavier to bear. "I'm . . . I'm going to go. I'm so sorry. To all of you. For lying and abusing your kindness and care and tragedy, and . . . for everything. I really am."

Marie is crying too, and Alice tries to give her another little smile, but she's not sure it works. She turns to go, already mourning that she'll never feel one of Babs's hugs again, never laugh at another one of Aunt Sheila's kooky jokes, come into this house and smell Babs's baking, laugh in the corner with Marie, get her eardrum licked by Frank's ridiculously long tongue.

Never have anything with Van but her memories.

Alice reaches the door, and no one does anything to stop her. No one even says goodbye.

It's all over.

TWENTY-SEVEN

Alice should go home and sleep, but instead she burns over two hours of take-home pay to get a rideshare directly to Isabella's house. It's a little after eight in the morning on a weekday, but it's luckily one of the days Isabella stays home with the kids instead of going to work. Something terrible must be clear on Alice's face, because within a second of opening the door, Isabella wordlessly takes Alice's arm, pushes her onto the couch, and buries her in a pile of blankets and small children still in their pajamas.

Isabella puts on *Moana* and Alice and Sebastian quietly watch it together, Sebastian curled up under her arm like she's not the worst, loneliest person in the world.

"You should get some rest," Isabella says when the movie ends. "I'm going to take Hazel up for her first nap, do you want to lay down with her?"

Alice absently wonders if she should be insulted at being told she should nap like a literal toddler, but she's so emotionally exhausted that she can't muster up even the tiniest spark of a feeling about anything. "No," she says, numb and empty. "I'm okay."

Great, now she's even lying to Isabella.

While Isabella brings Hazel upstairs, Sebastian, who somehow knows how to use the remote despite not being able to poop in the potty, restarts *Moana* again from the beginning. He drapes himself across her lap, a couple blocks in his hands, mindlessly humming along to the music, and Alice lets her mind go blissfully blank.

She might have slept for a while, she's not sure, but she knows that at some point Hazel is dropped in her lap, still warm and snuggly from her nap. *Moana* starts for the third time, and Hazel babbles to herself as she turns the pages of one of her board books. The first song is ending when there's a knock on the front door, and it isn't until Isabella says, "Oh," that Alice looks up from where she's been idly playing with Hazel's toes, making them dance along.

Alice freezes, Hazel's pudgy feet in her hands, her brain experiencing the blue screen of death.

404 Error: program Alice.exe could not be found.

"Minivan!" Sebastian says, jumping up to stand on the couch and looking at the crowd of people at the door. "Hi, Minivan!" Sebastian waves, adorable in his onesie pajamas, and Van smiles at him.

"Hey, buddy," she says, for all the world like this is a normal visit. Like it's regular for her to be dropping by Alice's cousin's house in the middle of the day, with two of her family members and a dog clustered up behind her.

"We're watching *Moana*!" he tells her as Aunt Sheila seems to give Van a hard shove from behind, forcing Van to trip across the threshold.

"Oh, I love that movie," Marie says, coming into the house

and perching on the arm of the couch next to Sebastian like she belongs there. Aunt Sheila lets go of Frank's leash and he beelines for the dining room, zealously vacuuming up the crumbs under Hazel's high chair.

All Alice can manage to say is, "I . . . what?"

What are they doing here?

What the fuck is happening? Has starting the same movie for the third time in a row created some sort of weird time loop, or opened a portal to a multiverse or something? She watches with a detachment she worries may be bordering on hysteria as her two social circles fully collapse into each other. Marie plucks Hazel out of Alice's lap and immediately starts tickling her tummy while dropping onto the living room carpet to chat with Sebastian like they're old friends, and Aunt Sheila is hanging everyone's coats up on hooks like they live here.

"Um, hi," Isabella's saying to Aunt Sheila, clearly surrendering to whatever is happening in her house. "Great to meet you."

"Look at this house!" Aunt Sheila says, louder than everyone else. "This is lovely! And it smells delicious! What are you making? What kind of stove is that? This sweater is so soft, where did you get it? Do you think it comes in orange?"

Aunt Sheila speed walks herself into the kitchen and Isabella follows her, shooting Alice a very confused and slightly afraid look over her shoulder as she goes, detouring around Frank, who is now licking her floor with great determination.

Alice finds herself standing up, somehow alone in a pocket of space with Van. Alice is wearing Isabella's soft joggers and one of Henry's ALL MUSHROOMS ARE MAGIC sweatshirts, and Van looks as gorgeous as ever in her favorite thick huntergreen flannel shirt and her dark jeans.

"Hi," Van says, and Alice wonders where her lungs have gone, her heart, her guts, because they're surely not in her body anymore.

"Hi."

Van looks nervous. She shoves her hands into the front pockets of her jeans, and the corners of her eyes are pinched in. She looks like she's trying to make herself less tall, take up less space, and it would make Alice's heart throb if she thought she still had one.

"Sorry for the entourage," Van finally says, and Alice feels herself taking a step closer even though she didn't mean to. "They got, um . . . a little excited when I said I was thinking about coming over here."

Alice doesn't know what to say to that. The fact that Aunt Sheila and Marie are here is confusing, of course, but Van being here—Van, who Alice just confessed her love to, Van, who Alice is fucking in love with—that's the only thing Alice can think about right now.

"Did you mean it?" Van finally asks.

Alice bites her lip, trying to figure out what specifically Van is referring to. She meant it all, but lord knows there's been enough miscommunication here for a couple of centuries at least. "Which part?"

Van licks her lips, and Alice almost passes out. She'd thought that she'd wanted Van badly before, but none of those times have anything on this one. She'd thought her final look at Van back at the house was the very last time Alice would ever lay eyes on her, but now, here she is. Tall and real, long fingers and chiseled jawline, inconceivably standing in Isabella's living room, and Alice is sure that the force of how badly she wants Van is going to kill her.

"You said you love me," Van says, her voice soft.

Alice hears Marie shush Sebastian, stage-whispering, "Wait, buddy, I gotta hear this!"

"Yes," Alice says, proud that her voice isn't shaking yet. "I meant it."

"Did you lie about anything else?" Van asks, and Alice tilts her head. It's not what she expected Van to ask. "Anything but Nolan?"

"No," Alice says quickly. "Nothing else."

And of course she technically never . . . whatever.

Van takes a step closer, and Marie starts making a low rumble of excited sounds, like a teakettle getting ready to hit a full boil. "What do you want, Alice?" Van asks. "Five years from now, what does your life look like?"

Alice can't help herself. She reaches out and touches Van's sleeves, the thick, soft material of her shirt and the warm strength of her wrists below. "You." Her voice is hoarse now, cracking again, but she doesn't let it stop her. "This. Us. Here, with my family, and yours. And Frank. Just . . . with you." She lets out a long, shuddering breath. "I just want you, Van."

The Marie teakettle squeaks—only once, but very loudly.

She feels Van's arms twitch under her fingertips.

"You know about the MS." Van says it like it's a factual query, but Alice knows what she's really asking. "It's a lot."

Alice nods. "I do. And it—to tell the truth, it freaked me out for a while. But I'm . . ." She takes a final step in, and she throws all caution to the wind. She reaches up and cups Van's perfect jaw in her hands, lets her thumbs brush against the soft skin of her cheeks, still cold from outside. "I'm all in."

Alice faintly hears Isabella make a little sound from where she and Aunt Sheila are peeking out of the kitchen, sees out of the corner of her eye that Bella has a hand over her heart and Aunt Sheila may or may not be beaming and excitedly shaking

Bella back and forth like a rag doll. Marie actually shrieks and Sebastian does too, likely for a different reason but it still adds to the festive atmosphere as the worry in Van's face slowly fades into the biggest, most purely joyful smile Alice has ever seen.

Van's hands are on Alice now, one wrapping around her neck and one warm and steady on her hip, and Alice hears what sounds suspiciously like Isabella whooping as Van leans down, as beautiful and strong and soft as she's ever been, and kisses Alice like nothing else exists.

"Fuck," Van mumbles against Alice's lips. "Me too, Al. I'm all in too."

"Mommy!" Sebastian yells as Alice finally, finally lets herself sink into Van's body, happily begins to be devoured by Van's lips and her grasping hands. "What does 'fuck' mean?"

It's less than a five-minute drive from Isabella's house to Van's. Van drives with one hand on the steering wheel and the other entwined with Alice's, both resting on Alice's knee like they belong there. Aunt Sheila and Marie have been relegated to taking an Uber home—although Alice has a sneaking suspicion they may end up watching all of *Moana* with Sebastian before they leave. Ani DiFranco classics are softly coming through the old speakers of the station wagon, Ani DiFranco himself is curled up in the backseat napping off his Teddy Grahams windfall, and every breath smells like Van. Alice can't take her eyes off Van, who can clearly tell, a smile tugging at the corners of her mouth even as she keeps her focus on the road.

She pulls into her driveway and Alice gets out of the car, inordinately pleased that Van hadn't done something idiotic like ask Alice if she wanted to go back to her own apartment.

If Alice had it her way, she'd never leave this tiny pocket of North Portland, would bounce between Van's and Isabella's and never get cold or lonely ever again.

Van has to jiggle the key in the lock a little because everything contracts in the cold, and Alice can't help herself. "Doorgasm," she whispers, and Van laughs.

Frank bounds inside and Alice follows him, kicking off her shoes and trailing Van into the living room. Alice has only been here the one time, but something about it already feels like home. Maybe it's how easily Van moves through the space, for once like she's not worried about being too big or knocking into something. Maybe it's how everything Alice sees is something she would have picked out for herself—the comfortable couch, the mismatched collection of round-bellied mugs with weird sayings on them like HAPPY BIRTHDAY GRANDPA, the pictures of family and friends and landscapes on the walls.

Or maybe it's just Van. Maybe if they spent more time at Alice's apartment, the place she's lived since she was nineteen and alone for the first time, it would feel more like home too.

Van makes them both tea before they go to the couch, and Alice gets to curl up into Van like she'd wanted to at Chanukah and every moment since, tucking her knees up to her chest and leaning her whole body into Van's. Van's arm is tight around her waist, and the kiss she presses to Alice's hair feels so good that Alice's eyes almost roll back into her head. Frank curls up next to Alice, his back warm against her hip, and something behind her heart that's been pinched and terrified since she was eight years old slowly relaxes, melting like it's finally in the sunshine.

"What about your next five years?" Alice asks after a while, trying to keep herself from falling asleep in case this is all a cruel dream, and she'll wake up alone in her cold bed. "What do you want?"

"This," Van says softly, the hand on Alice's thigh squeezing slightly. "You and me, here. I want—I don't want a flashy life, you know? I want to . . . take you on trips and cook dinner with you and see our families, and spend most nights just like this."

Alice drops her head onto Van's shoulder. "Trips, hmm? Where are you taking me?"

"I dunno," Van says, and Alice can hear that she's still smiling, even as she kisses Alice's head again. "Anywhere you want to go. Especially if I can see you in a bikini."

Alice snorts, burying her face in Van's chest, but she's suddenly seized by a vision of Van in a sports bra and trunks, sunglasses and trucker hat in the sunshine, and her throat immediately goes dry. She swallows thickly. Beach vacation is definitely an urgent priority.

"Do you think your mom's going to be okay with this?" Alice asks after a few minutes. "This" being Van not only bringing home a woman, of course, but Van bringing home the very woman who lied to all of them for months. She presses her palm to Van's chest, hard, as if to say, *I'm not going anywhere, no matter what she says.*

"I hope so," Van says, settling Alice a little more comfortably against herself. "She loves you, so that'll help, I think. Aunt Sheila's on board and she's kind of a force of nature, as you might have noticed." Alice laughs. She has, in fact, noticed. "And Marie's going to be insufferable, so I'm not sure Mom will have much of a choice, unless she wants every holiday to feature, like, a full-ass PowerPoint lecture about it."

Alice laughs. She can picture it perfectly. Marie cosplaying as a gender studies professor, smacking a ruler on her palm and pacing back and forth, quizzing Babs on queer terminology, they/them pronouns, and forcing her to admit that Van being happy is more important than Babs's vague, quiet homophobia.

"She's perfect," Alice says. She nuzzles her nose into Van. "You're perfect." She knows she's the one who brought it up, but she's suddenly very aware of the feeling of Van's hands on her body, her chest under Alice's palm, and she's ready to stop talking about Van's mother and baby sister now. She sets her tea down on the coffee table and then swings a leg over, straddling Van's lap.

"Hi," Van says, her hands automatically going to Alice's thighs, high enough up to be a promise.

"Hi," Alice says, already dipping her head down and letting Van take absolutely everything she has.

They move to the bed when Frank gets a bit too involved. Alice should have been asleep for hours now, but she's pretty sure she's never going back to her job. Not when it would keep her away from Van, would mean spending days alone in this bed and nights alone behind that desk, instead of nights here like this, with Van's lips pressed to hers, Van's hips pinning her down on the bed, Van's fingers slipping inside her.

No, she'll find another job. She'll put all of this behind her—the night shift, that lobby, Nolan, the enormous lie—and she'll stay right here. On her back, in this bed, listening to Van whisper encouragement in her ear and then slowly falling asleep with her legs still wrapped around Van's, Frank quietly snoring in the corner.

EPILOGUE

One hand interlaced with the other, Alice thumps down rhythmically on the middle of the chest, chanting out loud. "Stayin' alive, stayin' alive—god, I should work out more, why are my arms so weak—stayin' alive."

There's a muffled laugh that sounds suspiciously like her girlfriend, and the CPR teacher calls out, "Try to focus, everyone."

Oops. Alice concentrates on the dummy in front of her. Van and Stephanie are hosting a free CPR training for their clients, staff, and the local community, and while Alice is ostensibly the poster child for needing to know how to do CPR, she's mostly just embarrassing herself because apparently she has the worst technique in the entire class. Van and Stephanie were due to be recertified, and it had been Van's idea to drum up business for the practice by making it a public event.

"You're doing great, babe," Van says, supportive as always, and Alice almost laughs. She's not, but it's okay. The dummy doesn't seem to know the difference.

"When do I breathe into his mouth?" Alice asks the instructor. She's named her dummy Bradley, and decided he's been injured in a devastating water balloon fight.

"We don't recommend performing rescue breathing unless you're trained to do so," the instructor says. "Just keep going with the compressions."

Well, shit. Alice will take "Information That Would Have Been Useful Eighteen Months Ago" for five hundred dollars, Alex.

"Oh no," Van says, using the dry tone of voice that everyone thinks is serious but Alice knows is a joke, always accompanied by that quiet twinkle in her eye. "But you were so looking forward to playing tonsil hockey with Bradley."

The instructor frowns down at Alice before kneeling next to Van and readjusting Van's hands on her dummy's chest. She does not seem to enjoy Alice's jokes, and is apparently fixated on the nuances of Van's form, clearly having pegged her as the person with the best chance of actually saving someone if push came to . . . well. Not breath, apparently.

"Like this," the instructor says. "Harder."

Van's ears turn pink, and Alice somehow resists the urge to mount her then and there. "Yeah, Vanessa," Alice says, forgetting to thump on Bradley's chest at all, letting him go gently into the good night. "Give it to him harder. He needs it *harder,* baby."

The instructor shoots Alice a deeply disappointed look. "This is very serious," she chastises. "This is life or death."

Yeah, Alice knows that, actually.

The instructor is saved from Alice putting *her* in a life-or-death situation by Frank bounding up to the class and proceeding to lick every dummy in the face. "Frank!" Alice calls, hauling him off Bradley. "She said not to do rescue breathing unless you're trained for it."

Frank seems unperturbed, and Van quickly stands up and tugs him across the open space filled with exam tables and exercise mats, back into her small private office tucked next to the bathroom.

"Sorry," one of the kids in the circle says to Alice, looking embarrassed. "I went into the office to say hi to the dog, but he slipped out."

"That's okay," Alice says quickly. "It's fine."

The instructor, wiping dog saliva off her thousand-dollar dummy, looks like she might not think it's very fine. Alice would apologize to her if she hadn't spent the last hour glowering at Alice's jokes and only helping Van with her form. Yes, Alice is being stupid and Van is talented and strong and very likely to save a human life and is also super hot—which the instructor definitely has noticed—but, like . . . lady. Try to triage, damn! There is a teenager across the circle who had his dummy face down for the first twenty minutes. Not sure if she knows it or not, but this is, like, life or death?

Before Van is back in the circle, the front door to the clinic opens and twin tornados sweep into the building. "Minivan!" Hazel shrieks as Sebastian skids up to Bradley, kicks him hard in the groin with one light-up sneaker, and announces, "I have to pee!"

"My children, everybody," Isabella deadpans from the door, holding out an arm to hug Van.

"They certainly know how to make an entrance," Van says, hugging her tightly. The CPR lady looks like she might have a conniption, and Alice takes pity on her, scooping Hazel up into her arms and pointing Sebastian toward the bathroom.

"Hey, nugget," she says. "You ready to have a sleepover with Cousin Frankie tonight?"

Hazel nods. "He donna teep in my ded," she says. She's three now, and while her sentence structure is advanced, her pronunciation is still garbled enough that half the time Sebastian has to translate for Alice. She got this one herself, though.

"He's gonna sleep in your bed? That's so fun."

"Yeah," Hazel says.

"Yeah," Van says, coming up behind Alice and grabbing Hazel out of her arms, flipping her upside down, and making her shriek with laughter. The kids really like Alice, but they don't love anyone—not even their parents, Alice admits ruefully—the way they love Van.

Alice gets it. Van is the fucking best.

The instructor quickly wraps up the class. Alice spends a relatively chaotic twenty minutes helping both kids pee, saying goodbye to all of the existing clients, booking two new-patient appointments, and high-fiving Stephanie about said new patients. Alice steps out into the parking lot to load all of Frank's supplies into Isabella's car, but she gets distracted by drooling at the way Van manhandles the dummies into the back of the joyless instructor's truck. God, Alice's girlfriend really is devastatingly sexy, isn't she.

Alice finally wrenches her gaze away from Van's muscles. Or, more honestly, Van finishes loading the dummies, so it's easier for Alice to shift her attention back to the car. "We'll pick Frank up Sunday morning," Alice says to Isabella, helping strap a very wiggly Hazel into her car seat.

"I CAN DO IT," Hazel yells, which is untrue.

"Perfect," Bella says. "Just text me when you're leaving Corvallis."

Alice nods.

"Remind me, what's the play?"

"*A Midsummer Night's Dream,*" Alice says. "But set underwater? Marie's playing the donkey, but it's a seahorse? I don't know."

"Gonna be a loooong couple of hours," Bella cackles, and Alice swats at her.

Bella laughs so loudly that Van looks over from where she seems to be trapped in conversation with the CPR instructor. "I have to say goodbye to my family," Van says, way too loudly. "If you'll excuse me."

She stomps over to Alice and Bella, giving Alice a kiss that's significantly too long and wet for her work parking lot in front of two preschoolers and her business partner, but Alice certainly isn't complaining. Anytime Van wants to shove her tongue inside Alice's mouth, wants to hold her hips in a deathly tight grip, wants to make Alice remember why last night she'd panted and moaned loudly enough that the upstairs tenants gave her dirty looks this morning—that works for Alice.

When Van finally lets go, the instructor is already inside her truck, pulling out of the parking lot with what looks like a lot of pent-up aggression at the mistreatment of her dummies by the devastating combination of Hazel and Sebastian, Frank's enthusiasm, and Alice's general ineptitude. And also maybe the kiss.

Alice drops her head onto Van's collarbone, laughing, as Bella waves goodbye, closing the car doors on Frank and her spawn and taking all of them home with her. Alice locks the front door of North Portland PT, they say goodbye to Stephanie, and then she and Van climb into the station wagon for the trip down to Oregon State.

Van drives and Alice puts on a podcast about the sinking of the *Titanic*. They hold hands the whole drive.

There's an accident outside Salem that almost doubles the two-hour drive to Corvallis. Alice learns more about the *Titanic* than she'd ever wanted to. They meant to have drinks with the family beforehand, but they barely have time to slide into their seats in the theater before the lights go down and a bunch of college students do their best to bring Shakespeare to life.

Underwater.

Alice hasn't seen much theater, but she and Van read the play out loud in preparation for this, and boy. As Alice's dad always said about a truly terrible school performance: It's really something.

At intermission, Aunt Sheila grabs Alice into a hug and yells, "How are you liking it so far?" Van keeps trying to make her an audiologist appointment, but Alice is convinced her volume has nothing to do with hearing loss and everything to do with enthusiasm.

"It's . . . really something," Alice says. "Very creative. Not . . . um, what I'd pictured."

"No," Aunt Sheila agrees, positively shouting now. "But Marina is radiant!"

Now that, Alice can agree with.

"Hello, dear," Babs says, and Alice slips out from Aunt Sheila's clutches long enough to give Babs a hug. Things haven't been entirely smooth since Alice came clean, since she and Van decided to make a real go of it. The shock of Alice's lie hit Babs hard, which of course Alice doesn't blame her for, and the reality of Van actually being a gay adult who is planning to marry a woman seems to have only recently sunk in. Steve and Uncle Joe seem to be in a similar boat—while all three of them are nothing but polite and welcoming to Alice, it lacks some of the effusive love from before—but Aunt Sheila has been on board since that first morning at Isabella's house. Alice wouldn't be surprised if she and Marie had matching TEAM VANALICE T-shirts.

It's more than Alice deserves, an aunt and a little sister, and Van is convinced Babs will come around. "We just need to be patient," she says, and Alice can do that.

Alice can be patient.

Alice has Van, the luminous, solid, shockingly handsome woman next to her, who loves her and takes care of her and falls asleep holding her every night. Alice has Van, and Frank, and Isabella's family, and weird experimental theater, and a spot on Van's couch that is perfectly contoured to Alice's butt, and her job at the PT clinic.

She's good. When the rest of the Altmans come around she'll be even better, but yeah. She's good.

Seventy minutes and several questionable theatrical decisions later, the play mercifully ends. They meet up at a restaurant for a very late dinner after Marie has had a chance to shower off her seahorse makeup, Alice and Van arriving a few minutes late due to a poorly timed but essential make-out session in the parking lot. What can Alice say—high culture turns her on.

Inside the restaurant, the host, who can't be over twelve years old, with enormous pimples and an adorably cracking voice, leads them to a big table in the back. Marie jumps up, throwing herself into first Van's and then Alice's arms. "Hi," she squeals. "You guys! What did you think?"

She's bouncing on her toes, looking as young as the barely pubescent host, and Alice grins even as she searches for something to say. "It was . . . wow!"

"Yeah," Van echoes quickly, one hand on the small of Alice's back now. "Seriously. Wow."

Marie beams, and Alice bites her tongue. Sometimes evading the truth is a real kindness, right?

Alice is glad for her years of perfecting her receptionist fake smile, because the next few minutes require the Fake Smile World Series. The next person to walk into the restaurant is Nolan, and he has a girl on his arm. And by girl, Alice means *girl*. She's heavily contoured, wearing heels so high Alice wants to refer her to Van to get her ankles checked out, and it looks like her phone has been permanently grafted onto her palm. She introduces herself as Tansilyn, and giggles with Marie about their old freshman dorm, which Tansilyn lived in only a few years before Marie did. She's twenty-four, and Babs looks ready to murder her.

"Do you want to have children, Tansilyn?" Babs asks through gritted teeth, and Alice quickly turns her laugh into a cough, which sets off Marie so loudly that Van has to flag down a waiter and ask for water. She also asks for a tranquilizer for her mother, which the server seems confused by, but has Aunt Sheila digging in her enormous purse, muttering something about "must have some benzos in here somewhere."

Alice loves them.

After dinner ends—five inane stories from Tansilyn, eight selfies, both boomer men giving up and starting to do the crossword on their phones—everyone seems like they're in a great hurry to go their separate ways.

The goodbye hug Babs gives Alice is much tighter this time, and when she pulls away she cups Alice's face in her hands and looks at her for a long beat. "You're a good egg," Babs says, and Alice feels tears welling at the corners of her eyes.

Aunt Sheila breaks the moment, as she so often does, hugging Alice from behind while Babs is still touching her cheeks. "At least one of my nibblets has good taste in women," Aunt

Sheila yells, way too close to Alice's eardrum. "Have a good night, Rue Rue."

Alice feels, like she has so often for the past eighteen months, like her heart doesn't fit in her chest anymore, like she needs to find it a new, bigger enclosure, something expansive enough to fit all of the ways she loves her families.

The boomers trundle off to Babs's cousin's house, where they're spending the night, while Nolan and "follow me on socials, at TansiTot!" get back on the road to Portland.

Van and Alice kidnap Marie and take her to a bar, cosplaying as young, cool people who stay out past ten at night. Van pointedly ignores Marie's fake ID, and Marie spends the next two hours gushing to them about all the people she's dating. Apparently the polyamory thing isn't just a political philosophy for her, and while it all sounds profoundly exhausting to Alice, power to her. Live your dreams, girl. Create a color-coded Google calendar for dating. As Raisin would say, *Fuck the patriarchy by fucking anyone who wants you to!*

After drinks, they drop Marie off at the grungy rental house she shares with six other sophomores, Van advising her to get an IUD and make an appointment with her local Planned Parenthood to get screened.

"Okay, Mom," Marie says, rolling her eyes, and Van mimes being stabbed in the heart.

Fuck, Alice loves them.

They get back in the station wagon, Alice driving this time. Van puts on a quiet Taylor Swift playlist, and Alice follows her directions to a cute little bed-and-breakfast across town. The old woman at the counter blinks at their joined hands for only a second before her face breaks into an enormous smile, and she talks a mile a minute about her lesbian niece until they shoo her out of their lovely little room.

"It's like if Aunt Sheila were an innkeeper," Alice says dryly, and Van laughs.

Although, instead of continuing to talk about her family—her chaotic aunt, her baby sister's sex life, or Nolan's latest child-bride—Van simply collides her body into Alice's and keeps moving until Alice falls backward onto the bed. The comforter is a pure, snowy white, fluffier than any Alice has seen outside of a movie or a cartoon. Alice wants to burrow under it like a hibernating chipmunk, but, before that, she wants Van to do everything to her.

She wraps a hand around the back of Van's neck, pulling her down, and kissing her until her chest feels like it's going to explode from a combination of oxygen deprivation and love overload.

"I love you," Alice mumbles into Van's lips. Van says it back—strong and solid and true—into the skin of Alice's chest.

"I love you," Van says again, even when Alice kicks her in the stomach after Van teases, "Do you need it *harder*, baby" as Alice is writhing under her. She says it again after Alice has come for the third time. And again, much later, when her fingers are tugging Alice's hair and she's grinding herself into Alice's mouth.

When she tucks Alice into bed, the fluffy comforter perfectly wrapped around them, she says it a fifth time, her tone more serious this time. "I really love you, babe," she says, pulling Alice onto her chest.

Alice nuzzles into her flushed, warm skin, and tells the truth, the whole truth, and nothing but the truth. "Love you too, Minivan."

ACKNOWLEDGMENTS

I've learned that while drafting a book is a very lonely and solitary process, everything after that is dazzlingly collaborative, and I'm immensely grateful to so many people who helped take this book from two bullet points in my Note of Book Ideas (one of which super helpfully said only "hot butch with a big dog") into this beautiful book you're holding in your hands.

First and foremost, the biggest thank-you goes to my incredible agent, Courtney Miller-Callihan. I'm thrilled every single day that you plucked me out of the slush so many years ago and have stuck with me through all of the (infrequent) highs and (many) lows, including, you know, a global pandemic, et cetera. By your side and because of your gentle guidance, I learned how to write books, how to revise, and hopefully how to be an author, not just a writer. Thank you for saying things like, "Have you . . . thought about pacing?" because no . . . I hadn't. I wouldn't have gotten anywhere near this book without you, and being a handspinner makes me feel so lucky every day. Huge thanks to Cheyenne and Ben for all of their support on this book and the rest.

At the time, I really wanted someone to publish this book, but now in retrospect, I know that I wanted only Dial and my phenomenal editor Katy Nishimoto to publish this book. Katy, I cannot imagine an editor who would have been better suited to this story, or nearly as genuine, creative, kind, and wonderful to work with. Your insights and ideas are consistently brilliant and you've helped me make this into the book I've always wanted it to be. I am so very thankful for the magic that put me on your list.

Thank you to everyone at Dial for their work in bringing Alice to life, especially Whitney Frick, JP Woodham, Avideh Bashirrad, Raaga Rajagopala, Debbie Aroff, Jordan Hill Forney, and Hope Hathcock. You can see the full list of folks who worked on this book on the credits page. Thank you all from the bottom of my heart for your expertise and effort to turn this manuscript from a pumpkin into a real, actual book. Immense thanks to Donna Cheng, Aarushi Menon, and Jo Anne Metsch for the gorgeous interior design of this book and a cover out of my wildest dreams that I literally cannot stop staring at!

A massive, immense thank-you to my first readers, some of whom jumped in after only a few chapters and haven't stopped cheering for me and Alice since. Thank you to Elizabeth Holden (I will leave tracked changes in everything you ever write if you'll let me), Allison Hubbard (RIP Higgenplatz, the real ones know), Emily Joy Howard, my co-mentor buddy, Julia, Re, and Nick for your eyes and brains and feedback. And of course, thank you to my wife and my sister for being the first readers for everything I've ever written, and especially for doing Alice Book Club, in which we donned fuzzy children's blankets with hoods and you helped me figure out the third act.

My friends have come through for me and this book in so many ways. Thank you, Annie, for having a phone call with me in 2018 and explaining how publishing works. Thank you, Lily and Jonah, for adopting what turned out to be a very large, rather silly dog and letting me rip off literally all of his attributes to turn him into Frank. (Bowie, I love you forever, but please stop trying to lick my eardrum, it's quite unpleasant!) Thank you to Rashmi for doing the work to help me figure out that soap opera medicine is real and learn the incredibly surprising fact that what happened to Nolan is actually plausible. Thank you to everyone who has celebrated with me, or asked how writing is going and when you can (finally) buy this book. It's now!

Thank you to the teachers, booksellers, and librarians who instilled a deep love of books in my heart, even if they weren't allowed to teach me how to spell, particularly Ms. Gutierrez, Ms. Teplin, Ms. Lyons, Ms. Goldberg, Mrs. LaDuke, my badass aunt Sharon, and Diane from CBW.

And the people I haven't ever met: Thank you to all of the booksellers, publishers, agents, and writers who have helped to create the golden age of the sapphic rom-com; I know Alice and I wouldn't be here without you. Thank you to MUNA (the greatest band in the world), HAIM, and Sara Bareilles for the soundtrack that I wrote this entire book to. Thank *you*, person-who-is-reading-this, and ostensibly read all the other, more exciting pages too. I sort of can't believe you're here, and I love you for it.

My family has been so supportive of this weird, random dream that cropped up in my thirties, and I'm so grateful. Thank you in particular to my parents, and not just because every time someone thanked their mom at the Oscars, my mom would look over at me and say, "See?!" Thank you for your love, weirdness, and unconditional energy and enthusiasm for me. Thank you to my sister for being my first friend, my Portland sensitivity reader, and everything in between. You'll always be my gump-faced, blown-up, baboon-assed bastard.

Finally, and most important, thank you to my wife, my person, the one who makes everything better just by being there, who knew the word *mycological* without even thinking about it. I love you every second of every minute of forever. Thanks for kissing me back. I'm sorry you kept having to walk the dog while I was writing. Unfortunately, that is unlikely to change.

ALICE RUE EVADES THE TRUTH

Emily Zipps

Dial Delights

Love Stories for the Open-Hearted

A NOTE FROM THE AUTHOR

I was thirty when my hands started tingling. I figured it was from riding my bike over bumpy D.C. streets, or maybe holding my wrists weirdly while I typed. It seemed odd, but fine. Eventually I moved across the country, started a new job, got new insurance. I remember feeling calm when my new doctor told me she wasn't sure what the tingling was about, but why don't we get some tests to rule things out. Sure, I thought. I love ruling things out.

I don't remember what she said when she called me back a few days after the tests. That phone call is a black hole in my mind. What I do remember is sitting on my little blue couch in the apartment with the tilted floors, the one we had just moved into, and hanging up the phone. I remember sitting there and thinking, *I have to tell my wife.*

I remember walking into the small bedroom with the one window that looked into someone else's bedroom, and sitting on the edge of the bed. I don't remember what I said when I finally told her, if I cried then or only later. What I do remember is that last breath I took in, the last one before I changed my wife's life for the worse. I think a lot about that doctor, about that last breath she took in before she changed my life for the worse.

I was diagnosed with multiple sclerosis in 2018, and I learned how to spell it probably around 2020. I never meant to write a book about someone with MS—it was at least a year before I could even think about my diagnosis without wanting to throw my computer across the room or rip my brain out with my own two hands. There's nothing good about having MS to me. There's nothing about me or my life that's better because I have MS. To be perfectly clear, MS fucking sucks.

Romance novels are fantasy novels, where things are not supposed to fucking suck in ways that are permanent. Every romance, every rom-com, is a fantasy, just as much as the dozens I read as a kid where princesses perform magic and ride dragons. In a romance novel, every obstacle is surmountable, every crush can become a happily ever after. How, then, could I ever write a romance with a character with MS, when it has no cure, no happily ever after? I was convinced I couldn't, not if I wanted to write a realistic story with characters who respond to things in ways that are far from perfect, ways that are honest even if they're shitty.

I swore I would never write a character with MS, and then I wrote myself into a corner with *Alice Rue Evades the Truth*. I got halfway through the first draft of this manuscript, and the realization slapped me in the face, the idea already fully formed, like I'd spent the entire first half of the book writing with this twist in mind. Van had to have MS. Sweet, wonderful, soft, handsome, steady Van, the dreamiest love interest I've ever written, had to be fucked up just like I am. It was the only way to tie Alice's childhood trauma to the plot, to keep Alice and

Van apart in the second half of the novel. It was perfect for Alice, for the book, and hopefully for you, my beloved reader. Great news for everyone but me and Van, really. It killed me to do it to her, because I loved her, but almost more pressing was the practical question it raised. I had to get Van to her happily ever after with Alice, and how could I if she had MS?

I didn't want to write inspiration porn; I didn't want to downplay how terrible this disease is. I didn't want Alice to say, "I don't care, and no good person would care! This changes nothing!" because that's a lie, and even though this is a fantasy novel, that's not the part I want to be fantastical. I wanted this to feel real, to be real, which meant I had to get Alice somewhere I hadn't yet gotten myself: okay with the quagmire of shit that is this disease.

Could I even write this? What would it take for me to be able to write from the point of view of someone falling in love with the most damaged, terrifying, broken part of myself? How could I sit in Alice's point of view, inside her head, and look out at Van, with her tingling hands and quiet fatigue and light-sensitive eyes, and say, *Yes, this is the woman I choose. Of all of the healthy people in the world, all of the gorgeous, stone-cold butches in Portland, this is the one I want?*

How could I write a convincing love story when MS is the silent, lurking, nonconsensual third in their relationship?

Choosing this for my character, something I would not in a million years choose for myself, forcing myself to think about this during my writing time, which is my escape from everything else, is a very odd choice, and one I didn't mean to make. But I'm happy I made it for Van. And not only because it fits the narrative so well, that it challenges Alice in the most fundamental way, but also because it made me think a little differently about myself.

I am incredibly lucky to have been able to work with Katy Nishimoto on this story. For our first big edit together, Katy asked me to think about if there are any things about Van-with-MS that Alice likes, any good qualities in Van that are because of the MS, not despite it. If anyone else had asked me this question, I'd have punched them in the face. Well, in reality, I'd have stuttered out an answer and then cried later. Hashtag conflict averse! But because it was Katy asking, because she had asked it so thoughtfully, because I knew where the question came from, because I trusted her completely with my book and with Van, I thought about it.

I agonized over her question. I talked about it a lot with my incredible wife, who fell in love with me before we knew I had MS and hasn't wavered for a single second. I decided, we decided, that it's important that Alice loves Van as she is now—not *because* she has MS, not *in spite* of her having MS, not *regardless* of her MS, but simply that Alice loves the fullness of Van as a person. Alice loves how gentle and thoughtful Van is with her body, and who's to say if she was that way before she had to carefully measure all of her movements, manage her energy like water in a drought? Alice loves how caring and thoughtful and soft-spoken Van is, and maybe that has nothing to do with her MS, but maybe it has everything to do with it. Alice wants to spend her nights curled up on a couch in a comfortable living room, Van's chest under her ear and Frank nestled up next to her, and she's in luck, because that's something Van can do even on her bad days. Their lives are compatible, their wishes, their hopes, who their trauma and sickness and triumphs have made them into, and that works.

What I've learned from this book is that the fantasy some people like me need to see is someone looking at your disease and saying: "I don't see anything wrong with you. You're perfect as you are." The fantasy I needed to see was different. My fantasy, it turns out, is someone looking at your disease, struggling with it, and then being able to honestly say: "I see how shitty this is going to be, and I'm here for it. You're worth it. I can fall in love with a different kind of life if it means getting to be with you."

No matter how Van became this person, Alice loves her, and that's enough. That's enough to get Team Vanalice to their happily ever after, and maybe there's something beautiful in that. Maybe there's something I can take, from writing Alice loving Van, into my own life. Maybe I can try to care for myself the way Alice cares for Van.

I didn't set out to write an "issue book," and honestly I hope I haven't. Van and Alice are queer and Van is sick and those are things I love about them—not things I wrote for "representation" but things I wrote because they fit, because they're right, because this is part of the beautiful variety within the human species. I love queer people and I love disabled people and most of all, I love Alice and Van.

I would like to be more like Van. She's so dreamy! And Alice is infinitely braver than I am—and also a hot mess in ways I hope to never be—and I'm immensely grateful that I get to carry both of them around inside of me for the rest of my life, exactly as sick and ridiculous as they are. And that? That's progress, I guess!

ALICE RUE'S TOP TEN PHRASES FOR EVADING THE TRUTH

(Warning: Possible Side Effects May Include Everything Getting Wildly and Irrevocably Fucked Up)

1. Something like that. *(The perfect vague, nonspecific non-agreement that people take as a yes! This is the Holy Grail of evasion.)*

2. What did he say happened? *(This works very well for information gathering and also flows nicely into the next one.)*

3. That's not exactly how I'd have put it . . . *(Because I DO NOT KNOW.)*

4. *Laughs nervously* Is anyone hungry? *(Distraction works, and not just on Sebastian!)*

5. He didn't tell me about that. *(They don't need to know he never told you anything because you've never, you know. Spoken.)*

6. I think I might be missing some information. Why don't you start from the beginning and pretend I don't know anything? *(*Wink* pretend *wink* I don't know anything.)*

7. It was really something! *(RIP, Mr. Rue, you were a real one.)*

8. Wow! *(Simple, effective, classic.)*

9. Tell me more about that. *(People love to talk about themselves. Sometimes they forget to circle back and this is good news.)*

10. More or less. *(Less, so much less.)*

RAISIN'S TOP TEN TIPS FOR LOOKING HOT AND BISEXUAL ON A BUDGET

(Annotated by Alice for Realism)

Raisin's Tip 1: Do all your shopping at thrift stores (except for underwear, socks, and bras if you're squeamish). Don't buy shit there just because it's cheap; hold out for stuff that's actually fashionable and truly slaps. If a grandma would wear it—*any* grandma—do not buy it, Alice Rue. Don't do it. Just say no.

Alice's note: *First, rude. And second, Raisin, I do not KNOW what is fashionable, isn't this the entire problem??*

Raisin's Tip 2: Not all thrift stores are created equal. Try a bunch in different parts of town, and figure out your favorites. Sometimes stores in rich neighborhoods will have the dank stuff, but they may be wicked expensive. Try both Hawthorne and Lake Oswego and see what's up.

Alice's note: *This is going to be the number one benefit of dating someone with a car, isn't it?*

Raisin's Tip 3: Go multiple times a week (weekdays only), right when the store opens. That's when it will be the most organized and the least crowded.

Alice's note: *Dude, I have a JOB. This tip is canceled.*

Raisin's Tip 4: Put on a podcast and take your time. It's a marathon, not a sprint, baby.

Alice's note: *Honestly can't believe you didn't make a sex joke here, but I'll take the win.*

Raisin's Tip 5: If you see something you like, touch it like it's a lady to get a sense of if you like the way the fabric feels. Rub it on the inside of your wrist for the Tender Skin Itchy Fabric Approval Test. Only try on things that pass that test.

Alice's note: *I see I spoke too soon. Touch it like it's a lady? I'm sorry, but you might be touching ladies wrong? What I do with Van has* very *little resemblance to what I do in a thrift store. You might need to google some stuff if you think trying on a stinky jacket and doing the dirty are similar.*

Raisin's Tip 6: Check all the sections and all the sizes because stuff is put in the weirdest places. Always check the men's section because gender is a lie and their colors are always better.

Alice's note: *Preeeeeeeeeeeeeach, why are all of Van's clothes so much better than mine? (Don't answer that.)*

Raisin's Tip 7: Bring a fanny pack only. You don't have time for a big shoulder bag, please. We're homos! Strap it to your waist like God intended.

Alice's note: *Jesus fucking Christ, Raisin.*

Raisin's Tip 8: If you see something you like (NOT GRANDMA STYLE) and think you couldn't pull it off, buy it, you frumpy bitch. This is how you glow up. You can pull off anything if you act like it works. Gay people get a weird fashion pass; use it.

Alice's note: *This is stressful! What if it looks stupid! But I guess . . . in a fight between boring and stupid, maybe stupid should win? I don't know. I need a therapist.*

Raisin's Tip 9: Some of the cheapest stores don't have dressing rooms. Wear leggings, a tight tank top, and slip-on shoes with socks so you can get freaky right there in the aisle. Simply do not make eye contact with any other shopper. Be free.

Alice's note: *Well, this is horrifying but also practical, thank you.*

Raisin's Tip 10: Check for stains and missing buttons and other sus shit. Missing buttons you can fix, you can patch things if you're fancy, but armpit stains are forever and nasty and I personally would never be seen with you in public again if you wore something with SOMEONE ELSE'S ARMPIT JUICE ON IT, ALICE, THAT'S JUST NASTY.

Alice's note: *Why do you think I would do this?? What has ever made you think I would do this? Raisin, your low opinion of me is profoundly concerning, and also I will never unsee the phrase* armpit juice. *I hate you eternally.*

A COMPLETE HISTORY OF VAN'S AND MARIE'S HALLOWEEN COSTUMES

1991
- Van, Infant: Pumpkin

1992
- Van, Age 1: Cat

1993
- Van, Age 2: Ballerina

1994
- Van, Age 3: Nala

1995
- Van, Age 4: Woody

1996
- Van, Age 5: Witch

1997
- Van, Age 6: Batman

1998
- Van, Age 7: Ninja Turtle

1999
- Van, Age 8: Trinity from *The Matrix*

2000
- Van, Age 9: Neo from *The Matrix*

2001
- Van, Age 10: Darth Vader

2002
- Van, Age 11: Spider-Man

2003
- Van, Age 12: Captain Jack Sparrow

2004
- Van, Age 13: Kid from *ET*

2005
- Van, Age 14: McDreamy (*Grey's Anatomy* group costume with high school friends)

2006

- Van, Age 15: Agent K (*Men in Black*)
- Marie, Infant: Pumpkin

2007

- Van, Age 16: Han Solo (*Star Wars* group costume with high school friends)
- Marie, Age 1: Cat

2008

- Van, Age 17: Marty McFly (*Back to the Future* group costume with high school friends)
- Marie, Age 2: Ballerina

2009

- Van, Age 18: Ghost
- Marie, Age 3: Witch

2010

- Van, Age 19: Coach Sue (group *Glee* costume with college friends)
- Marie, Age 4: Princess Tiana

2011

- Van, Age 20: Mr. Montana
- Marie, Age 5: Hannah Montana

2012

- Van, Age 21: Bear from *Brave*
- Marie, Age 6: Merida from *Brave*

2013
- Van, Age 22: Jim from *The Office*
- Marie, Age 7: Great White Shark

2014
- Van, Age 23: Kristoff
- Marie, Age 8: Elsa

2015
- Van, Age 24: Kristoff
- Marie, Age 9: Anna

2016
- Van, Age 25: Kristoff
- Marie, Age 10: Elsa

2017
- Van, Age 26: Jim from *The Office*
- Marie, Age 11: Moana

2018
- Van, Age 27: Wonder Woman
- Marie, Age 12: Wonder Woman

2019
- Van, Age 28: Batman (with Frank as Robin)
- Marie, Age 13: Eleven (*Stranger Things* group costume with middle school friends)

2020
- Van, Age 29: Nothing (social distancing)
- Marie, Age 14: Ghostface

2021
- Van, Age 30: Pongo's owner (Frank as Pongo)
- Marie, Age 15: Cruella

2022
- Van, Age 31: Thor (group costume with ex-girlfriend, Frank as the hammer)
- Marie, Age 16: Harley Quinn

2023
- Van, Age 32: Ken
- Marie, Age 17: Barbie

2024
- Van, Age 33: Prince Eric (group costume with, ugh, Sarah as Ariel and Frank as Sebastian)
- Marie, Age 18: Olaf (group costume with high school friends)

2025
- Van, Age 34: The Wizard from *Wicked* (Alice and Frank as flying monkeys)
- Marie, Age 19: Elphaba

CREDITS

ART AND DESIGN
Donna Cheng
Aarushi Menon
Jo Anne Metsch

AUDIO
Abby Nutter
Kaitlyn Robinson

CONTRACTS
Janice Barcena
Erica Davidson

COPYEDITING AND PROOFREADING
Madeline Hopkins
Alicia Hyman
Kathryn Jones
Vincent La Scala
Tracy Roe

EDITORIAL
Katy Nishimoto
JP Woodham

MANAGING EDITORIAL
Rebecca Berlant
Leah Sims

MARKETING
Debbie Aroff
Jordan Hill Forney

PRODUCTION
Katie Zilberman

PRODUCTION EDITORIAL
Michelle Daniel

PUBLICITY
Hope Hathcock

PUBLISHERS
Avideh Bashirrad
Whitney Frick
Raaga Rajagopala
Andy Ward

SUBSIDIARY RIGHTS
Rachel Kind

ABOUT THE AUTHOR

EMILY ZIPPS grew up in Southern California, currently lives in New Mexico, and is a proud graduate of Mount Holyoke College. When she's not writing about queer women kissing each other, Zipps can be found overanalyzing reality TV, talking too much about women's sports, and spending time with her wife and their dog, who looks like a coyote and acts like a cat. *Alice Rue Evades the Truth* is her debut novel.

ABOUT THE TYPE

This book was set in Garamond, a typeface originally designed by the Parisian type cutter Claude Garamond (c. 1500–61). This version of Garamond was modeled on a 1592 specimen sheet from the Egenolff-Berner foundry, which was produced from types assumed to have been brought to Frankfurt by the punch cutter Jacques Sabon (c. 1520–80).

DIAL DELIGHTS

Love Stories for the Open-Hearted

Discover more joyful romances that celebrate all kinds of happily-ever-afters:

dialdelights.com

◎ @THEDIALPRESS

▶ @THEDIALPRESS

Penguin Random House collects and processes your personal information. See our Notice at Collection and Privacy Policy at prh.com/notice.